FOU

A
NOVEL

FOU

CHRIS WILSON

SINCLAIR-STEVENSON

First published in Great Britain by
Sinclair-Stevenson
7/8 Kendrick Mews
London SW7 3HG England

British Library Cataloguing in Publication Data
A CIP catalogue record for this book is available
from the British Library.

ISBN: 1 85619 189 3

Typeset by Phoenix Photosetting,
Chatham, Kent.
Printed and bound in England by
Clays Ltd, St Ives plc.

For
Diana Athill and Tanja Howarth

But as all several souls contain
Mixtures of things, they know not what,
Love these mixed souls doth mix again
And makes both one, each this and that . . .

John Donne

VIENNA
1909–1919
and
LONDON
1991

1

FOU, I was then. *Folle*, if you prefer the feminine form and expect the genders to agree. Crazy, anyway. Touched, la-di-da. *Tout change*. Now, I'm gone gaga.

I'm no literary lady, and I'm no spring chicken. My wrist tires easily. There's too much to tell. It is difficult writing stories and some things I must leave out, because I only buy one box of paper. There are only 500 sheets, and half the time I screw up.

First, I insist on your imagination. Picture me. A frail old bird, my face crumpled like a brown paper bag, as I glower down at my twitching left hand, propelling a pencil, scratching my story. Also I'm volcanic. There's the lava of reminiscence of ninety-odd years of hot life, bubbling and heaving, pressing to burst out through the small crusted scab of Literature.

Although I'm no author, I passed many years as a writer's model and got intimate with scribblers. I don't talk nobodies here. These were men who shared shelf space and touched covers with Stefan Zweig, Johann Wolfgang von Goethe, Arthur Schnitzler, Rainer Maria Rilke and Thomas Mann. But I never advise you to get intimate with writers, because they are dead, almost. And the small feeling that stirs in them is only their imagination. I tell you what they

3

do. They worm their way in past the lady's guard. They poke about inside her. When they are finished you feel sore and used. You forgive and forget. Then years later you find they have published you naked. They change your name without permission. They lend you a vain temperament. Then they change your appearance out of all recognition. And you are demeaned – no more than a caricature in a subplot, maybe, or torso in a love scene.

'Thomas!' I say, 'I read about this Elise woman in Chapter Three. Is that any way to treat a lady?'

'Lise, don't be vain. Whatever makes you think she is you?'

'The mole on her thigh,' I say. 'The tattoo on her left buttock. And her little peculiarity.'

'Well, yes,' he concedes, 'I did borrow a little from life, from you.'

'Me too, Thomas. I did borrow from you. I tear Chapter Three from your manuscript. It is shit, so I flush it.'

Artists I can't commend either. They're worse rogues. They take liberties with your flesh. They muddy the shades of your skin. They place your pretty head on another's flawed body, or flatter some rich matron of the arts by stealing your best features for her to wear. So Effi von Hofmenstal gets to rest on my butt, and flaunts my pubis and thighs – as if my lap of luxury were her own. Because her husband can pay a premium on a hefty commission to get her so improved. Pity the poor artist's model. Everyone else gains by the arrangement, by which are appropriated her choicest parts.

Egon does the worst; for he distorts and diminishes. Some blame his eyesight, and diagnose astigmatism. Myself I blame his mind. He narrows my hips and shrinks my breasts. By the time he has finished painting me I'm a chicken carcass. All bones and bloody sinews. To add injury to insult, he makes unnatural suggestions of an intimate order.

I haven't always been so wise like now. Frankly, I was foolish. I made plenty of mistakes in life. Also, I sinned some. A few of my sins were original, but the best part were banal. Mostly, I do things I shouldn't –

rather than not do things I should. I liked to try most things, once at least. I've never been shy or lethargic.

A dismal thing happened in our family in 1909, and we were never the same after.

Our domestic arrangements had a lot to do with it. I don't mean our customs and manners – though they surely contributed – so much as the allocation of rooms, and comings and goings.

Our home – a four-storey mansion in the Twenty-first district, inherited from Uncle Adolf – proved a poisoned legacy, perching us precariously above our station, encouraging pride, the employment of domestic servants, and *folie de grandeur*.

In moving into no. 19 Straußstraße, we took over a cook called Lux, and hired a tutor for my brother August to coach him for the *Gymnasium*. Soon Uncle Carl moves into the attic, attaching himself as fixture and fitting.

One afternoon, tripping into to my parents' bedroom to have a dab of sympathy and iodine applied to a graze on my knee, I spy Peter, brother August's tutor, rocking on top of Mamma, whispering in her ear as if confiding something or other, while she gasped, eyes closed, her face strained in an agony of concentration.

I was ten at the time, and though neither innocent nor stupid held a dark hole in my knowledge. Hanky-panky was the size of it. I'd never seen the like before. I couldn't gag my curiosity.

'Why, Mamma, what are you doing?'

Both parties cease wobbling, oddly frozen, and turn to look at me, complicitly flushed, blurting out together:

'Proving a theorem of Pythagoras,' said Peter.

'Turning the mattress,' gasped Mamma.

'It's no wonder you're in a tangle,' I remark, 'if you can't agree what you're doing.' And I spun on my heels, humming Schubert's *Arpeggione Sonata*; I left them to the jerky business. Of course, I guessed something was up, having glimpsed Peter's bare bottom. And that Mamma came scurrying after me, pink, panting and pixilated, to caution me to silence, only strengthened my suspicions.

One Sunday afternoon, two years later, when Mamma had gone to visit Aunt Edith in Berggasse, I was struck by the whim for an apple to gnaw on. Skipping through to the larder, I chanced upon Pappa and Lux the cook. They were shoulder to shoulder, cheek to jowl, pulling together, then apart, frenzied by indecision, gripped by the theorem of Pythagoras. But, there being no mattress to turn, they were compelled to do it standing up. Nonetheless the geometries of the conundrum looked similar – though rotated through 180 degrees.

I've always had a streak of mischief, so I couldn't resist the question, which earned me a fresh answer:

'I'm helping Lux with her dumplings,' said Pappa. 'It's a surprise for Mamma, so you mustn't tell.'

'And I'm helping the master help me,' said Lux, her eyes rolling a forlorn apology.

I kept mum, telling nobody about this calculus. Absolutely no-one except my dear friend Emmi Pappenheim when we were playing doctor and patient.

We take turns to examine each other. We start at the head and work down to the waist.

'Emmi, you have a serious case of elbows,' I observe. Truly, she is bony.

'Lise,' she warns, 'you're suffering a severe attack of nipples. And this ...' her fingers graze my budding chest, '... if you are not careful, may develop into an outbreak of fatal breasts.'

It is a sweet thing, this curious, innocent diagnosis. Our glancing, trembling fingers feel the pulse of private places. There is more to hand than meets the eye.

We are shaped, scented and tinted so different, Emmi and I, and yet we are both girl. When her hand discovers in the folds of my skirt the depths of my lap, I start to squirm and squeal.

'Don't,' I demand, pressing her fingers firmer on to me, to force them to still.

Then she tugs away, flushed and haughty, tearing the secret seal that binds us, so I whimper at the split.

'Wait,' I tempt, 'I show you what grown-ups do.'

'You know?'

'Sure,' I brag, 'I've seen it twice – upright and lying.'

6

By way of illustration, I direct a re-enactment, casting myself in the man's role – since his seemed the more dramatic and rewarding part – instructing Emmi to hoist her skirt, as I grind my hips against hers. I was not unmoved by it. Emmi blushed, as required, for her part.

'I'm going to grunt,' I said, 'be warned. Groan, if you like. It's optional.'

'Ugh,' she squealed, 'it's filthy,' and broke away again.

Later in Vienna it becomes chic to talk of the 'primal scene', courtesy of the jottings of Dr F—, who alleges witnessing this business causes terrible trauma. That was never my experience. But perhaps I'm a special case. For, though I saw my parents doing The Business, I never saw them do it together.

My body was too public. All privacy I have in mind. Yes, when I grew into a young woman I was too liberal with my love, fearing an admirer might kill himself if I ever denied him this, that or the other. Like most delusions, this sheltered a kernel of sense and earned plenty of trouble. You'll see.

But, despite a difficult start, I've enjoyed a lavish life on this earth. I've had a rich past, or two. I was intimate with the famous. I could tell you stories you'd never believe.

It all concerns me, body and soul; and the young woman I once was, in rude health and artless innocence. It's a nocturne for desire. A caprice with variations. A sonata for skin and soul. After the fantasia, there's a fugue. With three-part invention; for a well-tempered soubrette.

It's no easy thing to tell. When I seek the words, I find the winding cavern of language stretches, empty and echoing, the length and breadth of my desire.

In a way it's a detective story. I was the detective – also my quarry. For my conduct posed the mystery. I presented myself with certain symptoms that demanded my prompt enquiry. Things went missing –

hours, valuables, reasons and such – and I often spent my waking hours dogged by an unspeakable sense of loss, nagged by an ineffable guilt. It is a terrible thing to know you are vile, and yet never understand why.

None of us are perfect. Discounting my distinction as an actress, I never lay claim. Except in facing up to my looks. For, between 1910 and 1935, I am celebrated as a sublime beauty. You'll hear more of my looks by and by, since they're central evidence to the case. As was my crushing sense of personal squalor. Since the age of fifteen, I was yoked with the incoherent sense of having committed some unspeakable sin of choking vileness.

It's opaque. The erotic is ever cryptic. The most profound and befuddling travel is around another's flesh.

Suppose you recline on an ottoman at quarter past three of the afternoon, before a tongue has split your lips, or a hand grazed your breast, or a thigh strayed between your own, you are lain back in time immemorial. Yours is the first and most innocent flesh, pristine and untouched, devising desire afresh.

Yes. I delighted to touch and be touched. My flesh was woken early. Mine has been a sensual life. Often I felt too much. It was my inclination to list to the sinister, to veer to the left-hand side of life. A large part of it I cannot tell.

Skin became my sacrament. I could never know enough – of its secretive pits, enigmatic sheen, its cryptic grain, teasing down. I took it silken, velvet and furred. Blanched and flushed. Cool and arid here. But there damp and hot. I took delight where its tints flush to disclose – amber, umber, scarlet – and its textures startlingly transmute – so it suddenly stiffens or swells – or glistens dewy damp.

There are seams and clefts to it, chasms and voids, gorges and peaks, where it is delightfully imprudent to dwell. And there I perched, or sank myself. And lapped the saline, sour juices. And gulped narcotic tangs. Was fingered by knowledge and prostrated by touch. And hurt.

It is an ancient country – another's body, with its shrines to love and life.

Ah, if you won't forgive an old woman her nostalgia, then we can't proceed.

8

My lovers are long gone. Only memory remains.

Most of this happens between 1909 and 1919, in Vienna, when I was young.

Play our music – try Mahler, maybe, and Richard Strauss – to hear our voice. Schubert's was the legacy. Franz Peter truly understands. It is profound: our sensuality, languor and exuberance, joy and melancholy.

Regard our portraits. See the art of Gustav, Egon and Oskar. We were no pale watercolourists. Our hues were richer then, and our texture thicker; for we were rendered in oils from a lavish palate. The entire spectrum was ours. We had some colours you've never glimpsed – now irrecoverably faded and forgotten. Also we had our reasons: too slippery for you to grasp.

Myself, I laid it on thick, on the canvas of my everyday.

On the wall of my room are two portraits of myself -- a photograph, and a gouache sketch by Egon. Both capture my face at the same angle; my vacant gaze grazes the viewer's ear and then is lost beyond. These pictures are framed six inches and seventy years apart. I am aged seventeen and eighty-seven. A likeness lingers – the ghost of beauty – taking me back to my golden days. I run away with my years.

Unchanged is the central parting of my hair, the sweep of nose, delicately sculpted curves of nostril, chiselled groove between nose and mouth, those long lashes, that dimple overhung by my lower lip, the crease of my chin.

But age has hewn her depths in my face, casting shadows. The eyes are sunk now. My brow and cheekbones arch out. Some creases line my brow, and loose folds ring my neck. Thin puckers radiate from the slackened lips.

It is as if the skin has been tugged taut then released: and all the elastic has snapped.

My eyes don't glisten like they did. The cornflower pupils are dulled milkily opaque. Lessons of Love. Tutor is Loss.

Often I compare the two images; beauty flaunted, beauty lost. The wear and woe of seventy years separates them – the raisin and the grape. The young girl is yearning. The old woman is glassy-eyed, wistful and resigned. Her other life is gone.

9

Time has etched harsh marks on my face. But I have chiselled my penny's worth from time. Bargain. Don't complain.

I'm striking still, in a blue-veined, chalky, furrowed way – like a marble statue, eroded by a century of deluge and drizzle. I talk now of my face. My body is beyond compare. Discretion is the best part.

It is a thin tangled thread that joins us, the girl and I.

She and I, and the many who come between us, are Liselotte Felice Sophia Constanze Berg, born 14 November 1895, in Annakirche-strasse, off Neue Markt, Stammersburg, on the outskirts of Vienna, to Johannes Peter Berg, Third Assistant in the Ministry of Education, and Irma Kete, née Nadherny, in the Austro-Hungary of his Apostolic, Royal and Imperial Majesty Franz Joseph.

She is a very pretty child, in a plump, pink, dimpled way. Folk often remark she's lovely. Her golden hair is woven into two plaits which dangle over her shoulders, or swing down her back. She smells of cornflowers and sandalwood soap.

Oh, yes. She's returning to me. Now I have the scent of her.

2

POOR, dear Uncle Carl is at the root of it. I tell you shortly. Be patient, please. Pity an old lady.

Don't expect too much of me. For years I was a froth-headed actress. Sometime a jailbird. Now, a dotty old woman. My education was the stage, casual café conversation, loose pillow talk, and some belated reading I do in prison. I only just start writing more than cheques, shopping lists and betting slips.

By ninety, one gets careless and confused; but old age entitles.

'What's this?' asks Desmond at the grocers. 'Carnal Love. £1 each way.'

'Forgive, an old lady's error,' I say. 'I give you the likely winner, 2.30 at Cheltenham, instead of my order.'

Perhaps, patience is due. Maybe it takes a few weeks' struggle before I overcome Literature. Then practice makes perfect. I struggle to get it right, but I tear my hair and plenty paper.

Anyway, I mention this because there are some things I forget to say last chapter. But as I am a feeble crone, you won't insist I go back and rewrite, and fritter *élan vital*. Nor waste ten sheets of paper, not at my age in life. Instead, I'll tell you quickly now what

11

I forget to say last time. I'll do it all fast. Then we'll move on. Listen!

Mamma is tetchy because her hands and ankles are swollen from rheumatism. Pappa works in the Ministry of Education. My brother August is two years older than me – sixteen, sarcastic and sardonic. Emmi Pappenheim lives next door at no. 21. Marie-Thérèse, our dog, is a terrier.

Oh, yes! And Pappa has a terrible, fearsome temper. One time, he shakes my bicycle to pieces when – without first asking permission – I'd pedalled to the Wurstelprater to take a ride down the Tunnel of Fun.

He gets angry for all manner of reasons, and sometimes just on whim. Then the family creep around the cavern of gloom he has quarried, shivering in the chill, careful not to sound their voice or show their face, for fear of being provocative.

We have an entire house to ourselves in a leafy street in Twenty-first district. So we are on the outskirts. The house is too grand, and Pappa could never afford it on his salary as Deputy Third Assistant if it wasn't inherited from Uncle Adolf who got rich in the cheese trade. So, as a family, we live above our station and are very proud. Especially Mamma.

There, it's done. Now we're back where we finished. And all the gaps are filled in.

As a child I am touched too much. At greetings and partings, family parties, I'm lucky to escape unfumbled. My hair is stroked, my back patted, my cheeks pinched, thighs brushed, my rump fondled. And you know – but never say – that a hand strays too far from innocence, pushes its stay, lingering beyond nonchalance, grazing a girl's privacy, deceiving appearances, loitering behind her back in the pleats of her dress.

I learn to be elusive. I'm the canny dog that won't suffer a stroke. When the move comes, I sway or skip away. Hands slide out for me, but reach upholstery instead, or tweak the folds of curtain where they sought my skirt. Lips are pursed on empty air. At the supper table, I rest my feet on the bar of my chair, and watch, beneath the fringe of the tablecloth, as the gentleman opposite plays footsie with the table leg, supposing he touches me.

Unwittingly I attract. Men are always so touchy, I grow wary of their handicraft. So, I treat it as a game of tag – and pride myself I seldom get caught.

Uncle Carl is Mamma's younger brother. He comes to live with us when I am thirteen and takes residence in the attic, where he shuffles about on slippered feet, descending for meals pink-faced, whiskers twitching, his receding fluffy blond hair combed backwards to mimic the crest of a tufted duck.

Pappa will pass him a steaming tureen of vegetables with heavy-handed generosity, and watches closely that Carl does not take a potato too many, act too liberal with the gravy or get over-familiar with the red cabbage.

'I expect you found employment today, Carl,' Pappa observes.

Carl covers his twitching mouth with a moist pink hand, as if to excuse a flatulence, and whispers through the fingers. 'I was not so fortunate,' he excuses, 'but I rose early and composed a poem . . . on the theme of springtime.' All Uncle Carl's remarks sound like apologies for the most intimate misdemeanours, because they are voiced with shamed, quiet gravity. When he asks you to pass him the pepper, it sounds like he's confessing a mortal sin or worse.

'So,' resumes Pappa, 'I expect you promptly went out and sold it, this poem, to some poetry merchant, august journal or literary society.'

'I was not so fortunate . . .' Carl swallows, 'and after a brief snack for lunch, I found the garden looked so lovely I was compelled . . . to sketch the flower beds.'

'You mean *dig*, surely?' Pappa asks.

'Oh, no, indeed not. I sketched them. If I'm not mistaken.'

'It's lucrative work, is it? Sketching flower beds?'

'Well . . .' Uncle Carl looks downcast at his loaded fork, 'it does not pay financially so much as spiritually. . . .' Then he starts chewing in an exaggerated fashion, to secrete himself in silence.

13

'As I remember, Carl, you were a clerk by profession – when last employed – not a landscape artist or lyric poet? Correct me if I'm wrong.'

'. . . bread alone.' Uncle Carl mumbles on his mouthful, darting a pleading glance to his sister.

'I think we all understand you, Johannes,' says Mamma. 'Carl is trying. He will find some fitting employment shortly.'

'At the Ministry of Blushing, perhaps,' hazards Pappa, 'or perhaps he will get a Royal Commission from The Imperial Society for Locking Yourself in the Bathroom.'

'Might I be excused?' pleads Uncle Carl, laying his cutlery in neat alignment over his half-eaten meal, then rising hunched from the table.

'That is the general agreement,' says Pappa. 'Why change the habits of a lifetime?'

And it is agonising publicity for Carl to shuffle those nine paces to the door whilst all eyes lie heavy upon him. He is so distracted, completing this lonely pilgrimage with dignity and decorum, that he brushes against August's elbow in negotiating the awkward left turn at the end of the table, and upsets a glass of raspberry cordial on to the damask tablecloth, only confirming Pappa's low opinion.

All the time the girl is clearing the table, drying the plates, she wonders what words of balm she can offer to console dear Uncle Carl. Because, although he butters no parsnips, he's very dear to her. I bound, whistling, up to his attic room.

'Isn't it horrid! How the grown-ups are always picking on us?' I protest. 'Do this. Do that. Make your bed, Lise. Earn your living, Carl. And so on. Why can't they let us be?'

Carl lays aside his volume of Heine and runs a lingering palm over her crown. 'What shall you do, Lise, when you're grown a young lady?'

'Marry, maybe. Else be famous. And you, Carl, what will you do when you're grown a man?'

'I shall be a writer of some sort.' His face twitches an apologetic grimace. 'Perhaps a poet, or essayist.'

'How old are you, Uncle Carl?'

14

'Thirty-five, Lise.'

'Better hurry, then,' I advise.

He winces: 'Why do you say that, Lise?'

So the child explains to him that Our Lord Jesus, Wolfgang Mozart, Franz Schubert – to mention but three – had done their best work, suffered and expired by that age. Beethoven, Schiller and Goethe lived long, but they'd found their *métier* early.

I survey the room. I have in mind a green box, about six inches by nine tied by a gold ribbon, containing rum and raisin truffles. We pretend, Uncle Carl and I, that these are his indulgence which he'll grudgingly share. But, in truth, he buys them just for me. Which is very thoughtful, given they're expensive items, and he's poor as a church mouse, and reliant on Pappa's charity until he gets back on his feet, which may take time, for he's grown as tenaciously attached to his armchair as a barnacle to rock.

'I suppose we are best friends, you and I, Lise.'

'Yes, Uncle Carl.'

'I am moved to sketch you,' he says solemnly.

'I should like that,' I smile, 'you haven't drawn me for four days.' It is a fine arrangement. I can be be admired and talk grown-up. He can stare through narrowed lids, and tilt my head, or rearrange my hair.

'Where did you live before?' I enquire.

'Gurtelstrasse. But there was a misunderstanding with the landlady.'

'And you were a clerk, then?'

'Yes, but there was a misapprehension with the ledgers, leading to a misconception of my work.'

'Money went missing?'

'There was some misappropriation of postage stamps,' Uncle Carl concedes sadly. 'I thought it best to leave, lest suspicion should fall on me.'

'Will you get another post soon?'

'Ah,' he sucks the tip of his silver pencil, 'I have misgivings. It isn't so easy when your previous conduct has been so badly misconstrued.'

'Don't worry yourself,' I console. 'I understand you at least, Uncle Carl.'

'There!' he says, laying aside his sketchbook. 'Time for a truffle.' He reaches under his armchair to draw out the missing box.

I take two. And complete the ceremony with the customary peck on his fevered stubbly cheek.

Because we understood each other so well, and made a collection of dried flowers together, and could speak our minds candidly, and had no secrets one from the other, and both smarted under Pappa's sarcasm and Mamma's relentless demands, and I'd procure cups of Pappa's brandy for him, and he'd supply bonbons for me, we grew very fond. And most evenings I would spend an hour or two sprawled on my belly on the hearth in the attic room talking to Uncle Carl, naming him 'Duck', on account of his look of perplexed dignity and waddling walk, whilst he called me 'Warbler', on account of I was pretty, chattery and shrill.

I suspect he'd become tired of Pappa's pleasantries, for Carl stopped taking dinner with the family, preferring to sup a bowl of soup and two slices of rye bread alone in his room. So it was he withdrew slowly into himself, cultivating no company but mine. I noted his decline and grieved for him. He rarely shaved. The lapels of his jacket wore the spillages of his daily soup. His hair hung lank and oily over his brown-rimmed collar. He'd quite abandoned shoes, shuffling around in his slippers – as if he'd resigned any intention ever to venture out in life. There was a foetid taint to his shuttered room.

On Monday mornings Mamma would shoo him down to the parlour while she cleaned his room. She'd descend red-faced with an armful of yellowed whites, hissing like a peevish goose. Then Carl, who'd been sitting rigid, wincing at the sound of doors opening and closing, fearing Pappa's premature return, would scurry up the stairs to his room, quick and nervous as a squirrel up a tree trunk.

'Shall we go sit in the public gardens, Duck,' I'd coax, 'and enjoy the sunshine?' For I want to draw him out of himself and his attic.

16

He'd flinch at the dangers of this exposure. 'Perhaps in July, I'll come,' he'd promise. 'When it's warmer . . . besides, someone might see me.'

'So?'

'I'm vile,' he whispers, his red-rimmed sparkling eyes moist, 'I'm useless, dirty, disgusting. Everyone hates me.'

'No, Duck,' I protest, 'I love you. So do we all, except Pappa and August.' I sense it's diplomatic never to mention Marie-Thérèse, the dog, who delights to snap at his ankles, as if he were an incorrigibly wayward sheep.

'I'm dirty,' he murmurs, 'I'm loathsome.'

'No, Duck, no.'

'If you knew the thoughts I have . . .'

'Yes?'

'You'd never come near me.' The lids of his averted eyes are all aflutter. His hands are wrestling each other. He's commenced a noisome sniffle. 'No woman has kissed me on the lips for seven years, Lise. What do think of that?'

'Seven years,' I suck in my cheeks to consider, then whistle, 'is a long time, Duck.'

At that age, kissing bemused me. Frankly, I couldn't see the attraction. Yet it seemed a key to the locked caboodle of adult affairs. All the grown-ups were at it: Pappa with Lux in the scullery, or with Frau Kessel; Mamma with Peter the tutor; August with Lotte Weferl in the botanical gardens; Uncle Carl with absolutely nobody for seven years, but still avid for any woman's mouth; Captain Moser with Aunt Edith, beneath the canopy of willow in the garden.

And once mouths met, there was no telling what could happen. Buttons would pop, hand slipped from sight, seizing liberties. Underclothes rustled. There'd be wriggling and shivering, moaning and gasping, flushing and clawing. Strong men went weak at the knees, toppled by an invisible force, dragging grown women down

17

with them, curtained by the long grass. Now you see them, now you don't: every Sunday in the fields around the woods.

One warm June evening, when Uncle Carl is sketching me, he speaks some phrases and makes some movements. I experience certain emotions. In due course I leave the room. Next day, he's gone.

I have contrary recollections of what takes place as the waft of wisteria drifts through the open windows, and we hear August practising Mozart's *Alla Turca* on the piano below.

I'll tell you one of these versions:

'I am going to Budapest tomorrow.'

'Why, Duck?'

'To become a famous artist, kiss women and become very happy and famous.'

'Good luck, Duck.'

'I will miss you, Lise.'

'I will miss you too, Uncle Carl.'

But years later, I remember a different version.

He reveals certain ambitions to me. I give him certain advice. Later, he'll follow my suggestions.

Well, he has his feelings. I have mine. I walk slowly to the door and let it click closed behind me.

'How is Uncle Carl?' Mamma asks, dusting a ball of dough with flour.

'Quiet,' I say. 'Sad. Dirty.'

'You'd think he could rouse himself.' She observes, 'Pappa will lose all patience.'

That evening, as I'm collecting Uncle Carl's supper tray from the kitchen, to carry up to the attic, I sense Mamma's staring down. I supposed she'd noticed something amiss with the soup, beef broth with noodles, Carl's favourite.

'What's that . . .' she tears at the collar of my blouse, 'on your shoulder?'

But I see nothing unusual.

'A lovebite!'

'What's that?' I enquire. 'Is it serious? Infectious?'

'Vile girl . . .' Mamma is blanched, quivering her sincerest anger.

I stand rooted in the kitchen doorway, shivering, the spoon rattling on the tray. My hands resign all strength. The soup pours scalding down my shin. The noodles slither tangled, like blanched worms, over my boots.

'Lise!' Mamma howls. 'Who did this?'

I cannot tell. It is too shameful. I quake, head bowed, in her shadow. 'Uncle Carl . . .' I murmur.

For Uncle Carl is waiting for his supper. But Mamma never lets me finish my sentence.

3

THE fact is he's gone – Uncle Carl. Why, how? The girl cannot tell, for her mind burns delirious, her body twitches fevered.

She's fallen. From the bridge at Stammersburg. You'd have to visit there to see how this can happen. You cannot view the heady drop beyond the low stone wall. A foolhardy child could vault over, to get to the other side of somewhere to retrieve a something or other.

So I tumble. The bank of the river leaps up to wrap me like a blanket. I am lain out, face down, on the slope. A fearful gravity is tugging me deep into the ground. My teeth clench on rye grass, clinging to this world.

I have broken my hip and arm. But worse, I have struck my pretty head an ugly blow, splitting it open like a breakfast egg.

I shall be lucky to survive. There is nothing anyone can do. Anyway, I cannot speak. Only groan, yell or whimper. I am in delirium, in perdition. It is inferno, a district of hell. I never disclose how the goblins use me.

I must make my own way, in sickness and in health; I must secure my own salvation.

I come. I go. Sometimes, I escape by an unlocked door. I climb, panting, up the dark, dank stairway towards the glimmer of day. My eyes blink open to daylight. Mamma wipes my forehead with a vinegar sponge. I rest awhile. Then I hear the demon grunting behind me. He tugs me back, down and away.

After a month, the crisis is over. Then my condition stabilises to a mystery. Between lucid hours, I fall back again to reverie. In all, I perplex three doctors and two consulting professors. My reflexes are normal and anomalous. I am declared hysterical and somatic. Doctor Flugel diagnoses mine a rare case of Comatose Hypochondriasis, predicting I'll recover to a state of feeble health or robust invalidity.

I tease the medical mind. I lose function then promptly recover it. My body vacillates between convulsions and unstirring serenity, sometimes with spasticity. To bemuse the doctors further, I will neither get well nor properly die.

When I fall sick, I am fourteen. When I regain my health, I am fifteen. I am not so much recovered as transformed.

The girl awakes a woman. I am born again.

For eleven months my body writhes, thrashing beneath the quilt. It grows, it swells, inflamed by fever.

When my mind cools lucid, I find a stranger's body in my bed. And I am wrapped inside her, trapped in foreign flesh. She has plump breasts. Her hips arch out, smooth and gravid as sculpture. Tufts of wiry hair have sprouted in clandestine places.

'Mamma! Save me . . .'

My life blood leaks out from her, in clots of gore.

So Mamma explains the curse on me, and shows me how to bind the wound. It is a bane devised by the brothers Grimm. The hourglass of my figure is made a calendar of flesh. I am enslaved to the moon. Phoebe has cast her spell on me. And every month I must weep a tax of blood. To pay tithe and tribute to the Queen of the Night.

21

This is the fate of martyrs and heroines. Then Mamma quite mars the myth. She tells me I make eggs.

She speaks as if this were a natural task for a girl.

Lay eggs, indeed. Like a chicken!

No. Not Lise Berg, Princess of Night.

I prefer to be enslaved to Diana, who has fashioned the temple of my body as a secret shrine of love.

'Brush your hair and wash your face,' Mamma commands. 'Child, you look a mess. If only you could see yourself.' She passes me the ivory-framed hand mirror, and shakes her head with regret.

Well, it is eleven months since I see my face. When I confront the looking glass, a sullen angel's face returns my sorry stare. I look startled over my shoulder. But we are alone; cousin face, sister body, and I.

Oh, God. My countenance. My features. I am quite defaced by beauty. It was bad enough being pretty. Now, I am hideously lovely.

And everyone will see. And want to touch and such.

My flaxen plaits are gone. My hair burns bronze and gold. It is alive. It crackles. It glisters and glimmers, writhing, as I finger the sinuous coils. The afternoon sun through the window lights a halo around my tresses. It is a fearful, tangled burning bush. I'm condemned for life to take this as my hair. And wear it as my own.

My eyes are wide; the pupils the palest, icy blue. They are shocking. Startling in their candour. They seem to look through me, then further. I blink to win brief privacy.

She scares me, this lady. With her penetrating gaze; her long, flickering saffron lashes; her fine nose, and flaring nostrils. So proud, so haughty; disdainful as an adult.

Oh, worse. That mouth. So lewd.

22

Broad iridescent amber lips are pursed in embouchure. I look like some fat-mouthed, smirking flautist, relishing his cue. Or as though I'm slavering over a gâteau. No. I mustn't pout so. I look some saucy coquette. Besides, there is something to these fat, labile lips that betrays me.

My shame! I shrink from their suggestiveness. Their hue, their moist split. They whisper of shapes elsewhere.

I suck them in and bite them. They must not humiliate me so.

I wonder how I can ever kiss Pappa again.

'Mamma, I have a bad dream about Uncle Carl. Where is he?'

She turns away, folding a sheet, as though absorbed by this task.

'He's gone to Budapest,' she says. 'I pray he's happy now.'

But his attic room is always locked. On the mantelpiece in the parlour there's an empty silver picture frame. You see the iridescent purple silken lining where his face should show.

When I am well enough to descend the stairs, I spend my afternoons sprawled languid on the chaise. I conceal my body beneath a blanket. I hide my face behind my favourite book – Schroeder's *Classical Loves of Ancient Greece and Rome* – and ponder the plight of poor Proserpine.

But Mamma prescribes visitors.

'Lise . . .' Cousin Felix gulps slack-mouthed, 'is it really you?'

I flush, shamed and angered, because he's guessed my pact with the moon.

He inspects those intimate features that form my face. He blinks and looks away. Then, holding his hand to his brow, he watches, green-eyed, through the slits in his fingers.

Felix is my almost cousin. His father was Uncle Adolf's partner in cheese. When the father dies, Uncle Adolf adopts Felix almost as son. When Uncle Adolf passes away, we inherit him approximately as cousin. Whatever the temptation to decline, we must grasp the nettle of Felix, having embraced the rest of the legacy.

We play *tarock*. I am irritable, and cannot hold my concentration. For I must swivel my front towards him, where my breast slumbers beneath my chemise. And I must disclose the lie of my lap, which holds the shrine to Venus, whenever I lay my cards on the table.

'Your illness has been kind to you, Lise.' Felix eyes me askance. 'You're grown a woman, and look lovelier than Juno.'

'So?' I spit. 'Is it my fault? Men have whatsits too.'

I will not have him spout mythology at me. I know he slyly touches upon my intimate sculpture.

'I've heard tell of vile things in trousers,' I warn him.

'I only meant . . .' he breaks into a stammer, and wrings his hands, '. . . to say you are very beautiful. Forgive me. I do not have the words . . .'

Oh, my! What change. I am swollen powerful, magical and dangerous. I read this in men's eyes.

We are complicit in our shame, men and I. I'm elected to the red-faced club of guilt. There's a sly, delinquent regard in their eyes that I've never glimpsed before. It is as though I've always caught them out unbuttoned, committing an indecency.

If I am bold enough to return their gaze, they promptly look down or away. Some flush. Other become agitatedly preoccupied – absurdly emphatic in their movements, like children under the eye of a stern teacher.

I no sooner look at man or boy than he spills his coffee, blots his copybook, stabs his foot with a spade, topples from his bicycle or becomes jerky as a marionette. Else freezes like a statue, in an inane heroic posture.

It was as if man is trying his utmost to look foolish to my eyes. Not even Pappa is exempt. Supper becomes a trial. Soup suddenly squirts from the side of his mouth when I beam my daughterly smile. I find my brother August gaping startled as I bite through my *bratwurst* or lick some crumbs from my lip.

Imagine. Some peasant stumbles drunk into a ditch one night then wakes to find himself become Emperor Franz Josef, lying under a

24

goosedown quilt. He thinks he is delirious, or the world deluded. Suddenly all men are sycophants. The great and good queue to bend his ear. And they listen to every syllable he stutters, as though to an oracle.

So it was for me.

Men would follow Mamma and me, as she led me by the hand down Wahringerstrasse.

'Do not look around, Lise,' she mutters, 'it only provokes them more.'

By the time we enter Votive Square, there's a swarm around us – of insouciant clerks, whistling errand boys, smirking soldiers and assorted loud riffraff. I feel as conspicuous as the nut seller, who sports a marmoset on his shoulder, chattering and clanking its chain.

Mamma must turn and stamp her bootee to try to scatter the men, like startled pigeons. Or, if they are reluctant to be dismissed, she must ask help of some gawping officer of the Empire.

'I fear you encourage them, Lise,' Mamma chides. 'It is most unnatural, how men follow you. I am a beautiful woman too. But when I walk alone, men never follow me.'

'But, Mamma,' I protest, 'I never encourage. It isn't I that entices them. It is my body. These men are staring at it. I believe they desire me, Mamma. . . . For I am built as a temple, where men can worship love. Perhaps it's my destiny to be a *femme fatale*. Men will die for the love of me . . .'

I don't understand how they come, these words. It is as if an Other is speaking through me. I shudder at my mouth's profanity.

Mamma stops abruptly. Her face glows crimson. She commences to slap my face. 'Coquette,' she shrieks, 'strumpet.' She pummels me with her fist. 'You stupid, wicked, wanton child.' Then she begins to batter my shoulders with her parasol.

She would have hurt more than my pride, and dented more than decorum, had not a pair of mounted Dragoons – breastplates ablaze over jet-black tunics, clipclopping a zigzag behind us – interceded on my behalf.

A lieutenant waved his sabre at Mamma, dismounted like a cascade of pots and pans, and pressed his breastplate into my face, nobly to defend me against further assault.

25

I am overpowered by the stenches of horse, man and leather, terrified both by Mamma's wrath and the mighty cold metal of the Imperial Cavalry, and petrified to have pitched the one against the other in hand-to-hand combat.

'Don't hit him, Mamma,' I howl. I fear that, like Cleopatra or Helen of Troy, I should precipitate a war.

Mamma considers the matter some days. She pays me plenty of side-ways chilling looks. Then steers me aside to discuss fates feminine.

'I should not have struck you, Lise. Not when you are so delicate in your head.'

'No, Mamma.'

'But what you said was wicked.'

'It was, Mamma?'

'It isn't the first time. When you were ill, Lise. You rambled too. Your mind wandered. Your hands also. You said dirty things. I'm surprised a young girl knows . . .'

'I did, Mamma?' I prickle and redden, I prefer she doesn't tell. I am familiar with my fevered mind. And how the demon used me.

'And when I come to you in the morning, you've torn your nightdress off, and scratched yourself. And your mouth twists in an unpleasant expression. You are muttering vile things.'

'Please, Mamma!'

There are things between my mind and I that never concern my family. I have some intimate shame.

'You've always had strong passions and strange fervour, Lise. You've always loved another too much.'

'I have, Mamma?'

'Your fall, Lise. Do you not remember at all?'

'No, Mamma, what?'

'No matter, Lise. All's for the best.' She strokes my brow, to feel for fever, and shakes her sorrowful head. 'You are too passionate, child. It is extreme for a woman. It mustn't lead you astray.'

'No.'

26

'You have an odd, compelling beauty, Lise. Men will always look at you. But you must not encourage them. The regard of strange men is inconsequential. You must not let it go to your heart or your head. . . . We Bergs are not a grand family, but society respects us. We are well known for our *gross* decency and honour.'

'We are, Mamma?' I sip my iced cherry cordial and nod encouragingly. I far prefer she tells me her stories.

'Will there be a prince and some kissing?' I guess. 'And the theorems of Pythagoras?'

She frowns. 'When you are much older – eighteen, perhaps, or nineteen – you will meet your prince. But he will not be a real prince. A royal prince . . .'

'No?'

'He will be a prince of law, medicine or commerce. And, if he satisfies Pappa and me . . .'

'Yes, Mamma?'

'Then you may marry him. And kiss him – in private – whenever you like.'

'Don't bother yourselves, Mamma. I don't want him. I know already. Not a doctor, grocer or lawyer. I should much prefer some artists, musicians or soldiers. There is romance to them.'

'But, yes, Lise. You will want him. He will be the one man in your life. You will love him to distraction. You will give him your precious body. He will adore you. Your life will be very happy.'

'One, Mamma? I am allowed only one?' Ditto with marzipan bonbons. At first she says: 'Only one.' But if I coax and plead, she lets me have another. Then one more. And so on.

'One,' she declares starchily, and raises one stern finger.

'But, Mamma . . .' I coax, 'suppose I get tired of the first? Or suddenly spy one better? Or have the whim for a different kind?'

Just suppose; if I'd already lain with a man, then I'd have used up my lifetime's supply.

She pales, still. Her mouth twitches mute. Her eyes close. Her twitching fingers worry the lace neck of her blouse.

At last she speaks: 'Lise, I hope you will not bring grief or disgrace to Pappa and me.'

27

But I would, I knew. It was my fate to become a beacon to men, and enjoy their attentions. My poor, dear parents would never approve. My beauty was a terrible thing. It caused suffering to me and many.

One admirer shoots himself in his parlour. Another cuts his wrists in my bath. The life blood squirts out from him, curdling in the scummy water. So when I come upon him, he's blanched as a dumpling floating in a bowl of *borscht*. A sorry sight. I never forget.

4

SINCE I first stumbled shakily from my bed of sickness and shuffled to recovery, peculiar, fanciful events had begun to trouble me.

I'd become a puzzle unto myself. And Mamma and Pappa worried for me. They thought that my sickness had gone to my head. They feared that I was touched.

And so I was, fingered by knowledge, hounded by doubt, teased by desires and discontents. But vague and innocent.

'How are you today, Lise?' Doctor Flugel asks, his ham-coloured face beaming, as if all were well in this world, and everyone healthy.

'Fine,' I murmur, 'only a little sad.'

'Sad! Sad?' He laughs a bronchial rattle, indulging my heresy. 'What do you have to be sad about?'

'Something is missing,' I say, 'in my life.' I name the lonely place.

'And yet she remembers nothing of her *accident* . . .' Mamma adds.

'This is how the mind heals itself,' Doctor Flugel announces. 'The young are so resilient. . . . Good. Wonderful. Fine. Well now. . . . Yes!' He and Mamma exchange glances. They suppose I never see.

'So you have no problems, Lise?' Doctor Flugel persists. He rummages inside his leather bag, rattling his hideous curved steel tools, such as are used for ripping babies out of women, sawing off limbs, or slicing you open from your belly-button up to your chin, to extract a septic liver. His hand emerges brandishing what looks like a timpani stick – dear God, I trust for external use only – and commences to tap my joints, as if I were some rickety furniture.

'No headaches, no pains, or disturbances of sight? No bright lights, strange sounds or smells?'

'No.' But I wonder how he peers so into the gloom of my mind. Does he also divine that seam of guilt, splitting me from head to toe? And my rattling emptiness?

It is too humiliating to be seen through, when I'm so debased, degraded inside. From now on, I shall never confide. I'll mist the window of my face.

The doctor insists to prick my palms with a pin, rap my knuckles with his wooden hammer, shine lights in both my eyes, click his fingers behind my ears. He has me close my eyes then tell him how many of his fingers are pressing into my upper arms.

'Curious . . .' he tells Mamma, 'the left-hand side of her body has rogue reflexes all of its own. Quick-witted but maverick. Whereas the right-hand side behaves quite properly.'

Later I'm to discover that the right-hand side of the brain controls the left-hand side of the body, and vice versa. Of course this confuses. But it's the same lifetime's handicap for everyone.

'When you write, Lise,' Dr Flugel enquires, 'which hand do you use?'

'Either. Both. But the left is clumsier. It always lags behind, and never forms its letters neatly.'

'Show me,' demands Dr Flugel.

So I arrange two pieces of paper before me and, taking a pencil in each hand, commence to write. By the time my dextrous hand has finished two lines of the Lord's Prayer, the sinister is still scrawling the third word of a naughty limerick, in shamefully large, gawky script.

'Extraordinary . . .' Doctor Flugel sighs, staring transfixed. 'Her hands work independently. Your daughter's in two minds.'

'Lise!' Mamma scolds. 'Don't act unnatural!'

But my laggard left hand is the least of my problems. I suffer mental symptoms.

I have blackouts. Hours go missing from my recollection. Sometimes, I mislay an entire night.

And, when Mamma reports I misbehaved myself, I simply cannot believe.

'Are you ready to apologise?' Mamma demands.

'Apologise, Mamma? For what?'

'For smashing the crystal fruit bowl. Spitting at August. Biting Pappa.'

'Mamma? I did all that?' It sounds *extrem*, as we say in Vienna: no compliment intended. My face giggles helplessly, my skin chills with goosebumps. This bowl was Mamma's choicest wedding present. I've injured the entire family. 'How can I ever repay?' I sob.

There is something most alarming.

Coins flee Mamma's purse and hide away in mine. Pappa's cufflinks go missing, and his diamond tiepin. He rages two days. The whole household is cowed, until he resolves to dismiss Lucie, the cook. Poor darling Lux. Who will make our dumplings now? And I feel – without knowing so – that I'm somehow to blame.

Weeks later I discover Pappa's valuables in a drawer, nestling shamelessly in the crotch of some camiknickers, where a gentleman's thingies never belong. I resorted to burying these resurrected items in the garden to conceal their second coming.

So a part of me is a sly thief; another receives stolen property; a third conceals the criminal evidence. *Mea culpa*. Forgive me, father – for I know what I have done.

Waking in the morning, my body informs she's been touched – felt. For I'm moist here, flushed there, throb somewhere else. I feel clammy, soiled and sad.

As in the delirium of my illness, my nightgown has been torn from me. When I sleep in bloomers, these get shed too – or fall from grace to shackle my ankles. Yet I can lock my door from the inside, and all the windows are quite secure. I've read *The Mystery of the Locked Room*, but there's no comfort in conspiracies.

31

It is a terrible and futile thing to try to spy on yourself, to keep abreast of your doings. There is a furtive part of you that does not want the rest of you to know.

Suppose you start keeping a secret journal which you hide beneath your bed. You write it diligently each day.

'Helped Mamma peel the vegetables. Polished the parlour furniture. Denied myself a second helping of lemon pudding. Practised my clarinet. Will try earnestly to be good today. And suffer a little for Jesus' sake.'

But next evening, you open the book to find an Other has ripped out the prior entries and scrawled – in a childish travesty of my own neat hand – a chilling warning.

—Snot ball. Slimy turd. Farty pants. I've broken your crucifix to teach you a lesson. And bitten your precious Pappa on his ear. Sore? Haha!! If I catch you spying on me again I'll stick your shitty clarinet up your guess what. Be warned!!!—

Also there are some lewd observations. And anatomical drawings.

This you read as a caution. You only trick yourself if you try to catch yourself out. And you've only yourself to blame.

The girl is naïve, but not so stupid. She knows her plight. There is an Other within her, who's wormed under her skin, who wills squalid actions and conjures vile thoughts when her wholesome mind is wandering.

This is a chilling discovery – that there is an enemy within, at war with yourself. However lovely my surface looked, it hid a hideous, vicious core.

I shuddered. Flushed with shame. And despaired. For I couldn't fathom the dark depths of *her*.

There were warnings of her comings. Golden starbursts would dazzle my sight. I'd smell scorched skin and singed hair. Also a whiff of cordite. There are shooting pains down the left side of my body.

The taste of Allgauer Bergkäse cheese on my palate. Then my feet are locked leaden to the floor as I turn heavy and frozen as marble. Then all goes dark — and my Other strides off in my flesh.

But sometimes she doesn't want my whole body — only my mouth. And she'll suddenly utter something too too shaming. I flush horribly. For everyone thinks it's me.

She speaks squalid blasphemies, pertaining to bodily functions (none exempted); or else makes candid observations about a person's appearance (comparing bits in view with the out of sight, separated by a torso). Or mortifying suggestions (bodily openings as storage spaces etc.). And cackles satirically for no apparent reason (when adults are voicing some heartfelt homilies). She insists on blurting — and in the rude vernacular — what others might think, but have the tact to leave unspoken.

'She's got a mouth like a drunken sailor.' That was Pappa's pained opinion.

Also she scratches me, unladylike, in public.

— Ooh, but my fanny itches, — she squeals as Mamma slaps her hand away.

Dear God, there's a trapdoor in my fate, leading to dark burrows. Like poor Proserpine, I must be split between the light and Shades, and live half with Mamma and half in the underworld.

When she is finished with me, I wake blinking with a migraine headache, and a sense of scorching shame. There may be scratches to my right wrist and arm. Sometimes, dribbles and stains. Her personal hygiene is never fastidious as mine.

Mostly, she comes in the evening. If I get those golden flashes in my vision, I'd hurry to lock myself in my bedroom. And toss the key on top of the wardrobe and throw myself on to my bed.

Once I wake sobbing at three in the morning, with blood flaked in the palm of my right hand. The gaslight is still aglow, so I see at once that she's bitten me horribly. Damp on my pillow is a note she's left for me, blotched, smeared by my tears.

—Shitbag! Sanctimonious bitch! Think you can can hide the key from me? I see everything you do! Take care. I'll do worse than bite if you try to cross me again. PS Pappa will have words to say in the morning, on account of what *you've* done. Can you guess? It's terrible. But if he gets beastly, remind him about doing *bumsen* with Lux in the larder. Haha!!—

Pappa and Lux, indeed! Haha! This trollop has some imagination.

I moon about. I gaze hours into the mirror, reflecting upon my narcotic face, searching for myself behind the stupefying image.

Or I lie on the couch, mournfully watching through the parlour window the traffic of the streets.

I watch the men pass down the pavement, sorting the beasts into types. The brisk pompous penguins. The shambling shaggy bears. The swaying, burdened oxen. The pink, snuffling swine. The sly, slinking dogs.

Ah, yes. And occasional lions and tigers. I am content, maybe, if in one day I see two tigers or one lion.

Beneath their different pelts – mangy or sleek – they share a sordid secret. Underneath their clothes, each and every one is nude.

The women chatter, so prim and correct. Yet they have breasts and such. But, watching their eyes, you'd think butter wouldn't melt in their lap.

Once you learn the uses men and women find for their private portions, you see the world anew.

There aren't signposts or hoardings but, everywhere, the trade's in skin. A prima ballerina costs two hundred crowns for a night, so brother August says. But he knows a Hungarian maid that can be had for an hour for one.

I narrow my eyes to watch. I imagine glistening trails of slime on the pavements, like the smears of snails. They crisscross and inter-sect, these shimmering mucus lines of love; betraying juices of the body, the weave and warp of desire.

But the maps of the city never chart these paths of passion. In Königstrasse, Herr Klingmann enters Frau Glanz, intersects the maid, then doublecrosses both with Fräulein Gott. But I should never have known – if I had not heard Aunt Edith whisper so to Frau Krebs.

And down the banks of the grey-green Danube, in the shadows of bridges, lie marshy lowlands, quicksands of desire. Couples come and go. They meet, combine, then briskly part. Some women are sucked into the mire. So Emmi says.

How strange. And, as a child, I never see the geography of the city. Never glimpse the sordid routes.

I've lived by declared rules. Pork goes well with cabbage. But Mamma cannot stomach lies. Men and women seldom mix. It is enough that Jesus loves us. Mamma told me so often that Pappa commanded five clerks and two accountants. She took such pride in saying so, I supposed a short chain of command from Pappa to God – with angels and saints as middlemen.

But now, I saw we answered downward too – to our flesh, its itch, flush, tremors and throb.

And, even if a man like Pappa is Emperor of an entire office, still he is laid low by twitchy, shuddering skin.

So I learn there are the spoken laws of day, and the whispered rules of night. There is civil order. But desire is rude.

There are public lectures and private lessons. There are train timetables posted for all to see. But the summons of passion are secret. There are menus on every restaurant table. And unspeakable appetites.

And in the juice and flesh of us, the unmentionable finds voice. Desire is the unspoken language.

The sham. I was deaf but now can hear. I was blind but now can see. Love makes us jerky mutes.

Ach, I am bewildered. I am beguiled. It is so squalid and so rich.

I know the corruptions of my body make me sumptuous and powerful, give me sovereignty over men.

My face twists mens' heads on their shoulders and dizzies their minds. I know that when men gawp at me their thoughts are turned elsewhere. Their imagination wanders down below; they poke their fancy beneath my skirt and petticoats.

All my life almost, Cousin Felix disdains me as a child. Now I am bleeding he slinks towards me, like a dog sniffing hidden meat.

Young man, you come on time. And so, you are too late. I am too lavish and rich a fruit for the likes of you. If I ever give myself, it will be to poet, prince or artist. A cheese merchant will never do.

'Felix. You've come again. It is the third day this week.'

And yet for fifteen years he stayed away.

'It is always a delight to talk with you, Lise. Alone.' He's hunched, eyes downcast over that gross beak of a nose, shifting his weight between his splayed feet, wringing his hands. Like a too, too shamed cormorant. He waits on my invitation for him to sit. I never give. Not to him.

He's clutching some strands of vegetation, and twittering proudly. Maybe he intends to build a nest.

'And you've brought a flower. For Mamma, I suppose.'

'For you, Lise. It is a narcissus.'

'But, cousin. Yesterday it was an orchid. If you keep bringing me a flower each day, I shall shortly have a bunch.'

He flushes. I believe he glimpses my silky, plump, pink thigh. For my dress has bunched beneath my rump, and so I'm exposed. Yet I did not seem to know.

Really! Such a flow of blood. The veins to his neck bulge and throb. All for a flash of lace and a squint at flesh. He's lost all bearings, gazing stupefied at a glistening triangulation of my skin.

'Felix, I do believe you've caught the sun. Do you not feel yourself? Perhaps you'd care to loosen your clothes and lie down.'

'No, Lise. But it is a sticky, torrid day.' He fidgets with his starched white collar. 'It makes me restless.'

'Then why do you not take me for a promenade? Mamma will not care.'

'A walk?' He considers the novelty. 'Where?'

'The Museum Café,' I say promptly. There and only there. Where K——, Loos. and Z—— gather. I have read of it in the *Neues Wiener Tageblatt.*

36

'Ah, Lise. That is unsuitable. It is a place for artists.'

'I do not mind,' I say, 'I could learn to tolerate artists. And I hear they serve a *parfait Palatschinken*, with oodles of *Schlagobers*.'

'I fear your parents would never approve . . .'

'Café Pucher, then, on Kohlmarkt, or the Frohner Bar in the Hotel Imperial?'

'They are not quite respectable, Lise. I am surprised you know of them.'

'Floge's Fashion Salon, then.' I concede my final lowest offer.

'Another day, Lise. Can we not enjoy a quiet talk together?'

'Very well, Felix.' I tug the hem of my skirt out from beneath me. It falls down to my ankles. If he will not take me somewhere smart or saucy, where I can enjoy some choice confection, with poppyseed and plum jam, and lashings of cream, or if he will not allow me to learn how artists dress, drink coffee, and eye me, he shall not enjoy the sight of me either.

'What shall we talk about?' I yawn. I hold my hand to my face, quite obscuring my left profile. 'Emmental, again? Or another cheese entirely?'

—Would you care to kiss my breasts?— *She* enquires quite conversationally.

'Pardon?' asks Felix, bemused, but strangely animated.

'I said nothing,' I remark severely, pinching my left hand, below the knuckles, 'you must be imagining things.'

—. . . or fondle my silken inner thighs?— *She* invites.

'Lise!' He lays a clammy hand in my lap. I feel the heat and moisture of it athrob through the cotton.

'Never . . .' I jerk up like a jack-in-the-box, and stride for the door '. . . touch me so again. Beast!'

I am locked in the dark closet of home. Now the world looks upon me so eagerly, Mamma hides me from its greedy eye. I am not to be trusted out, unless chaperoned by family. There's a supposition here that I'm safe from men at home. Myself, I have my doubts.

Only, I cannot be sure what is fact and which is fancy; in the narcosis of delirium, when I lay ill, possessed by a grunting demon, fevered, frenzied, I imagined he came to my bed, pulled back the quilt and lay down beside me, snuggled into my back, nuzzling the nape of my neck, reaching round my back to my breasts. So I'd turn on my front and push myself into the mattress. Then strain tight my thighs as his hand pushes to part them, or insinuates down through the cleft of my buttocks. All I can do is wriggle and moan, and turn to claw him or bite, if he will not desist.

5

I WAS troubled these nights by recurrent nightmares. There's a fat, fleecy, ginger rat, with red ember eyes, pink gums and chiselled, yellow teeth. Sometimes it hides in my petticoat, clinging by its claws; other times it nests in a drawer of my dressing table – leaping out squealing when I look for a personal item. We terrify each other – rat and I. Yet I sense we are kindred spirits; that there's a yen to be friends. But I can never bring myself to touch it. So we can never come to terms.

Also I dream of knocking on a bolted door. At my feet blind worms writhe through the eye sockets, wriggle through the mouth and nose, of a rotting skull.

One night, I'm woken shivering by the creak of my door. A finger grazes my brow, then presses across my lips, to caution me to hush.

'August,' I sigh. 'It's you. I thought it was another . . .'

'Hush, Lise. You were wailing in your sleep.'

His sombre face is hewn from dark hollows. Only his eyes glint. The gaze descends, glissades my slopes, down from my neck and shoulders to my breasts which shudder, night-veiled by my chemise. All glimmer is gone. I am eclipsed. His looming shroud on my bed overshadows my gloom.

Forgive, I write purple over black. But nighttime is my home.

'Go,' I say. 'It isn't right . . .' I am grown a woman now. Besides, he is my brother. An Other might not act so coy and proper, but then she isn't me.

— Kiss me though. Like a brother. Before you go. —

One afternoon, I am seated on my bed, tugging a brush through my coiling hair. My chemise, unstrapped, falls to girdle my hips, so I twist my trunk to watch the judder of my breasts. Oh, imperfection. The left is larger and hangs lower than the right. I cup it in my palm to assay its weight and worth. Its nipple rises inflamed by a touch. I splay my legs to spread my lap. My pointless finger skims the smiling lips of innocence. I don't know quite what to do with myself.

I watch the sober reflection of this in the chest-top mirror. It is important I know if a woman's desire is betrayed by her face.

In the yawning gape between door and frame, behind my naked back, brother August's hazel eyes regard me. And behind his still beguiled stare, I see another face. In the glass looms Mamma's grimace, as she spies August peeking at me.

Oh, the games we play before mirrors, in all innocence, with images, reflections on our impressions.

Mamma turns the key on us. She locks us in my room. She rages and sorrows over me. She shouts and sniffles by turn. It is her opinion I am turned wicked and vain.

She calls me a flirt. She howls that I am become a hussy and a Jezebel. She swears she will not allow me out alone, for fear I'll disgrace the stiff reputation of dead Uncle Adolf.

I'm neither vain nor proud. Merely astonished by flesh.

Mamma tells drily of woman's part, skirting the juice of it. But Ilsa Schroeder tells rich reports of what transpires when man and woman meet.

40

I am gorged and swollen to a woman's shape. This mysterious weeping realm, this body of rumour, is mine.

My blank face provokes fervour. It directs a man's mind elsewhere; there, between this and that, where a coy girl is loathe to disclose.

And this swell chest of mine that grew on me, to suckle babies, entices full-grown men. I see gentlemen squint at my front. So I shudder at this scrutiny, and blush. There is some proverb in the Bible to warn men off women's breasts – '. . . when I became a man I put away childish things' – but this I never say.

Yet the taut curves, silken touch and lustre charm even me. I shiver to the feel of them. Sometime, somehow, perhaps, I share . . .

'Do you want to be a *maderl*, a harlot?' Mamma demands.

'No, Mamma. That would never suit me. I shall be . . .'

—An actress, instead.—

Yes! *Quelle joie.* It comes to me insistent, that instant, out of an Other's mind. Certainty screams in my ear. Suddenly, I know my fate. I shall not be denied.

I recognise the Other's voice now, whenever it interrupts. It has a lower pitch than mine; and a rasping metallic timbre. Her voice sounds like a viola to my violin. There's a sneery suggestive edge, as if she knows more than I.

'Actress!' Mamma squeals. 'A painted woman. A lady of the chorus. A show girl. And make an exhibition of yourself. To an audience of hundreds!'

'Ah, yes, Mamma. If you please. That would be enchanting . . . I have the talent for it.'

Truly, for I fluoresce in men's eyes.

'Actress,' Mamma spits. 'Disgraceful!'

'No, Mamma. Actresses command royalty.'

'What?' she splutters.

'Kathi Schratt!' I explain. Enough said.

She goes sombre and quiet. 'Who talks about Fräulein Schratt?' she hisses.

'Everyone, Mamma. All Vienna knows . . .'

— . . . she does rumpty-tumpty with the Emperor. —

True. It was common knowledge that the Emperor Franz Josef was ruled by the actress Kathi Schratt, and lived in fear of her regal whims and tyrant's temper. And Kathi was fat and fifty – not a jot or smidgin as lovely as I.

'First spit on my corpse!' says Pappa. He is ominously solemn.

'The shame of it,' moans Mamma. 'The thought of it . . .' She cradles her head in her hands. 'A daughter of mine on the stage. I make all manner of allowances and indulgences for you, Lise. But that you become an actress I never permit.'

Our garden is fenced on both sides and to the rear. To the left, and friends to us, are the Pappenheims. On the right, shaded in their privacy, behind a canopy of honeysuckle and wisteria, are the Wolfs, secluded and haughty, shrouded in wealth. Rumour has it that they have two pianos and a harpsichord, maid, butler and cook.

One day Pappa dons his best suit and silk cravat. Mamma burnishes his gold watch and chain with chamois. He calls on Herr Wolf and invites him to contribute to a charity for Catholic Orphans. Pappa returns promptly, flushed. That is an end to the matter, or trade with the Wolfs.

Only, in summer we hear murmurs, peals of disdainful laughter, and clinks of porcelain as the Wolfs take afternoon tea in their garden.

I turn my back on them, to repay their insult to Pappa. You can imagine my dismay and annoyance when I am struck between the shoulders by an object; hard, small and forceful. I twist about and spy a small rosy apple on the ground. Elementary geometry tells enough. It has been thrown from the Wolfs' garden. When I hurl it back, I hear soft, mocking laughter.

'I can see you,' whispers a voice. It is a boy's. His tone is teasing and coaxing.

'Where?'

'Here.' There is a rustling, a limb of honeysuckle is quivering. And beside it, through a hole in the fence no larger than my hand, a pair of eyes regard me. Also protrudes a nose.

'I'm Lucian,' adds the mouth. 'Shall we be friends?'

'I'm Lise,' I say. 'And I cannot decide if I'll be your friend. I don't like boys who throw things. Also, I insist on seeing your face, before I promise anything.'

Oh, but his eyes are most persuasive; a deep turquoise, steadfast, inquisitive.

'Shall we "*du*" each other?' he enquires.

'Show me your hair first,' I demand. His eyes dip down from sight, as he displays a nest of raven ringlets above a high white brow.

'I must examine your hands also. Hands are very telling,' I warn him. And, polite and docile as can be, he extends a limp right hand. The fingers are fine and thin, like a pianist's – scrupulously clean and perfectly manicured. It is a hand I shake with equanimity.

'I can like you . . .' I admit it. 'Only, if we are to be friends, we must find a larger hole.'

'No,' he says, 'I have looked the length of the fence. This is the largest.'

'Dear God,' I sigh. 'Oh, cruel hedge! What will become of our passion?'

'Love will find a way,' he murmurs.

'Oh joy! Sweet Lucian!!' I confide to my diary. 'What great and innocent love we share.'

—Oh aren't we demure? Smug toad,— was scrawled the Other's reply the very next day. —Why do we peer through holes at boys when we can have whatever man we fancy? When do we get some fun? Why don't you let him touch your . . .— And so on.

We met secretly twice a day. Before breakfast and after supper. The evenings were most perfect. Yet we both needed the brief morning tryst. Just to soothe the chafe of yearning.

A hole in the hedge is not the most accommodating meeting place. But ingenuity and human hands can enlarge it. Lucian carved away at the edges with a horn-handled hunting knife. But we feared to make the breach too broad, lest we expose it.

If one stepped back, the other could view them. If both knelt close, their lips could brush. A girl could pass her tresses through: the boy could stroke and admire them.

'Pass through your hand,' urges Lucian, 'and feel the throb of my heart.'

'Now yours,' I say, 'and feel the lump in my chest.'

'I yearn . . .'

'And I!'

'Pappa!' I demand at supper. 'What do you know of the Wolfs next door?'

'Their religion is not ours. Herr Wolf is a banker,' he says, 'and rich as Croesus. And don't eat with your mouth full.'

I gulp down a forkful of cabbage. 'Would you say, Pappa, that it is correct to call you a *petit bourgeois*? And boorish bigot?

'Certainly not. That's Red-Party-Jew-piffle.' He turns to raise eyebrows to Mamma, and inadvertently spits a lozenge of spinach, which glistens pretty as an emerald in her hair. 'Who could say such a thing?'

'Just asking,' I say. 'I was curious, that's all. . . .' For I will never break the confidence by telling what I hear through the breach in the wall.

One evening I sense the Other is coming, from the telltale golden tadpoles wiggling at the edge of my sight. I slump forlorn on the stairs, tugged by a leaden despair.

Imagine my dismay when I wake blinking amongst the lupins in the flower bed – with no memory of going there – to observe a disembodied arm reaching through the hole in the hedge, its hand lost from sight beneath the folds of my skirt. I shiver as unseen fingers meander, beneath the lace hem of a girl's last defence, reaching to the depth of her purity. I sense an intrusive digit wiggling moist, smooth and sly.

Worse. My left hand is obscurely engaged, poking through the hedge, touching upon something firm and fleshy, I know not what, there on the other side.

I watch appalled, struggling to grasp the meaning besides. My thighs are splayed wide, jerking purposefully beneath my skirt to a private rhythm of their own.

'Aagh!' I pull away my hand to slap his down. 'Never take advantage again,' I hiss.

'But Lise . . .' Lucian's lovely sea-green eyes peer through the gap, rolling bewildered. 'You said . . .'

'Never,' I howl. 'Not I.'

Life gets so awkward when you share your flesh with another. You are always called to account for things you never said or did.

I suffer a bad attack of duplicity. There used to be one of me. Now, this intrusive double-crosser makes it two. People cannot trust me. Nor do I trust myself.

Some other symptoms I'd noticed, concerning the conduct of my left hand:

At supper, when I'd eaten a satisfying sufficiency, I'd lay my knife across my plate. But the left hand *will* continue shovelling food with its fork, stuffing my mouth, though I'm already full. It's *her* – greedy girl – that goes on gobbling at the trough.

And when I open my wardrobe, or drawer, to choose my clothes, I find that both hands have plucked an item, or are wrestling to secure their preference. Flimsy items get torn.

Invariably, I side with the sensible right hand, agreeing with her selection. For the taste of the left is for anything gaudy, or the violent cymbal clash of colours. Yes. Cerise skirt and saffron blouse. Together!

A hole in the wall gets you so far. No further. Yet I never tire to crouch there, in the flower bed, behind the purple and yellow irises, whispering to Lucian, my love.

45

'Shall we marry?' asks Lucian. 'When we are older?'

'I am sure of it. For I have never loved another like you. Never in my fifteen years.'

We lay fingers on fingers. Then retract our hands, so our lips can meet and part in the frame of the hole.

'Yet so much keeps us apart . . .' sighs Lucian.

'The fence,' I agree.

'Our families. My parents' respectability. Your family's reputation . . .'

'Yes, Lucian?'

'If only we could be together . . .'

'To hold each other,' I improvise.'For life.'

'Yes, Lise.'

Perhaps we are slow on the uptake. Else, secretly, we embrace the barrier, and must be separated to stay together. But it is three weeks and four days before we devise our assignation: to meet, in clandestine night, beyond those walls that heartlessly divide us.

'Midnight. Yes, Lucian, at midnight. In the park.'

'By the fountain. Next to the statue of the lion, there's a mulberry bush . . .'

—Mm!—

6

LOATHSOME things! Bestial! They terrorised my youth. I only had to hear that sudden swish, like the drawing aside of a curtain, or casting off of clothes, and my heart would hammer my breast. The startling abrupt erection, the taught silky sheen, made me gasp and shudder as the dismal shade falls over me. Somehow, a lady's parasol never caused the same alarm. Umbrella!

There. I've scribbled it. For you it's easy enough to write that word. For me it's a triumph of will. For a long time in my youth I couldn't abide them. You can imagine my agony to be caught walking the streets of Vienna when it suddenly starts to rain. You find yourself fleeing through a forest of the beastly things. No direction yields relief.

Poor Psyche, so lovely she makes Venus cast her jealous spell. All eyes admire her, but none – neither prince, king nor commoner – will ask for her hand in marriage. So it was with me.

Another coincidence! Like Psyche, I am visited by a phantom lover, at night, as I toss delirious. Yes! Strange. But I never see his face. For he comes in my dreams, and deserts me at dawn. Ten or a dozen times my demon Cupid came, feeling me with his fevered fingers, splaying my thighs, thrusting deep within my surrendered body, releasing me abandoned and shivering at dawn.

Yet in the lunacy of hallucination, I mark him out, that I'll know him should we meet in a sane and lucid time. Every time he comes my nail carves a notch in him, gouging the skin of his shoulder. Because, when he touches me in my delirium, it is as though he moves me for real.

One night, I dream I wake. And see his golden locks, and snowy face. Immediately, he's gone. And never comes again. The most shaming part of it? Though he's used me so lewdly, I'm desolated by loss. It is a tragic fate. I know from Schroeder's *Classic Loves*, Psyche must undergo fearful tribulations before she regains her Cupid, and bears him a daughter whose name is Pleasure.

It becomes an affectation men later remark on – when I am a woman of the world – how I am avid to examine and finger their shoulder, to search for telltale signs.

Of course, at fifteen, I know nothing yet of Historical Materialism: I must wait ten years before Bertolt tells me the good news about the Utopia consequent on Inevitable Socialist Revolution. But my diary becomes an unwittingly dialectical document; what with my thesis, the Other's antithesis – not to say antipathy – reconciled in some synthesis of my doings.

At first, I was cowed by the Other. I was a prim, decent girl. But she was so bold and brazen – the pushy strumpet. No! Worse, perverse.

How else to describe a voice that cackled obscenities, an eye that perturbed passing pastors by winking at them, fingers that pocketed whatever came to hand.

And what injustice! She could do whatever she fancied. Always I carried her can. Struck dumb by her unspeakable doings. But answerable for them.

She slyly slinks away, leaving me to bear the blame.

Yet, in the contest for my conduct, I held the stronger hand. Mine was the right. Hers the left. I kept control in the daytime hours. She woke late at night, and was drowsy by the morning.

I confided to my secret book, 'You vile, horrid part of me. I'll give you no encouragement. Pray God, you'll go away, and leave me pure as Mary.'

The Other was quiet and thoughtful for two days, before scribbling a brazen reply.

—Hypocrites! Whited sepulchres! They're as bad as me, only they won't admit it. Piss, snot and shit, to the lot of them, — she scrawled, —I'll do as I like. And no-one will stop me. —

Innocence comes in many unlikely guises, so when her Lucian stumbles through the haze for their midnight assignation, Lise does not recognise him. She is conjuring in her mind a different boy, composed only and entirely of his glistening curls, complexion white and damp as dough, those cherry lips, turquoise eyes, and absolute devotion.

'Oh, Lucian,' she gulps, 'save me. There are demons abroad. Wrap me in your arms. Clutch me, save me.'

The grass sparkles dewy. A gauze of mist is hung over the ground. Her fingertips clench a crevice in the bark of the oak. It is a sinister hour to wait.

For a bow-legged dwarf with a huge square head is hobbling towards her.

'Lise?' he hisses.

God spare her She has pledged herself to a goblin!

'Lucian!' She steps out from the shadow of the tree, into the gloom of her predicament.

They embrace. But she cannot cling to him with the rapture she'd imagined. Rather, she enfolds him loosely in her arms, patting his back with cautious restraint, as if burping a puking baby. How, she wonders, do so many pretty features combine to contrive such an ugly whole?

She gazes down sadly on his flat, matted scalp, pressing itchily on his neck. She inhales his odours of wet wool, herring and camphor.

'Lucian . . .' she says, 'don't gasp so.'

'It's my weak chest, Lise. This damp night air is bad for me.' He breaks into a racking cough, summoning up some reluctant phlegm, by way of illustration.

'Help me, Lise. I slipped on the path and grazed my wrist. I've lost a glove in the dark. We must find it, or Mother will surely scold me.'

They were the last lucid words she hears from him. She cannot bear this disenchantment. For she came to bask in a radiant passion with a hero, not skulk in the dark with a panting dwarf. She came to grasp a great love, not rummage around for a mitten.

She's a practical girl. She knows the course she must take. Promptly, she's spun on her heels and is scampering homeward, leaping puddles, gulping the frosty air.

Poor Lucian! He cannot keep abreast of her. She hears his heavy trudge and receding breathless yelps. But she never looks back.

The next few days, she never visits the garden. She fears to see the recriminatory hole in the fence, and desperate rolling eyes peeping through.

When Mamma insists she gets some parsley from the herb garden, to garnish buttered potatoes, she sees from the safe distance of the path that the hole in the hedge has been blocked; patched over from the other side.

The next time she meets Lucian Wolf is five years later. He has become first violin in the Metropol Orchestra.

It makes me weep some, for he plays the Brahms *Concerto* like an angel. He even composes his own cadenzas.

The girl begins a long campaign to convince Mamma and Pappa of her sincere ambition – to act. There are plenty of shouting matches, tantrums, and long quiet intervals broken by the tinkle of falling glass.

The girl and her Other act in concert for once – sharing a dramatic ambition.

'Let her apply then!' Pappa concedes. 'Please God we'll get some peace at last. How does she summon the strength to kick through a door panel?'

'Like father, like daughter,' sighs Mamma. 'Temper, temper.'

So the girl earns her chance to present herself for competitive examination at the Dramatic Academy, where the pupils are brilliant and the professors were once luminous stars of the dramatic stage. It is nearly quite more fabulous than the Conservatoire in Paris, almost.

The panel of examiners have her wait three hours to see them. When her name is announced, she is led into a large studio. It is a charming room. On three walls there are mirrors, reaching from floor to ceiling. She can see the jury from all angles, front, side, and back. They are two bulls, a dog, a tiger and a weasel. She studies their stares with some satisfaction.

'Why do you wish to become an actress?' barks the dog.

She owns up to a profound talent and great beauty. She confesses an ambition to win the love of monarchs. The jury mistakes this for wit.

'What are your talents, girl?'

She confides that she can command the admiration of men, cry at the drop of a hat, imitate all manner of persons, and is expert in all deceptions. Also her voice is beautiful and loud. Of course, she never mentions she is vile to the core.

'Very well, Fräulein. You may recite for us.'

'Recite?' she asks. 'What?'

'Your piece!' growls the cur. 'Surely you do not come unprepared?'

But she has no piece. Her Mamma and Pappa did not warn her. She is livid at their betrayal.

In Theatre, Despair is never allowed. Instead you must Improvise.

In her hand she clutches the Prospectus. She opens it at page 2. This declares the rules of the Dramatic Academy. She sings the first five regulations, concerning attendance and the prompt payment of fees. She renders these in the manner of Marcella Sembrich, as if written by Hugo Wolf, to a tune by Richard Strauss. It is very melancholy, and makes her sniffle. So she is startled, then, when the jury chuckle.

'Cry, Fräulein!' shrieks one. 'Weep buckets.' So provoked, she does.

'Laugh!' commands another. She cackles so loud that the door rattles on its hinges.

'Show us your legs!'

The child reveals more than her willing nature, drawing up her skirts above her knees like a theatrical curtain. But she fears they are making free and loose with her. She draws a mental boundary – a no man's land – above her garter, level with the hem of her bloomers. Beyond, she won't disclose. But the gauche hand suddenly jerks her skirt higher.

'Recite . . . the Catechism!'

Well, she cannot remember the part exactly. But she speaks her abridged, unorthodox version. The first portion she tells, blankly confused, like a station announcer. The rest – to display a dramatic range – she tells in the wheedling tones and ripe patois of Herr Schramm, when he is hawking elderly fruits from his barrow.

The jury dismiss the ingenue in high humour and with an impromptu burst of applause.

Her Mamma and Pappa are smug and content with her breathless, blurted story of the examination. Imagine their consternation when, within two days, a letter arrives awarding her a scholarship.

For a week, battle rages. She must blubber and snivel, roar and rant. Though the efforts drive her ravenous, she forgoes three lunches and two suppers. She shivers, vomits, coaxes, pleads. Mamma raves. Pappa is implacably cold. She returns their coin, acting them by turns. Only, she's more more vigorous and heartfelt. For she grapples for her fate. Frankly, she strains her voice. It is as yet untaught. But she must force it to extremes – from *sotto voce* sincerity to fortissimo frenzy.

She swears she'll fall ill again. She has several blackouts to show so. It is reported she breaks seven panes of glass in her bedroom windows, but this she never remembers. It was never her, but an Other.

—I know all about you and Peter the Tutor,— she howls at Mamma, when Pappa is out.

—Not to mention Lux!— she raves at Pappa, when Mamma has gone shopping.

She retreats to the top landing of the house, and sits for hours sobbing by the locked door, until Pappa and August wrestle her down to her room.

Next day, her parents declare peace. But on certain conditions. According to this Treaty of Vienna, she has to promise piety to God and chastity to Mamma. Also absolute obedience to Pappa. She pledges not to talk to men, except if they address her on stage, and always to be back by eleven. Finally, her parents warn, they expect her to grow out of it – this passion to display herself.

There are practical problems in getting to the Academy. The family home is too far away from Lowelstrasse for her to attend punctually in the morning. So, during the week, and when she rehearses weekends, she must stay with Aunt Edith in her apartment in Berggasse.

She eavesdrops her parents' talk of it.

'If she has to invent and act up,' sighs Pappa, 'better she does it on stage than in the parlour. Perhaps it's good, after all that's happened here, if she lives elsewhere for a while.'

'But I fear . . .' sighs Mamma. 'She hasn't come to terms . . .'

Oh, joy! They are very fond, Aunt Edith and Lise. They compete to see who can gobble most *Linzertorte* or *Marillenknödel*. Sometimes at a family party Aunt Edith will furtively dose Lise's raspberry cordial with schnapps. Although Edith is forty-eight, and a widow, she is not quite grown up. She is much given to winking. Her laugh is too loud. By evening, her voice is often slurred. She is more indulgent and liberal than Mamma.

'You must not take advantage of Aunt Edith's good nature,' says Mamma, 'nor abuse our trust in you.'

'I abuse, Mamma? What can you mean?' Lise smiles, already plotting her liberty.

'You know!' says Mamma. But she does not elaborate for fear of giving helpful suggestions.

Of course, the girl intends to keep her promises – insofar as is proper and practical. Yet she's fearful for the conduct of her Other side. For if the love of princes is at stake, and there are liberties to be taken, then there's no accounting what *she* might do.

When she begins at the Dramatic Academy, she takes classes in Melodrama, Declamation (including Tenderness and Fury), Deportment, Fencing, Comedy, Voice, Sincerity and Cosmetics. The second term, she adds Character, Mime, Dancing and Classics.

She is brilliant. In her first-year examinations, she takes the gold medals for Female Character, Emotional Volume, and the silver plaques for Comedy and Melodrama. Also, she's Commended *Cum Laude* for Conviction. Only the Sash for Subtlety eludes her greedy grasp.

7

OH joyous times, of luminous happiness. When the girl is on stage, she's never afraid to be entranced or lose herself. The Other and she act in concert once the curtain's up.

Years later, when I tell friends about my time at Drama Academy, they barely believe.

'I knew Herr Hitler then. . . . Yes, the *Reichsführer* was always pestering me.'

'Lise! All lies,' they splutter. 'You're surely fibbing.'

'It's true,' I protest. 'I give him some career advice.'

'And?'

'Unfortunately he takes it.'

'What was he like, in those days?'

'Much the same – sly, sullen, gawky and stupid. He had a big problem with his personal hygiene. And a bad stammer. Big difference, I notice now, is he's gained a lot in confidence. And people don't laugh at him like they used to . . .'

Between classes, Minna Levy and Lise sip tea or cordials at the Museum Café, by the small oval oak table to the right of the door.

Here all must see them: all customers who subscribe to the door. These chirruping girls become known as afternoon decorations of delicacy and charm. They are much appreciated. Kessel buys them eggs and sausage, Kosmak always bows to them, Osen does a jig for them, Rainer sits alongside, sketching their giggling faces. There are many and varied invitations. Often they are distracted by pleasures and must forego their late class in Deportment or Dramatic Feeling. Still, it is Education.

Surly Adolf Schickelgruber hawks his postcards from table to table. Lise never buys, because she heard Loos say they are *kitsch*, and a discredit to art. But it is a sad story for too many. Schickelgruber applied to the Academy of Fine Arts as a Painting student, the same year as Egon Schiele. They would not take him. Neither would *Kunstgewerbeschule*. This makes him bitter.

He rolls his eyes and pleads for Lise to buy.

'Ten thalers each. A crown the set,' he wheedles.

She knows he needs a friend. But she despises his weakness – callous girl – and can't abide the taint of rancid oil and onion that lingers in his wake.

'*Klein Dolferl*, face facts. Find another craft. You aren't an artist. Better chance you get to be Chancellor.'

He winces and shuffles away. After some months he disappears entirely. There's no sign of him. Not a sniff.

He changes his name to Hitler. Makes a fresh start. Years later, he is too well known in politics. Then the former customers of the Museum Café regret they never bought his postcards, nor encouraged him in art. Too late. Another story. You never can tell.

In the girl's class at Drama Academy there is another beauty besides her, named Karl Graf. Lise cannot believe his self-regard. Always they are paired as leads in a play, so she must spend a deal of time watching his hideous, hateful, arrogant looks – his mane of gold coils, his uncanny violet eyes, taut cheeks, dimpled chin, lewd split lips, ivory teeth, muscular torso, narrow hips, bulge of buttocks, lithe legs, strutting turkey walk.

56

He is too vain, on account of his superficial resemblance to Adonis and his lucky proficiency in making an audience weep at tragedy or cackle in comedy. Often he offers Lise advice as to how she might play beside or behind him, react to his lines, keep out of his spotlight, and decline to trespass between himself and the spectators.

'Fräulein Berg . . .' says he, formally – for he never calls her Lise. He speaks with quiet, peeved gravity, in a throaty purr that can – by some freakish resonance – make timber tremble, glass whine, and novice actresses shiver. 'Why do you brush your hair whilst I am in my death throes?'

'It is a dramatic conceit I just invented, to show the callousness of Medea's character.'

'If you persist in it, you will draw the audience's eyes away from me.'

'Yes, Karl. This gives contrast and interest. For you spend a long time dying.'

He nods, flickers his eyes, and reveals his teeth in a way he supposes entrancing. 'Perhaps, then, I should add my invention too. I could walk on my hands during your monologue.'

'All right, Karl,' Lise concedes, 'I let you die in peace.'

Though he is pushy and vain, and has to be nudged to move from centre stage, there is something to him that attracts her. Offstage, too, they are often together, side by side at the mirror, preparing their performing faces.

Shoulders or hips brush, her reflection smiles at his. His eyebrows arch momentarily.

'You look handsome tonight, Karl.'

'Perhaps, I looked finer on Tuesday. There is a blemish below my chin.'

'*Ach*,' she consoles him, 'only a pimple.'

'No, Fräulein Berg. My skin has *never* suffered a pimple. And where . . .' he demands, 'is my comb?'

'This?' She hands him the one she uses. She grazes a finger down a groove of his knuckle.

He shudders. 'Please, Fräulein,' he fastidiously flicks away the keepsake of some golden strands she's left for him, trapped in its teeth, 'use your own. Not mine.'

And she wonders how this man can respect a woman when he so disdains her tresses. Intimacy must be a distasteful business for a man who can't abide the touch of another's hair.

'Minna and I take refreshment after the show. The Museum Café. Perhaps you care to join us?'

'I do not drink wine or spirits. Alcohol can diminish an artist.'

'A coffee, then?'

'It is enervating.'

'Warm milk?' she suggests. 'It's very calming.'

'I do not trust the glasses in cafés. They are seldom clean. Another's mouth has . . . Anyway, I promised to meet Oskar.'

'Don't bother yourself,' she spins away, flushing, leaving him to the regard of his own impassive image, 'I don't care for you myself. Not a smidgin . . .'

—It's Minna, not me, that wants to hump you. —

But it isn't just Minna. It is all the girls, and the wardrobe mistress, the prompter, Professor Burckel, the cleaners, and Otto Kautsky.

Lise, herself, is not immune; she'd like, perhaps, to rehearse with him a little. Brush dry lips, lock fingers, run a hand through his mane, open a little to his touch. She is a bud that will unfurl.

If Karl knows this, he does not show it. Only the audience may have him. And he keeps a sanitary distance from them, lest any of their number are dirty. It is sufficient for him to be popular with himself. Oh yes, and with Oskar Kesselman.

'*Quel dommage*! What a waste!' says Minna. 'I blow him a kiss. And he frowns and looks over his shoulder.'

'You'd think he'd like *me*, at least,' says Lise. 'But perhaps he envies my beauty.'

'Mmm?' observes Minna. Lise scents a doubt, whiffs a challenge.

'Myself, I don't care for him a jot. His beauty is only skin-deep. His genius is shallow. But I bet I can win his regard.'

'Bet what?' says Minna.

'Lunch. A platter of *Schweinsjungfrau*, with *Spinat* and *Rotkraut*, and a bottle of *Zierflander* to boot.'

'Done!' Minna giggles. 'I give you a week.'

58

Well, she wants to persist with this boy, and will not resist his challenge. She imagines how he might press upon her heart, and taste his mouth in hers. It is certain that he will desire her, once she draws open the veil of his vanity to disclose herself to him.

Tuesday, she gives a muted, depressed performance, so Karl gets all the applause. He nods his approval as they exit right.

On Wednesday, the good is undone. Her chest is bursting its bodice as they stand powdering themselves at the mirror. A nipple blinks out, crimson-eyed, startled erect by the light of day. Of course, it is the left one.

Karl grimaces his distaste. Lise is distressed and bemused. No-one has ever had a bad look for her chest before. Most men cannot see enough.

Next night, she simpers her admiration and dresses demure. She ventures to Karl he has great projection and forceful presence. He is not surprised. He nods his assent.

Lise begs he coach her. He regrets he hasn't the leisure. But he mentions four defects and suggests she secures the professors' corrective advice.

Thursday, Lise ignores him: he doesn't care. Friday, she competes to act him off the stage. After, he asks her why she mispronounced some syllable in scene two.

Well, she concedes defeat. There is only one more thing she has to give him. It is a pointed gesture. Subtlety isn't her strongest suit. She shows him what she thinks.

'Here Karl,' she mutters, 'I have bought a small gift for you. I believe you'll never tire of looking at it.'

It is a small gilt mirror in a leather purse: pigskin, to labour her point.

'Lise,' he purrs, he glows, 'it is exquisite .' He shows her how it fits snug in his jacket pocket, and how well the leather matches his wallet, how the mirror stands steadfast and upright – courtesy of a folding stand at the back.

His cool dry lips graze her cheek. His hand pats the small of her back. They go for a celebration drink. He hazards a glass of mineral water.

She has an hour of crystalline contentment before intoxication blurs her evening.

Minna has to buy Lise the platter of pork. 'How did you do it?' she gulps. 'He can't stop smiling at you. And twice I see him wink.'

'It wasn't cheap. This is no free lunch. To win that man, I have to give him everything he wants of me.'

'Oh, Lise,' she whinnies her disbelief. 'You tart.'

But, in truth, she disclosed no more to him than his own reflection. She'd never met a man who liked himself so much, or was quite so blind to her beauty.

Of course, there's a moral to the tale. Otherwise I'd never waste your time with the telling.

A year later, Karl is killed in an automobile accident. He is crossing Babenbergstrasse when he freezes, struck by his handsome reflection in the smoked glass of a limousine window. He who hesitates is lost. Promptly he is struck again – from behind – by a vegetable lorry, turning right out from Getreidemarkt.

Lise doesn't see it herself. But, by chance, Otto Frank is in the front row of spectators. He reports that Karl gathers a big audience and dies theatrically, like a real trooper.

'The crowd were mesmerised,' Otto remarks. 'Karl gave them everything, bar an encore.'

The advantage of being an actor is that you get to practise all of life's blows by proxy, before they strike you for real.

Of course, when she hears the news, Lise regrets she ever bought Karl a mirror. But she knows his self-regard was well established by then. And she only encouraged him a smidgin.

8

I WAS properly flummoxed by my innocence, I can tell you. It was such a curious, complex conundrum, vague and tangible – both abstract and fleshy. Mamma had instructed me most particularly to hold mine untouched for a husband and, meanwhile, wash it every day. And afterwards I'd pat it dry in the plump pink folds of its tufty hideaway. A girl thinks how droll of the Good Lord to cache away purity in this little purse. Out of sight, out of mind. At least it doesn't clutter a girl's head.

She's well instructed by her mother's metaphors. Virtue is fresh air. You can't see it; only splutter breathless when it's gone. And virtue is like the foil cap on a bottle of schnapps or the gummed strip on a box of cigars. It is a seal of sorts, to be broached by the man who has procured it, at the price of marriage. Once the vessel has been opened, its value tumbles on the open market. For it can no longer be traded as new and intact. So it is with the innocence of girls. As for men, Mamma told her, they had no virtue to lose. Only they take advantage.

It's fortunate that we women bear our virtue, or conceal the loss of it, down below, wrapped beneath films of starchy cotton, ultimately veiled by lace. Because we'd be in a sorry state if we wore it naked on

61

our face. And supper talk might be very different, if the female countenance was so revealing.

I imagined Mamma's howl as she ladles out the noodles: 'Lise, where has your innocence gone! I cannot see it any more. Has it been mislaid in the woods?'

I'm suffering; confused. I am mind and body, both, also myself and an Other, and struggle to reconcile the two, or three, which seem so separate and contradictory.

My face and body belong to a lovely lady. But my mind is a gawky girl's. Whilst *my* intentions are honourable, the Other always intrudes.

'Mamma,' I ask, 'could a girl lose her purity by accident? Quite innocently? Not knowing what she's done?'

'She'd have to be very foolish.' Mamma batters a veal cutlet with her wooden meat hammer. 'Never dare bring that excuse to me. Not knowing? By accident, indeed! Breadcrumbs, if you please.'

But I am sullied, by my vile, putrid, festering core. A secret secret, part-concealed even from me.

This is my Other, and her horrid, vile whims. And desire: the bite and scratch of it: the voracious mouth, the burning touch, the caustic juice, the violating fingers, the savage rousing hurt.

Often it slices through the gauze of my contentment, the razor edge of desire. I conjure indecent thoughts, and scandalous images of twining legs, writhing bodies, pulsing pink parts, mucus-moist, and such. I don't deserve any innocence. All purity is lost to me.

So no decent man can marry me. I shall have to make do with cads. But there is part of me that delights to be depraved. A part of my conscious mind is siding with the Other.

Emmi and I often discuss girls' affairs in her bedroom.

'You must think of *it* a lot,' says Emmi, 'and yet you never mention . . .'

'What, Emmi?'

'Nothing, Lise.' She flushes scarlet, gnawing her nails. 'Sorry. I never say again . . .' Odd girl. So hesitant, she often loses her thread.

'You mean *it* – the love business between men and women? Doesn't it sound odd? But it must be very wonderful. Everyone gets involved.' We are sprawled, legs entwined on her bed. I lick her neck, to encourage. She shivers and wriggles, as I press her thigh tight up between mine.

Her eyes flicker. She turns away, apart, and gazes blankly at the pillow as I massage her shoulders, pressing through her soft pliancy to clutch the cords of tendons below. I know she likes it.

She shudders and looses small squeaks of pleasure – sounding off like an exuberant dormouse – as I nuzzle the nape of her neck. My nose goes twitchy on the milky scent of her skin, and the ripe must of her hair.

As my hands reach round under her arms, I sense the quake of her heart through the persuasible slopes of her chest. My hips press into her rump.

I know why man loves the tremulous silk-smooth contours, moist, furtive folds, revelatory perfumes of woman. I wonder what man offers in return.

I go misty and clammy at the very thought: of, I know not what; except I have suspicions.

'Do you suppose,' Emmi twists away, casting my hand out from her lap. She sits up, arms folded, 'it is nicer than a plate of chilled fresh raspberries, sunk in cream, rippled with honey? . . . Or when you take your first bite of a *Powidltatschkerl*? . . . You are savouring the butter and sugar, then the centre of hot apricot jam explodes in your mouth . . .'

'Well, Emmi . . .' I am surprised by the sweet confection of her comparisons, 'perhaps it's more like when you discover you've gone wet, for no reason, there, and accidently you chance to touch upon . . .'

'Lise!' Her face creases. 'You are a dirty girl. I don't want to hear.'

My face burns under a baste of shame. Really, if Emmi thinks me dirty, what would she make of my Other? It is so disconcerting to realise you are so much viler than the next girl.

Everywhere the girl is held and embraced by the swivelling eyes of men. At the Academy, professors watch her unblinking. In the street, men feast their glad eyes, ogle, gloat and leer. Men peek in cafés, round the fluttering edge of newspapers. From every passing car or tram she sees hungry stares. At home, brother August holds her under shifty surveillance. He has taken to dropping his fork at supper – to steal glimpses upward of what lies in the shades of her skirt, and tuck suggestive notes beneath the snap of her garter. Only Pappa is pained to look at her. His daughter's loveliness frightens him.

She is a spectacle for men, an object lesson. When she isn't acting in theatre school, she's performing on the stage of life. Typecast as Beauty. In the mirror of her face men see reflected their desire. They gawp and gulp.

'Lise,' demands Aunt Edith, 'what's the matter with your left hand?' For often I'm clutching it with the right, imprisoning the wrist.

'It goes numb, Edie. Sometimes. Or I get pins and needles.'

'You must see a doctor,' she says. 'Your Mamma would never forgive me if I don't look after you. Not when you've been so ill before – in your head. . . . Perhaps it's a nervous thing.'

'No matter,' I say, 'it isn't serious. It comes and goes.'

But Aunt Edith insists. Next door, at no. 19 Berggasse, there is the well-known nerve specialist Doctor F—, whom I've often met walking his Chow.

Our encounters are always shaming. For Aunt Edith's Pomeranian will insist on sniffing the doctor's Chow's bottom. There is too much tugging on the leash, some yelping and dribbling, and the Chow tries to mount Mitzie. All is a swirling ball of straining, quivering fur.

I take it too personally, as if responsible by proxy for the rude doings of my dog. As if Mitzie's nose were mine, her bottom were my bottom, the doctor's dog's whatsit the doctor's thingie . . . and so on. So we are already too, too familiar.

So when I consult doctor F—, I cart some shame along. Also, the occasion is wasted, for I was unconscious then of his original theories.

There is no transference, not even of money: a long story.

'Ah, the young Fräulein with the Pomeranian.' He nods, and directs me to a chair.

I explain my hand to him. He nods impatiently, then observes he must peer up my nostrils. As he leans over me, he smells too much of tobacco. His shoulder presses my chest, and he spills cigar ash in my lap. When the nasal examination is finished, he asks me about my monthly cycle. I reply that this is my concern, not his. I am grateful for his curiosity, but it does not connect to my fingers.

'Fräulein Berg,' the doctor chides, 'all parts of the body are joined. They are nervously attached to the mind.'

I nod, mute. I have noticed myself how a body is well connected. I will not dispute the phenomenon, least of all with a well-known doctor.

He tells me there is no shame in nature. Only in men's minds.

'And women's minds?' I ask.

'Ah,' the doctor chuckles. 'She is a special case.'

He reports to me his particular interest in my nose, declaring this a significant diagnostic organ, and disclosive of the uterus. He confides that he had a colleague, called Fleiss, who pioneered nasal surgery to cure all manner of feminine complaints.

'I've no shame, doctor,' I blurt, prickling so far as my belly-button. 'And this Fleiss is badly informed – about a woman's body – if he thinks to reach a womb through the nostrils. Really, doctor . . .' I tell him, 'you say it is all in the mind. This Fleiss says it is all in the nose. But, for my part, I *know* it is in my fingers.'

'Have you no other complaints?' asks F—.

'None. Except numbness in fingers. Otherwise all is perfect.'

'Perfect?'

'Well, can you not see my appearance?'

'Your face is plain for all to see,' says F——. He taps the tip of his cigar on the onyx ashtray. 'But it is a mere façade – with windows. It is not my task to remark upon your appearance. If you want reassurance, go consult a looking glass, not a neurologist.'

We sit silent some moments. Then F—— breaks more ice.

'Excuse me, Fräulein, but it is imperative I know this, before we continue. Are you a virgin?'

Of course, an innocent girl is bemused by his enquiry. Some men protest an interest in a woman's hand, then try to rummage in her lap. F—— is quite contrary. He proceeds in the reverse direction.

'Doctor,' I say, 'if a woman had been intimate with the entire cast of *Die Entfuhrung Aus Dem Serail*, at the Stadtsoper, it would not affect my fingers, unless . . .'

I pause. I don't want to pursue this. I begin to suspect a practical joke.

'Yes?' The doctor's eyes are narrowed around glittering sparks of pupil. 'You said "unless" . . .'

'Unless she used my hands.'

'First you say "a woman". Then you say "my hands". So we must assume it concerns you,' he observes. 'Now, for what would you use your hands?' he enquires.

'To touch.'

'Touch what?' Doctor F—— feigns ignorance.

'This and that,' I confide.

'Including?'

'Private bits. Thingummies. Whatsits and so on. You doctors know the names.'

'Try, Fräulein.' He smiles. 'Name the bits.'

Well, it is not my job to teach anatomy to a doctor. My mouth locks mute on this matter.

'I think you sometimes touch yourself, in a manner for which you feel ashamed.' The doctor nods soberly. 'Am I correct?'

'Never,' I protest. 'Who says I do? Emmi Pappenheim?'

But he will not betray the betrayer. The man who demands I name names will not disclose when his turn comes.

His silence discomforts me.

Then, in the painful hush, I hear *her* blurt, —So what if I touch my magic button?— I bet you fiddle with your magic wand . . .—

'Magic wand, magic button, Fräulein?'

'All women have . . .'

'All women . . . have a magic button?' The doctor looks concerned. His eyes go wide. He sneezes. He has a fit of sneezing. I advise he should consult Doctor Fleiss, concerning his nose. This I intend as a pleasantry; a joke that stumbles short of satire. But he does not laugh. Instead he frowns and blows his nose.

I take advantage of his downcast eyes to raise a matter that concerns me.

'Doctor, you know the world. Have you heard of a kind of demon that visits women at night and makes love to them?'

'Are you thinking of *men*, perhaps?'

'A man indeed. But this demon does his wicked business when the woman's asleep.'

'An incubus.'

'They're well known then?' I'm reassured.

'Indeed,' confirms F—.

'And they are real?'

'Everything in the mind is real, Fräulein. Even our imaginings. Why do you ask?'

'Emmi Pappenheim imagines one. I ask only as a favour for my friend.'

'Emmi Pappenheim, you say?'

'Yes. Two "m"s, two "p"s in the middle. As in "Mamma and Pappa". And . . .'

'Fraulein?' He halts his scribbling hand.

'While we are on the subject of Emmi, she has another problem, poor girl.'

'Yes?'

'Sometimes, some hours are lost to her. She cannot remember what she has done. It is like a trance. When she wakes, everyone is frosty and accuses her of naughty things.'

'Naughty?'

'Breaking and stealing valuables, screaming and howling, talking dirty, biting . . . the usual things.'

'She is a lively character, this Emmi, your friend.' F— smiles. 'What else does she do?'

I rub my brow. Sometimes, it is a struggle to remember. 'I mention most. Only sleepwalking I left out. And going out of her head. And writing rude things to herself in her diary. Oh, yes . . .' I wince.

'What?'

'A few times she finds lovebites on her neck or shoulders, although she's slept alone.'

'Odd,' the doctor stares intently, 'not to say impossible.'

'Strange, indeed,' I concede. 'Poor Emmi.'

He flexes his fingers as he regards me, all sombre intensity. 'I will say some words, Fräulein. You must reply with the first word that comes to your head.'

'Like consequences?'

'Exactly so . . .'

'With points and forfeits, then?'

'Without those.'

I enquire how we know who has won, if there is no score. He says there are no winners in a doctor's consulting room. This I can believe.

'*Button?*' F— begins, innocent as cheese.

'Hole,' I promptly reply.

'Yes! Explain.'

I disclose my association. A button fits in a buttonhole. He nods wearily.

'*Hole?*'

'Finger.'

'Why "finger", Fräulein?'

'I play the clarinet. On my clarinet are fingerholes . . .'

'*Father?*' F— persists.

—*Bumsen,*— she says.

I hold my hand to my mouth, having uttered a dirty word. There is no exact translation. But it refers to intimate business. It is more affectionate than 'fuck', less competitive than 'screw'.

'Please tell more,' smiles a forgiving Dr F—. He is avid to hear the obvious explained.

'Well, doctor,' I improvise as best I can, 'Mamma and Pappa do the business. So I am conceived. I am always grateful. I never forget.'

'Really, Fräulein. Isn't there more than that? Perhaps you get angry that they do *bumsen?*'

I do not see why he singles out my parents for censure. This man has children of his own, contracted, I suppose, in the popular fashion.

'Doctor,' I say, 'don't you tire of this game? Better is Hunt the Garter,' I advise, 'or do you know Candour?'

He says he is unfamiliar with Candour.

'We must each say what we truly think of the other. We offer adjectives. They must follow on in alphabetical order . . .'

—Arrogant, bald, conceited, dirty-minded, egocentric fart, and so on . . .—

He blinks at this, then glances at his watch.

'All right, but consider. . . . Demons emerge from guilts. Hurts interred juvenilely kindle latent maladies. Non organic, psychological quandaries rouse symptoms totally unexpectedly. Vitality withers. X-tinguishing your zest.'

Well, I'm impressed: even if he cheats on the 'X'. But, then, everyone cheats on the 'X'. It's only human nature. X is always the unknown quantity, unless you care to mention X-rays, Xmas or xylophones. I clap my hands delightedly. This man isn't half so slow or foolish as he pretends.

'Liar,' I giggle, 'you've played Candour before.'

'We make progress, Fräulein. But our time, alas, is over. You must come again on Thursday. My schedule is crowded. But . . .' he stares at my bust, unsmiling, 'I will find the suitable spot to squeeze you in. We have urgent business to conduct. It is imperative I see you very soon.'

Men have often said as much to me before. Though seldom so directly. A man's public respectability – I learn – gives scant private protection.

'Of course, I will call again.' My face strains to sustain its smile. 'We can play some more parlour games. It has been too, too *amusant.*'

But out on the boulevard the fresh breeze, the birdsong and afternoon sun restore her good sense.

After all, if a doctor spills ash on a lady, demands she play risqué word games, asks impertinent questions and confuses various well-known bodily openings, she is wise to secure a second opinion.

Anyway, I promptly discover the cure for myself. The gold bracelet given to me by Pappa for my fourteenth birthday is pressing too tight on my wrist, strangling the circulation. I get a jeweller to stretch it. This cost me thirty thalers. But, if I'd waited for diagnosis from Doctor F—, maybe I'd have gone hysterical . . . or been struck down by gangrene whilst still protesting my innocence.

The girl was naïve, but she had sound intuitions to goad her.

Only, when she gets home she feels an unexpected wet-tipped item leaking in her pocket. It is a tortoiseshell fountain pen, with an inscription, 'To the Master from C. G. J.'

Yes! The Other had pocketed it, when Lise was busy discussing psychology with Dr F—.

But that's never the end of the matter.

9

'**H**OW did it go? Your consultation with the Professor?' Aunt Edith asks.

'Odd,' I concede. 'He asks me about my periods. He accuses me of playing with myself.'

'What business is that of his? What we women get up to is our concern.'

'Exactly, Edie. And at the end, he insinuates things. I think he makes a pass at me.'

'Well. . .' Aunt Edith shakes her unshockable head, 'they remark he's original, but this sounds all too familiar. I won't have him take advantage of a niece of mine. Let him submit a bill, but I'll never pay. If he asks, I'll tell him why.'

So when the Doctor writes to tell Aunt Edith of my missed appointment, and arrange another time, we enjoy ourselves composing a candid reply.

Thereafter, I am careful to cross Berggasse, and pass on the other side, whenever I see them – the shuffling doctor and his black-mouthed Chow. Once, he trotted, panting and wheezing, after me. But he cannot catch me up.

Years later I must confront him again, twice at *soirées* at the

Schnitzlers. You could never coax him to do impressions or sing a comic song. He stood too much on his dignity, and so he stood alone. When I winked at him, he blinked and gazed away.

I concluded he didn't care much for women or pleasure. You could see as much from the face of his wife. Poor Martha, with those weary, wary eyes, sunk in her gander's face.

Nature spared her the burden of beauty.

It is hard to bear – beauty. It is a terrible thing. There is too much low traffic over your skin. You are like a honeypot at a picnic. Like an exquisite bloom – a lone orchid amongst thistles. Men swarm and buzz like wasps. Each must have you. Must poke his proboscis between your soft, moist petals, drink your precious essence, suck your nectar.

Still, you must make the best of it; grin and bear your beauty. But at sixteen I still have to get reconciled to my skin.

The girl rejects compliments, frowning or blushing.

'You look radiant today, Fräulein Berg.'

'No, Professor T—' she insists. 'My skin looks pasty.' Or, 'How can you say such a thing? My lip is cracked.' Or, 'No, my hair needs styling.'

Truly, she is infuriated. For she knows on Saturday in her turquoise taffeta gown, with her hair fresh from the curling papers, she looked seven times more stunning.

And yet, she knows, her skin is only a cover. Inside, she feels ugly, clumsy, unworthy. And she has a hideous, hidden centre.

She resents the hungry stares. But she won't forgive the man who disdains her.

I would relish some of those squandered compliments, now, at ninety. Desmond in the Spa Grocers says, 'Lise, you're a frisky filly.'

But frisky doesn't flatter. And I resent comparison to a horse, even if the intention is innocent.

I whinny and hobble out.

Suppose there's a trollop who looks the spit of you, wandering your home, throwing tantrums, acting vicious to your loved ones, bringing you into disrepute. I fancy you'd become concerned for your good name. And you'd pay your face a second, and quizzical, look in the mirror.

The girl took to keeping a note of her movements – not in her diary, which the Other had found and desecrated – but in code, in tiny crabbed letters, in the margin of the Gospel According to Matthew, in her Bible, where a lewd character would never have a mind to look. A desperate condition demands a drastic prescription.

She'd review her previous day each morning, till she had satisfied herself each and every hour was accounted for. Or, if she chanced upon some hole in her time, she'd document any evidence around the frayed edges.

You'll imagine. It's a dreadful thing when some sneak thief steals into your body, making off with your time. Apart from the loss, there's a foul sense of violation.

'Thurs. 4 May. Two hours lost between supper and bed. Edie says someone's secretly drinking her brandy. Suspicion – as always – falls on me. Why won't she leave me be? Another vile night. Woke sweating at 5 a.m. Sheets tangled. Nightdress gone again.' Or, reassuringly, 'Fri. 5 May. Entire day to myself. Slept quietly.'

I get a feeling for this Other, the ebb and flow of her whims. I've become a natural scientist of myself. Then, I'm forced to revise my opinion, when I find scrawled across Chapter 2 of the Gospel:

—A virgin with child? No hanky-panky? Phooey!! You can't fool me. And quit your prying or it'll be the worse for you!! PS I spit on your Bible. Why don't we have any fun?—

73

The girl despairs of keeping herself good. Whatever she tries, the Other catches her out and trips her up. The harder Lise tries to commit herself to right, the worse behaves her left-hand side.

The girl has to come to terms. If she has a frog in her throat, she has to cough it up. All sort of nastiness must leak from the inside out.

Evidence accumulates. Scratches, stains, headaches and such. You can only control this Other by feeding it a little. Otherwise it will revolt and take over. Like when the mob lynched Graf Latour. Better by far to make a few concessions. Be liberal, not repressive. Like Mayor Karl Lueger and his Christian Socialists.

The secret of being largely good is to let yourself be bad, a little. Otherwise, perhaps, you might even go crazy, a little, maybe.

Looking back, I don't cast blame. Mamma and Pappa had their own cause to wipe the traces, so no signs remained to be seen. The attic room stayed locked. The picture frame stood empty. A certain name was never mentioned – as if to mend by silence.

And Mamma was always houseproud; she'd never leave blood to dry crusty on her carpet.

Maybe they supposed my complicity – that I was mute from sorrow not ignorance, and really knew more than I said. But we all turned our blind eyes, deaf ears, and careless backs. I on them, they on me, all of us on *him*.

The cause of my illness? In hindsight, I believe it was part mental, part physical, aided by natural talent – a heady cocktail, mixing a blow on the head with emotional trauma, all in a cracked vessel. Yes, I was fragile, chilled, shaken and stirred.

Oh, foolish child.

Lise lies warm and drowsy in Kretschmer's studio. He invites her after buying her lunch in the Pandora Café. Oh, happy bargain! First

74

she gulps a bowl of *Gulyaschsuppe*. On the steaming surface are the chef's initials floated in sour cream. Then she wolfs down smoked goose with red cabbage, sliced roast potatoes and horseradish sauce. To drink, there are two bottles of *Gumpoldskirchen*. Kretschmer pays. No expense spared. So she is cajoled to have a mocha soufflé, too, washed down with coffee and orange liqueur.

'Come, come . . .' coaxes Kretschmer, 'to my studio. I shall sketch you. Here! Take my arm.'

He plies her with apple juice. He does not say, and she cannot tell, that it is laced with something stronger. Maybe, aqua vitae. Later she remembers a peppery aftertaste, and oily film lining the glass.

He is a distinguished sculptor. He has molded that bust of Kathi Schratt. The girl is honoured to sit for him. Or, rather, sprawl on his chaise.

He remarks upon her fine features, strokes her thighs, murmurs his reverence.

Oh, but she is gorged. Warm, drowsy, content. Talk on, Herr K. Do not mind me if I close my eyes. Sketch away. Let your hands reveal my loveliness.

On the border of sleep is a magic stupor. You lie warm and safe, preparing to dream, closing the door on the logic of day, yielding yourself up to desire.

Inconsequential thoughts snake through your mind, sinuously profound. Artists are the aristocrats of love. A famous sculptor reveres you. The body is wiser than the mind. Feel how she moves, gorged by the great man's touch, melting moist. The time has come. This girl has nothing to lose. And everything to grasp.

—Now is the time!—

A wise girl heeds mother's caution. But a bold woman of the world tosses herself into the maelstrom of passion.

—Take me, Carl, — a voice sighs, — make me drunk on love. Move me to ecstasy. —

'What, Lise?'

'Do the filthy business, then,' the girl slurs, 'dirty man. If you must.'

'Well, now . . .' Kretschmer detaches his monacle and lays it studiously on the table. 'I never make rash promises. But I'll see what I can do for you. But I must warn you, Fräulein . . .'

'Yes?'

'My name is not Carl, but Heinrich.'

Kretschmer knows his way around a woman's attire. He has inside information. The girl does not need to direct him where are buttons, what to unlace, or where is a hidden catch. No, she's promptly peeled – plucked, blushing pink and helpless, like a prawn from its shell. The sculptor has deft hands.

But when he reveals himself, I commence my doubts. Of course, I know it is only willing flesh. But it has the look of a raw, mad thing; a startled stranger. This is no magic wand, but a grotesquely swollen finger, pointing most accusingly. As if it will never forgive.

She is struck by a disproportion. Her own small fingers fit. But this, she fears, she cannot admit.

'Must you use that horrid thing?' She winces.

'I must, Lise.' He taps the lurid glistening tip. 'It is the only tool I have for this task.'

He kneels between her splayed legs. A private smile lights his face.

As his chill hands palp her chest, she stiffens, sobered and shocked.

She is too revealed. She has no hiding place. This is all too intimate. This man is a stranger. Her body is hers – and most parts none of his business.

She looks sadly down her torso, beyond the swell of her belly to the tufted ridge. She reminds herself of nothing so much as a plucked trussed duck, whose carcass will be wrenched open. So she can be stuffed.

'Rude,' she gasps, '. . . my bottom,' for his hands have slithered beneath her buttocks and are frighteningly close to her privacy.

She thinks of the last time a man handled her intimately; when Doctor Hess lanced a boil on her thigh. She clenches her hands and

76

closes her eyes tight. One stab and it is over. Then it only stings and smarts.

There comes a surgical intervention between her legs. She yelps like a puppy when you trample its foot. And, yet, there is something strangely familiar.

She feels very much put upon and done to. Her blinking eyes regard the crush of flesh. Kretschmer's bristly belly is overbearing upon her, and he is crashing her hip bones with his, in his impatient staccato jerks.

'Wait.' She recants. 'Herr Kretschmer, I change my mind . . .'

Pinioned beneath his pressing chest, she squirms and moans. He whimpers in reply, so she senses she's only encouraging him.

To have him off, she takes desperate measures, but as she claws his shoulder, he only quickens.

Having begun, he seems adamant to finish.

'Very well . . .' she decides. First she reclaims her tongue, whose tip had somehow meandered into his ear. She grits her teeth, then bites his nipple, and – for a reason best known to her left hand – pushes a finger into him, repaying the hurtful invasion as best his body allows.

The effect is prompt and striking. And yet the damage is done.

He makes a strangled howl. His eyes meet hers, then swivel away vacantly. The party collapses, quivering, quite crushing the fragile maiden-no-longer.

Now she howls in discomfort, and rolls him off. He lies heaving on his side, like a beached porpoise.

She is sore. And sensual delirium seems far away.

Kretschmer is an adequate draughtsman. He can sketch a good likeness. But when he lays down his pen, he has no further craft to draw upon.

'Herr Kretschmer . . .' She pats the folds of his belly. Her words slither slurred from unwilling lips. Her chest is tender. Her body lies leaden.

'Lise?'

'When comes ecstasy?' Lise asks. 'You owe me, I think.'

77

For it is so brutal and brief. Having suffered this, she now requires her due; the treasure of pleasure – those feelings that poets rhapsodise, the stuff of romantic ballads.

His eyes roll shamed, like a trapped puppy who has done a piddle on the carpet.

'It was not good for you, Lise?' he asks earnestly.

'Not yet, Herr Kretschmer.' She looks at him as straight as her bleared eyes allow. 'I still await bliss.'

He had her. Yet he withholds her rapture. He has spread her legs; now she requires he makes her split her lips.

Yet the only movement to him is a quivering of his breath, stirring the forest of hairs over the pink hillocks of his belly.

Lise nudges him. Perhaps he has forgotten something. Maybe, there are things undone.

'When comes woman's pleasure?' she asks. 'When happens my delight?'

—Come on, fatty. Pull your finger out.—

He fondles her lap with fumbling hands. This adds insult to injury. And some tacky opalescent mucus stuff is seeping out of her to glisten viscous on the chaise.

So Mamma was right to warn her. Only they take advantage, and inflict this damp indignity. And she can tell no-one of her shame.

She turns from him, sobbing. He strokes her shoulders to soothe her. She sweeps his hand away.

Lise considers her loss. She is used, soiled, alone. It was like this when the demon left her at dawn. She rises, wrapping herself with silent speed, all the while keeping her back to him. He shall have no further glimpse of her.

—You've seen the last of me,— she hisses.

'Me too,' Lise agrees.

As she leaves, he slouches by the door, smiling smugly. He presses twenty crowns in her palm, then hands her a painting of the bridge at Muhleng. The girl remarks that he has got the better bargain.

'Next time, Lise, you will enjoy it better.' I swear he winks at her. He presumes too much if he thinks she'll acquire the taste with him.

'Next time, Herr Kretschmer, I will enjoy it with someone else.'
Outside his apartment, she slams his painting down on the railings.
The skin of canvas rips, impaled on the prongs.

Oh, how she regrets him. First time should be sober with a conspicuous artist. She'll never sit for him again.

In the apartment in Berggasse, she watches herself in the mirror for telltale signs of change. You cannot see in her eyes what has happened. Her image is enigma. This self-regard is never revealing. Her wide-eyed gaze is aloof. The beauty will not confide, nor yield her secret. Lise is always surprised that this is she.

'Beautiful lady, what do you want?' she whispers. Her breath clouds the glass pearly.

'Wait and see,' she murmurs, 'the mist will clear.'

'There! see what you made me do?' she writes in her secret diary. 'Are you satisfied now? You've probably ruined my whole life! For ever! You slut!'

Then she runs a steaming bath, slumps listless in the scalding water, gazing sadly on the lie of her flushed, dishonoured body.

Presently, she feels cleaner and calm.

She chuckles at the perfect foolishness of the sticky business. So that is it? A man squirms on your belly, jerking – in there, with that – with solemn intention to squirt.

Not so much dirty; more absurd.

She lathers Kretschmer from her with Aunt Edith's lemon soap and steps dripping from the bath. Then she dabs dry her chaste body with a crisp, clean towel. She sprinkles cologne on her neck and pats herself with powder. Dressed in fresh chemise and drawers, she is back as she was. A little broached, but barely sullied.

I take pride in it. Whatever I do, however dirty I get, I always clean up well.

79

10

AMONGST the spectres that spooked the girl were certain shadowy suspicions. For reassurance, she resorted to elaborate precautions. These measures mortified her. She'd never disclose them to another soul. Now, shameless in my dotage, I'll reveal. Frankly, I conceal nothing worth knowing or seeing.

That afternoon in Kretschmer's studio gave her inklings, put her on the scent of it. A nod and a wink. A bare suggestion, no more. Innocence is a tenuous, fragile thing.

It had been the way her body behaved. How her legs splayed, hooking ankles around him. How her hands clutched his buttocks, as if reaching out for the familiar. Her numbed head blinked bemused, as her body led her on.

Had the Other done this business before, behind her back, without her knowing? Else, having done it the once, would she try, in her furtive way, to repeat the misadventure?

It is a dismal thing – to have your purity and character dangle by so fine a thread.

So! Two pairs of knickers, at least. The top pair secured by a length of string through the waistband, knotted tightly. Or else a girl can sew the top of her bloomers to the bottom of her bodice, back and front, with a few quick tacks. Also, it's sensible to pin the back of your bandeau. Good idea, too, if you scribble a brief warning note in pencil, on a small slip of soft paper, and stow it where it matters – 'To whom it may concern . . .' etc.

And if you tuck a five-thaler coin under your garter, you can tell – if it's gone, when you come round again – that you've meantime had it off, maybe shedding your stockings.

There were more radical remedies. These I leave to your imagination. Anyway, what attractive girl wants to paint her private beauty with gentian violet, just to discourage admirers?

But diagnosis poses a problem. Just because a pair of bloomers are missing, a pin is shed, or a coin, or you've come untacked or unknotted, doesn't mean *she*'s been naughty. For the Other might have been taken short. Yes. Or changed her clothes, or taken a bath.

Yet certain bodily cues, you can't help noticing, alert a girl that something untoward has gone on. It may not look very wise, down below, but it says enough, when its bloated lips are split to a crooked gooey smile.

But if that hair – which she'd glued across the crack between the panel and frame of the door – is unstuck in the morning, it doesn't mean the girl has gone sleepwalking again. Or someone has entered her room. No. She might have wandered barely awake to the lavatory, sometime in the night. And afterwards forgotten. It happens.

But that gastric burn waking you in the morning to your thirst and headache is a sure sign she's been tippling the brandy, getting drunk whilst she's out of her mind.

Of course, I simplify the business. But at least you get an inkling. As does the girl. And the greater her suspicions grow, the more convoluted becomes the ritual of investigations and precautions.

It is a family joke that it takes me an hour to prepare for a ten-minute walk. And they laugh at how I am always fingering my waistband, cadging five-thaler coins, borrowing pins, mislaying knickers, or disappearing red-faced with needle and cotton to tack myself up again.

But it was no joke, I can tell you.

At the Dramatic Academy, the professors are tyrants. They humiliate students, butchering their confidence. They aim to break you, then rebuild you in their image.

Fräulein Allers,' they say to Anna, 'you have no voice. You have the sensitivity of a corpse, the charm of a cow-pat and the deportment of a rhinoceros. You do not breathe properly. Your hands are inelegant. Tomorrow, bring some talent along. Otherwise, stay away.'

Naturally, she's discouraged. She freezes. She dare not move for being derided. Her hands she clutches behind her back, lest they are again insulted. All her energy and intelligence are spent in trying to resolve the enigma of where in her abdomen is lurking her diaphragm.

'Fräulein Berg,' shouts Professor Bernheim, 'discipline your face. You are playing a nun, not a courtesan. You must not flirt with the Angelic Chorus.'

Or: 'Fräulein Berg, I won't tell you again. You enter right. Speak one line. Then exit left. You must not hog the stage, or drag it out, by affecting a stammer and limp.'

Theatre is a hard school. It teaches the girl humility and discipline.

They have her stand, still as a statue, for seven minutes, with her back to the audience. All the while her face is sprayed by the actor's spittle.

Minna and Lise sit side by side in the Museum Café, staring across at the Master.

Oh, the rogue. K— worships women. But it is more evident in his paintings than his manners.

He always gives them gorgeous robes: purple and crimson silks and satins. A lady never lacks for gold and jewels – not in Gustav's paintings. He reveres every pore of their body. His brush, his stroke, ravishes every snatch of her skin. Enlivens her whole being. She enacts myths for him. Her face speaks ageless truths. Eyelids flutter closed in bliss. Mouths split in delirium. The lady's legs are splayed in rapture. 'Oh, Gustav. Ah, what a marvel to lie on the sheets of your canvas.'

They are at their place by the door. Minna's elbow stabs her ribs. Herr K— is rising to leave.

82

The romance of the man is not only in his art and reputation. It glisters oily in the creases of his face. It shines in his gipsy smile.

He looks older than his fifty years, and yet he looks a rascal child. There are mad tufts of hair above his ears. His scalp is bare, except for a triangle of wild, wiry hairs above the creased brow. Imp eyes glisten a taunting, teasing enquiry.

Lise too has learned to tease. She controls her breathing in a manner taught by Professor Schlick. She won't be disconcerted by a famous audience.

'Soda water, please, with a slice of lemon,' she calls out as he passes, 'and my friend will take a raspberry cordial.'

K——'s face creases like a rapscallion in mirth: 'But I'm not a waiter, Fräulein.' He pulls out a chair and slumps facing them, spreading his arms on the table and cupping his bearded chin in his hands.

His eyes narrow and he peers at her intently. 'I could draw you, Fräulein.'

'I heard this story once before,' says Lise. 'It nearly cost me my innocence.'

'No, Fräulein. I do mean *draw*. Your features are very fine.'

'So, you're really an artist, then.'

'Engelhardt says not. The Ministry of Education do not value my work. But I believe I'm competent.'

'You must persevere, sir. If you have any talent, you will get recognition sometime. You must believe in yourself. I know this from my acting. Soon I'll be celebrated. Because I have genius.'

He nods sagely. 'It's a privilege, Fräulein, to meet a genius. In my whole life, I have met only . . .' he pauses in reminiscence, counting his fat fingers, 'two or three before.'

'I am perfecting the part of First Siren in Schramm's *The Sphinx*. Do you wish me to recite for you?'

'Please,' he says, 'a small portion, perhaps – an hors d'oeuvre, a taster.'

'If you insist. But you have to imagine my wig of silver strands, and my cape of black velvet. And in your mind's eye you must summon up a desert in Egypt at midnight . . .'

His lids fall to curtain his glistening eyes. 'It is done. We are in Egypt. It is eerie here on the lonely dunes.'

83

Though Minna pleaded for her to hush, she orated her piece with a forceful projection.

Herr K— interrupted with a wave of his pudgy hand.

'You are right, Fräulein. The stage is the only place for you. Your confidence is prodigious. Few audiences will deserve you. None, I predict, will forget you.'

'Lise Berg,' she offers her hand, 'and you are Herr . . .?'

'K—.'

'K—!' She beams. 'But you are a genius too. And, I swear, you've painted me already.'

'I have?'

'*Danae*. Do you not think the model is the spit of me? Her hair. Her face. And . . .' she blushes, '*Nuda Veritas*. Not to mention *Goldfish*.'

K— clamps a hand to his brow. 'It is astonishing. It is uncanny. But, yes. You are the beauty in those paintings. And I thought I had imagined her . . .'

It was a fabulous moment: Lise meets Gustav K—. He finds in her his fantasy incarnate. Within ten minutes, they have known each other aeons. Shortly after, she sits for him.

At first she declines his offers of any drink or refreshment, and keeps herself entirely buttoned, from collar, yea, unto bootstud. And carefully checks the integrity of her intimate clothing as soon as she returns home. This way she gains trust, then relaxes. In time he will paint her as *The Virgin*. Also *Jealousy II*. And *Pensive Actress in Flowered Hat Reading a Letter* . . .

Oh, but now comes Felix. And it is not his scene. There is no cue or call for him. Always he draws the focus or interrupts. Lise heckles from the audience.

If this was theatre, not life, an usher would eject him. Too often he is hovering. He chooses disconcerting times and improbable places. He stains the good name of coincidence.

Lise is scampering for a lesson when he seizes her tight by her arm.

'I cannot stop now, Felix. I'm late for Dramatic Sincerity.'

'Ah, but you've flunked that class, Lise. Sincerity is beyond you.'

'What?'

'I know your secrets,' he hisses. This is not his usual solicitous manner. No, he's insolent and belligerent. His face is drained white. His mouth twitches disagreeably. The eyes are narrowed hatefully.

He says he has followed her. Here and *there*. He tells it as if the shame were hers, not his.

'Felix, cousin, you're always poking your nose where it never belongs.' Lise has been practising the part of Frau Macbeth, so her contempt comes fluent and withering.

'My nose is not the issue. We discuss your conduct instead . . .'

He reports he has followed her. On Tuesday to Bognergasse, to the appartment of a Herr M—. Then on Thursday to the Thirteenth district, to a certain sidestreet in Hietzing, where he watched for her several hours. He remarked that he was compelled to sit on the bare earth behind decorative shrubs, azaleas, ferns and vines. Through the windows of a particular house he had seen a black and red suit of Japanese samurai armour. And her naked back. Then curtains drawn.

He sought to impress her with his command of detail. Well, she has never been to Bognergasse. Nor does she know Herr M—. But to say as much would be to sanction his prying.

'Just suppose it is so, Felix. What is it to you?'

'What is it to me?' he bellows. 'We are almost engaged to be married.'

'We are?'

'You know it.'

'We are almost cousins. You are not quite a fiancé. You are not exactly a gentleman, Felix. Sometimes, your face seems nearly pleasant. Why do you never do anything thoroughly?' She laughs in his face frankly and, pulling his ring from her finger, casts it bouncing down the pavement. Both watch the gold band roll into the gutter.

'Suppose I tell your Mamma and Pappa?' He tugs violently at her wrist. 'The people you see. The places you go.'

'I should prefer you didn't,' she softens, 'cousin, dear.'

'Ah!' He senses a hold on her. His eyes are slits, like a weasel's observing a fieldmouse.

'Why do you deny me, Lise? When you give yourself to other men, to worthless artists . . . dirty bohemians?'

'I do not,' she spits. 'I sit for an artist. I do not lie with him. I am innocent. He paints me as the Virgin. He is most respectful. Herr K— has never touched me.'

Well, hardly.

'What do you want of me, Felix?'

'You know what I want, Lise. And I will have it.'

'Are you blackmailing me, Felix, over the matter of my virtue?'

'Exactly, Lise,' he nods, 'I am. I know you know how to please me. Give me what you give Professor T–!' He says this with sly relish, as though playing his ace of hearts.

'Professor T—,' I giggle, 'teaches me the clarinet.'

'Yes! I think you play duets when his wife is out.'

But I never do. He's confusing me with another.

Then he is leaning forward and scowling at my neck. 'Who gave you that string of pearls?' he demands.

I reach up and, true enough, around my neck I'm wearing an exquisite chain of the darling things!

Unhooking them, I feel their gravid cool loll in my palm.

'Aren't they charming!' I sigh to myself – quite forgetting Felix. I've always lusted after a string of pearls. 'Aren't I lucky, the Jewel Fairy has come again. What would a girl have to do to *earn* these?'

But this is shocking new evidence. My Other has been playing games behind my back once more. And I thought we'd reached a *rapprochement*. I believed I'd paid her off – through that tacky transaction concerning skin and Herr Kretschmer. But here she is, paying me.

Immediately the gilt of possession is tarnished. Perhaps they are stolen? Or has she done something awful to gain them?

11

'D precise tastes in men. Names meant a lot to me – though it takes me a while to learn the logic of my prejudice. I was specially fond of Carls and Gustavs. But it never adds up – a Carl Gustav would have to be very special for me to love him twice as much. As to physique, I prefer them tall and lithe. Ebony or dark-brown hair attracts. I'm a sucker for olive eyes. When I tour Italy with Molière, I can't believe how beautiful men are. Artists and writers have been dear to me. A little fame never comes amiss.

Yes. In my time I've known important and original men – not least Max B—, the celebrated physicist, who discovered the smallest elements of our world and choreographed their intricate dance and miniature motions. He pursued me all through 1927, flatteringly calling me a phenomenon.

By conventional count – totting time – I was then thirty-two. But Max assured me my years were not fixed. He insisted I should become younger every day. This redress is permissible by quantum physics, he promised, because the age of a woman can't be summed up by remorselessly adding her years. No. Age is a volatile maverick number, relative to her vitality and mass.

'Lise,' says he, 'my electron. Yours is a body of peculiar charm.'

This is how physicists flirt. Their compliments go abstruse and technical. They suppose you're intimate with their smallest particles.

Max said that the more I disclosed my movements, the less he knew my whereabouts. And vice versa. Electrons do the same. Like me, they're contrary, caught in two minds, finding devious routes to privacy, deceiving even themselves.

'Don't blame me . . .' I'd sob, 'it was never me, but an Other.'

Frankly, I'm as tired of saying it as others are of hearing it.

'Very convenient, you little madam,' Mamma says, sour and tart as a pickled walnut.

Convenient? I think not. It is an appalling arrangement, by which I do all the giving, and the Other only takes. She has the pleasure, I take the blame and shame. She flounces around town, but, suddenly shaken from a trance, it's me with the splitting headache, and sour taste in the mouth, that has to pay for the taxi, or trudge home in the rain.

I'm forced to a dark corner of solitude, secrecy and guilt. Nobody will trust me. At drama school it goes quiet when I enter the rehearsal room, bar some whispers. At home, Mamma and Pappa have turned incurably severe and frosty, all on account of a tantrum and two thefts. Aunt Edith locks her alcohol in her desk drawer, and ostentatiously slips the key down her bodice.

Also I get troubled by *déjà vu*. Perhaps you've suffered this too? For instance, you walk down a street and gaze up at a window, certain you've once been in the room. Or a man looks across from a nearby café table, with a suggestive smile. His needle eye is piercing, tying us by a thread of innuendo. I can't put a name to his face, or place to either. Then I hear in my mind's ear, with chilly clarity, some endearment spoken in his stranger's voice, or visualise his freckled shoulders. Then I worry about my imagination, or else shudder that my Other has met him already.

Three times now, men have addressed me in the street as 'Felice', which sets me thinking. For, by cute coincidence, this is my second name. But I never pay any regard. I stride past, my complexion burning. They look perplexed or hurt.

Worst of all, she suddenly left me stranded, this Other, after midnight, without rhyme, reason or overcoat, in the drizzle in Michaelplatz, with nothing solid to hang on to, bar a bouquet of roses. From somewhere. So it was me that had to tramp back in the chilly damp, and fabricate a story to ping the elastic goodwill of Aunt Edie.

Now comes decision time. Who controls – I or *she*? I must confront the Other, if I'm to remain mistress of my life and salvage the flotsam of my reputation.

'This is war,' I declare to myself – and to the Other if she cares to listen – and bolt myself into my bedroom.

First, I'll make a thorough search and audit. She'll get no peace or privacy from me. I intend to look everywhere; especially in the inobvious places which seem infinite in a cluttered bedchamber of ample proportions.

Aunt Edith knocks on my door, wakened by my loud endeavours, to enquire if I've taken up cabinetmaking.

'Only spring cleaning,' I call.

'In December?' she demands. 'At quarter past one in the morning?'

'Some things are lost, Edie. I really must find . . .'

—No!— howls an inner voice. —Don't dare pry behind the wardrobe. —

'I look wherever I choose,' I resolve. 'Don't try and bully me, you bitch,' I spit.

Piece by piece, I assemble a mosaic of her – this Jewel Fairy, my sinister side – from the Other things she has cached through a hole in the lining of my bag, or squirrelled away inside a pillow, or secreted beneath the lining paper in my drawers, pushed beneath the bed, or lain beneath the carpet.

Within an hour, I've found plenty of incriminating evidence.

There are tram tickets to places I've never been; there is a sepia photograph of a rakish German subaltern, and another of an older fellow the spit of Peter Altenberg; a brandy glass engraved with the legend 'Sacher Hotel'; a box of fifteen Papirossi cigarettes, of which seven are missing, presumed smoked; eight plumstones and two rotting apple cores; brother August's mother-of-pearl penknife; Minna Levy's missing belt with the snake's head buckle; a red box labelled 'Humbolt's Prophylactics', containing balloons shaped like sausage skins; Aunt Edie's cameo brooch; two telephone numbers scribbled on torn paper; a douchebag; a business card of Herr Sigmund Tazker, carpet salesman of Bucharest, supplier to the aristocracy of seven nations; a sensational novella entitled *Houri of the Opera*, with some romantically eventful passages underlined; a gold bracelet, inscribed 'With devotion from your loving Gottfried'; a purple velvet garter with sequins; a pair of lace bloomers – more air than fabric – with scarlet edging; an open box of *marrons glacés* heavily overlaid with bedroom fluff; a tin of perfumed cachous; a dinner napkin from the Hotel Dionysus; a small ornate bottle of mimosa scent; some soiled, intimate items; Karl Graf's address book, without an entry for my name; an end of salami, discoloured but still edible; two ticket stubs for the Stadtsoper; and a few personal items I'd prefer not to mention, notwithstanding the intervening years.

Also there are four separate bundles of banknotes. The combined sum, I'm appalled – yet delighted – to discover, exceeds Pappa's annual salary.

I mustn't forget the letter:

Felice, *chérie*,

Ah, yesterday! And next week? S must visit her mother in Melk. So we might spend the whole afternoon together!

Of course, I do not hesitate to lend you money. But you must recognise my resources are limited. Let us pray your sick brother recovers soon. And that your Pappa is reformed when he's shortly released from prison.

I carry your garter next to my heart, in remembrance of your thighs.

Your adoring D.

I do not know who D is. But I do not like the sound of these insults to my family. And I suspect he's after some humpety, by snaring a poor girl with money.

In a small cavern in the plaster, behind the loose wainscot, there is a cache of a different order – a tin box containing a yellowed roll of paper, tied by a faded, crimson ribbon; a pair of gold-rimmed glasses; a silver-backed gentleman's hairbrush, trapping in the bristles, tangled and tormented, some wavy blond hairs.

It felt a violation to look here. As though I was toying with some revered relic. I sniffed the hairbrush and promptly dropped it with a start. A wave of vomit surged up my throat, then ebbed back, leaving an acrid taste and burn.

Then came the golden flashes, and stench of singeing hair. My Other always comes this way.

—Be gone,— she howls, —damn you! And leave my belongings alone.—

'No,' I'm decided, 'I stay and finish what I start.' So I sink my upper teeth into my lower lip, tasting the warm, sickly flow of my blood, force open my eyelids with my fingers, and crash my head on the wall. All this keeps my attention, and reminds me who I am.

'Lise,' I wail, 'I am Lise. Lise. No Other,' as the flares and flashes explode in my sight. When the firework display is over, it is dismal and gloomy in my mind's eye: a metronome clicks the rhythm of my migraine, the angry nerves in my left cheek pierce like burning needles. And though I am weeping and heaving, it is me, Lise, that remains. For once I've repelled *her*.

I untie the ribbon around the scroll of paper. There's a musty waft as it uncoils crackling to show a charcoal drawing of a girl's head. The hand is not an artist's. The image is gauche, sentimental and clumsy. A naïve and doting hand has stylised the mouth, eyes and nose within a flat oval. But it is recognisable as a rendering of me – as the girl I was, maybe – from the parting of my hair, and the distinctive almond nostrils within the blotch of nose. Anyway, the self-deprecating hand has labelled the picture 'Dear Lise', lest there be further misunderstanding. And, in the top right corner, it has enclosed the signature 'CGN' within three concentric circles.

It is very touching and beautiful in its miraculous ineptitude. For this hand reveals itself so shamefully, outlining its ungainly designs. I'm drawn to its devotion.

91

Whenever Gustav sketches me, he masters me so readily. I'm earmarked, commandeered and impounded. But this cack-hand captures nothing.

I retie the knot, lay these items in the tin, and stow them again behind the wainscot. Then I'm shaking and heaving, lost shuddering through surges of retching.

Of course, Detective Inspector Stern and his sharp-nosed shepherd dog Fritzie, of *The Mystery of the Post Office Savings Bank Robbery Resolved*, could have made more of the Other's possessions than I. But I was led to certain conclusions: part reassuring, but largely shocking.

Here is a light-fingered body, intimately clad in lurid lingerie, who stays out late, keeping cheap company in expensive restaurants, harshens an ingenue's voice with tobacco, is careless with her money and valuables, and has a hygiene problem of an intimate nature, and a disregard for waste bins.

I had thought of the Other as a domestic shame, who knew her place and stayed at home. Now I find she's all over town. Do you wonder I was alarmed by her? I suspect I'm dealing here with an unreasonable character. The greater the trust I give the Other, the more outrageous are the liberties she takes.

And Gottfried? What are the expectations of a man who gives a girl a gold bracelet?

How does a girl get enough money to deck herself out in the new season's fashion at Floge's Emporium, then spend the season in Cannes? And why hasn't she started spending her fortune?

On the other hand – it occurs to me – this other has a touching, sentimental side. She's an enterprising character. She goes to plenty of interesting places. And she seems to know how to enjoy a good time. And gets into less trouble than one might suppose.

Her cigarettes and *marrons glacés* I cast on to the fire. The coals flare. No loss – for the girl never gained the taste for either. Gold flames char the cardboard. The air is scented with caramel. She'll get no more pampering or privileges from me. That'll give her something to chew on. She can put self-denial in her pipe, and smoke it.

The underwear I fold neatly and stow in the bottom drawer of my chest. It seems a pity to waste it: though vulgar, there's something pretty too. Maybe I can wear the oddments sometime in the theatre – and feel myself in the part, if I'm ever called on to act a tart.

But the photos I burn. The subaltern's eyes betray him as a rogue. And the older fellow has a beard – and I can never abide facial hair on a man. Except in Gustav, when I forgive it.

Her coins and banknotes I confiscate, to lodge in my savings account. It's the least she can give to repay me.

This Gottfried alarms me. I want to know what he is doing giving a young girl a gold bracelet. I demand to know his intentions, then insist that he abandons expectations. I will go so far as to give him back the bracelet, if the cad insists. Only, I don't know where to find him.

It occurs to me that I stand in relation to the Other as parent to rogue child. She's mine. Flesh of my flesh. So she is vile, vicious and lewd, but I'll never admit as much outside the kin of my skin. And – whatever my private opinion – I'll protect her, and have none take advantage or abuse her.

Anyway no-one's all bad – as Aunt Edie is overfond of remarking. Maybe this Other works some spare hours in an orphanage, or donates a good fraction of her income to charity. For all I know she could tramp the streets, serving soup to the homeless and needy.

But Gottfried? Perhaps one of the phone numbers is his. Twice I set out for the post office, to make discreet enquiries by ringing the numbers. But the first time I set out I am poleaxed by a blinding migraine and must limp home to bed moaning. My second attempt is stymied by shooting pains of paralysing severity in my left arm.

I guess that the Other is trying to stop me. Indeed, she slyly succeeds – behind my back – shredding the slips of paper on which the numbers are written.

12

So there I was on the track of her. In my witless innocence, I thought she'd wilt away, or wander off, once I'd exposed her. To find another skin to lodge in; someone else to live off.

'Be gone!' I'd evict her, showing no particle of pity. 'Never darken my desire again. And take that douchebag with you.'

—But who'll buy my truffles now?— she'd whimper.

Then my silence would be absolute and eloquent.

'Edie,' I ask at breakfast, 'do you know anyone of the initials "CGN"?'

A rat on the mat would have won a warmer welcome. Edie blanches, and her hand is rattling her cup against the saucer. 'Yes,' she gulps, stiffened mechanical, 'I did.'

'Who is it, Edie? Forgive my asking.'

She narrows her eyes, and looks through me, as if focusing on a far thing. 'We never mention him now,' she remarks, hushed but harsh.

Well, I'd never seen Aunt Edie meet an unspeakable before. Nothing intimate ever daunts her. Her wry tolerance is legion. She was the sort of charitable soul who'd find a good word for diphtheria.

And sympathetic! When she showed me how to make pancakes, and explained that sweet and savoury rarely marry, tears came into her eyes.

'Family?' I ask, forcing my luck. 'Was CGN a Nadherny?'

She nods, glassy-eyed.

'A skeleton?' I guess. 'In the family cupboard?'

'Lise . . .' she's starchy and resolute, 'I know what I know. You know what you know. Let that be an end to the matter.'

Next day in my clarinet lesson with Professor T—, my mind returns from reverie, scalded by intuition.

He is accompanying me on the piano in the Brahms F minor sonata, *allegro appassionato*. There is a cloying intimacy to our music that quite disconcerts. Professor T—'s dancing eyes in his swaying head are too intrusive and familiar. Whenever I look toward him his eyebrows arch, and his lips purse as if for a kiss.

I go all breathy, and start meandering an inadvertent tremolo.

'Dearest,' he whispers, 'what's wrong?'

'Gottfried?' I groan. A terrible notion has struck me.

'Shh!' He winces, gesturing over his shoulder. 'Emilie,' he hisses, 'she'll hear.'

'Aah!' I gasp. 'It's you! *Quel dommage*! How vile.'

Professor G. T— is Gottfried? He is the Other's furtive paramour?

This weasel, this failed soloist, with a limp, always reeking of rum, with a wife, two sons, a stutter, bald patch, frayed cuffs and a smirk, has been taking advantage of his lovely young pupil.

I am shivering from rage, shot scarlet with shame, wrenching my clarinet to pieces.

'The pearls?' I quake.

'What pearls?'

'The gold bracelet, then?'

'Aah!' This pierces him. He is tossing his head in alarm, a demented finger stabbing towards the open door.

95

'Yes! You have a wife,' I scream. 'Pity you didn't consider that before . . .' I advance on him and commence to whack his ear with the curled score of Brahms. 'You start . . .'

Well I can guess how he starts. But how far does he go?

'Beast,' I howl. I calculate that must cover most possibilities. 'Satyr, goat, deceiver, baldy . . .'

His head is sunk over the keyboard now. He is crashing a discordance with his crown, whilst his wife sobs hunched, poor frump, in the frame of the door.

'This libertine,' I warn her, 'tries to compromise me by pressing jewellery on me – whilst you're forced to clodhop around dressed like a scarecrow. It is quite enough to make a girl sick and . . .' words fail me, 'abandon the clarinet entirely.'

Of course, that's never the end of the matter. You can't better an Other so readily. By nightfall she's counterattacked. I return to find my room ravaged. My First Communion dress has been hacked to ribbons, my dressing-table mirror is shattered, the message 'Lise Berg is a bitch' is smeared in scarlet lip colour over my new mousseline blouse. The tip of my left index finger is stained the same hue. And I discover myself prostrate, heaving, choking over the bedroom carpet, retching up the best part of a bottle of Edie's cognac.

Truly, she's rabid when you cross her. And she won't be conquered in a single skirmish. Only now I'm keeping an eye on her whereabouts, she won't ambush me so easily.

Ach, Gustav is slow. It is half a year, perhaps, before he is finished with a painting. The girl swears he takes his time just to tease her. And he is unfaithful to her image. He sees other models behind her back, and never troubles to hide them. Lise sees the trollops, sprawled shamelessly across his canvases.

When she scratches an itch, sticks out her tongue at him, or rises to dance a polka with his model skeleton, then he bawls at her, partly playful, but also angry.

'Lise, lie still!'

'Three months in this position, Gustav, with my legs so. And you tell me to stay still!'

She rises, stretching, knotting her kimono tight, to examine his canvas, to find he isn't painting her face or body – which are quite dry and untouched – but some intricate purple patch behind her head.

'Gustav! You are detailing the background. And you promised you'd put some colour in my chest.'

'Lise, I'm working on the allegory . . .'

'Gustav!' She stamps her bare foot so hard it makes her squeal. 'I will not take your symbolism lying down. Liselotte Felice Sophia Berg prostrates herself for no man. She stands entirely for herself.'

Because, frankly, she finds his wandering eye insulting. She does not bare her breasts for him, and spread wide her legs, just to remind him of something else – mythical, abstract or dead.

Then her curiosity compels her tongue. 'What do I personify, then, in the painting?'

'You are *The Virgin*, Lise.' His eyes sparkle his impudence. 'You are sensuality – asleep. Soon I shall be finished with you, and then you can wake up.'

He understands a girl's innocence, dear Gustav, sweet man.

Desire is a deep, dark pond. She fears to dunk herself. Perhaps it is unfathomable. Suppose she loses her footing? Maybe she'll sink from sight? So she perches shivery at the edge, watching the surface ripples made by her waggling feet.

Each time, she keeps her eyes wide open, for fear of losing herself. She is a poor audience for men's pantomime. Though she casts aside her clothes, she cannot shed her disbelief.

Ach, it is preposterous. And yet, being so unlikely, it is beguiling. Oh, mischievous, and wayward, too. There is intimacy and juice. So much to see and feel, she had not known before. There are textures and shades of skin you do not find elsewhere, in this moist tufted land.

And swollen reddened weeping glands. Here, in the monkey house. Aromas she had smelled faintly before, without knowing where they fully belonged. Sometimes she falls into a trance, waking blinking and lost.

She says this for Gustav, he reveres a woman's form. You would not believe the respectful scrutiny he gives to a knuckle here, a knee there. He is like a child with a new doll, laying it wistfully upon the bed, fondling its hands, tweaking its hair, stroking its curves, fingering its seams, arranging its arms, spreading its limbs, delving all around. 'Ah,' he sighs, 'oh, my,' or 'there!', 'now, what have we here?'

'Don't! Tickles!' she screeches. For there is no part too small or reclusive for his scrutiny. He insists he sees everywhere, however out of the way.

'But, Gustav,' she protests, 'don't peep.'

Yet he enjoys a lady so much. It it as if she is the first he has ever seen, and he cannot believe his luck.

Gustav strokes her into torpor. She closes her eyes, as he fingers her awake, entranced.

She purrs. There is a thing deep within her that commences a distant throb. She goes deliquescent, touched by melting warmth.

Gustav quivers, grunts and gulps. She fears for his old heart, as it batters his ribs against her breast.

He touches her: she reaches to his root. Her chest flushes a coral pink. She feels all tingly and aquiver. It's an odd sensation. And not at all unpleasant.

—Mm, — she sighs. —Aah. —

One day I raise an intimate matter with Gustav, when his private parts loll prominent to view. I'd have mentioned before, but it never seemed germane.

'Forgive a personal remark, Gustav. But you only have two testicles.'

'Yes, Lise. Since birth.'

'Never mind,' I console, 'you're man enough for me.'

'Thank you,' he says, peering puzzled into my eyes. 'Two is the popular number. Did you not know?'

Yes, Kretschmer too had two, now I think of it. I feel very foolish. Some demon of my dreams it was who had three.

Maybe theatre helps me some with my Other, just as my Other lends me drama. If you can act up and act out on stage – poisoning a husband here, challenging the gods there, howling some rage, spitting on decency, seducing a baron entr'acte, or demanding John the Baptist's head on a platter – you're part way on the path to contentment, by giving some voice to your sinister side. The stage is a magic place, floating between desire and life, where your fantasy and fate can greet at least. Also you get paid. And gentlemen leave you flowers.

And there are things my Other knows already, or learns on her travels, that enrich my conscious range. When rage or passion are called for, none can project so strong or loud.

Over the years I collect plenty of names for my condition. Every doctor awards me a new one, till I've collected a clutch of titles, wearing them with nonchalant pride, like honorary degrees or campaign medals.

'Lise Berg,' I introduce myself to some new psychiatric practitioner, 'dissociative personality, multiple hysteric, confabulist, depraved character, pixilated paranoiac, ecdemiomaniac, poriomaniac, erotic pervert, pathoneurotic, borderline schizoid, gephyrophobic . . . Need I say more?'

One quack says I suffer from *fugues*. Well, I never mind. I've been called worse in my time. And it's a perfectly respectable condition – unrelated as it is to any popular madness or disease (except epilepsy, maybe). It's just an extreme form of absent-mindedness. You simply go walkabout from time to time, forgetting who you are. Stress or worry are often to blame. Mine is a mild case compared to others'. Poor Friedrich Vögel – the textbooks tell – left his home in Stuttgart, as a pastor, one morning in April 1903. Next thing he knows, it's June 1929 and he's a side-order chef at the 'Halfway House' motel in Cleveland, USA, known as 'Spike' to his friends. He's bigamously married to a Chinese–Mexican woman, and has fathered five children and converted to Christian Science.

Fortunately, I never do anything so extreme. I never lose more than nights, or occasional daytime hours.

'Aunt Edie,' I interrupt her reading one Sunday afternoon. We are seated alongside on the sofa. 'Can I ask your advice?'

'I'll do anything,' she clucks, 'to stop you making that infernal tapping.'

'Tapping?'

'Clattering your spoon on my Meissen porcelain.'

'Oh Edie,' I giggle at her naïvety, 'it's not tapping, it's *ragtime jazz*. Don't you like it? It's all the rage.'

'What do you want to ask . . .' She folds over the corner of a page, to mark her place, and lays aside her reading spectacles.

'This girl I know, Edie, at the Academy. She is always acting badly, going wild, disappearing with men, getting drunk and so on . . .'

'A familiar story,' Edie clucks. 'I dare say she's from a bad family.'

'No! Her family are very proper. And her twin sister is respectability itself.'

'Well? What's she to you?'

'We're always fighting and bickering. The bad blood makes me sick.'

'There's good in everyone, Lise. Everyone has their reasons to act as they do. Maybe you irritate her too. Perhaps you don't look hard enough for her good side . . . If you show someone consideration they'll invariably repay it.'

'Really, Edie?'

'It never fails.'

'Perhaps I could buy her a present, then, a peace offering?'

'Yes,' Edie beams, 'what does she like?'

'Cigarettes, brandy, gaudy clothes, saucy lingerie, vulgar jewellery, racy books, naughty postcards, kissing, stealing, doing rumpty-tumpty.'

'Mm,' Edie strains her smile, 'nothing else?'

'Chocolate bonbons. Marzipan and truffles.'

'Yes,' Edie nods, 'that would be best.'

So, on Monday morning I went shopping for the Other, buying a sumptuous box of rum and raisin chocolates, individually wrapped in gold and purple foil. There was a lurid picture of a Turkish belly dancer on the lid; and the whole box was swathed in pink ribbon. Naturally it offended my fastidious tastes, so I felt ashamed to buy it – explaining to the shop assistant it was a gift for a country cousin. But I sensed it would delight *her*. At least, that was my intuition.

I left this gift, with a brief, friendly note, on my bedside table – in case the Other took hungry in the night.

Within two days, all thirty-six chocolates had been gobbled.

Did she show any glimmer of gratitude? She never did.

All I gained by this generous overture were chocolate smears on my pillow, and a sickly taste in the mouth on waking.

Nonetheless I persevered, leaving cigarettes, perfume, and aqua vitae where the Other would be sure to chance upon them.

This was the phase when I tried to win her over by bribery and sundry indulgences. As things turned out, it proved a mistaken policy.

13

NOW, in my dotage, I'm alien – exiled in a foreign land. If I return to Austria, maybe they remember to arrest me for some mistakes I make in '53.

I've rooms on Rosebery Avenue, near the Sadlers Wells Theatre in Finsbury, London. *The King and I* now showing. It is precious for me to live close to drama, now I am not acting up on stage. Saturday midday, I go to the food hall in Chapel Market. It is not my business to advertise the shop's name: they do it too much themselves. But at the end of the week they sell off their old fresh food cheap. A third of the former price, maybe. What does it matter if a peckish old bird scoffs stale feed?

On the side of the package of grocery are instructions – saying open this way, eat like that. These I ignore: if I buy it, I feel free to open and eat just how I choose. Near the impertinent information, there is a sell-by date: 'best before . . .' it says.

Makes me chuckle. I am still out on display, dried and wrinkled, beyond my shelf life.

'Lise,' I tell myself, 'you were best before August 1934.'

Then my eyes moisten with memory, sometimes, maybe.

Sometimes odd thoughts of hers would trespass through my mind.

—Ah, there goes sweet Frau Ligetti, back from laying flowers on her husband's grave. Wouldn't it be too, too delectable to hack her shins and gob in her face?—

And I have to stiffen my legs and clench tight closed my mouth, for fear they'll obey the vile intruder's whims.

Or when brother August is stretched out reading on the rug at the hearth, she thinks, —Oh, how perfect. Shall I boot him in the mouth? And kick out his horrid teeth?—

'No!' I wince, turning abruptly away.

—God, I've suffered!—

'Suffered? You?'

—Poor Carl. I killed him.—

Truly, it sounds as though she's just chanced upon her conscience. 'Carl who?' I demand to know.

But you never get a direct reply to a question, for she rambles incoherently.

—Now this!—

'What's happened?'

She doesn't tell. All I know is the relentless burn of her caustic anxiety. Something serious is awry.

Suppose a young girl misses her monthly visitor and resorts to an unofficial doctor for deliverance, and is discovered by the law; then the consequences are terrible. She faces a confinement of up to five years' hard labour.

It's no wonder a girl is wary to disclose a haemorrhage to family or Doctor Flugel – for fear of arousing untoward suspicions. Anyway, another's involved. I owe her my protection. So when I go faint, descending some staircase in a tenement in 8 Bezirk, and blood is dripping dark and thick in a shameful private way, and I know no-one in the building, I stagger on to the street, racked by cramps, and hail a fiacre to take me home. I leave a curdling puddle beneath my feet, and sinister footprints. And a hefty tip. And say nothing until I develop a fever, accompanied by anaemia, exacerbated by infection, leading to melancholy and languor, confining me to bed for five weeks. With me, there are always complications.

As I remember, through the gloom of this sorry period, it isn't until the spring that I regained the vivacity to resume my former life, act, or sit again for Gustav.

'Gustav, darling man, you are old and yet I'm grown very fond. How does that come about? You are not handsome, are you? Not so much lion, more chimpanzee.'

'Perhaps I remind you of your father, Lise . . .'

'*Ach*!' She giggles at the thought. 'I never want to hump Pappa, Gustav. What droll ideas you have.'

'Then, perhaps you like men who are famous and wealthy?'

'Yes, Gustav, that must be it. Now paint me famously, will you? Hurry, please!'

Because, to her mind, there is no comparison between Herr Fischel's photographs and Gustav's portraits. And, if she can contrive it, she would like to be immortal in art.

Mamma scolds that she is vain. But she's never vain – not in her own regard. No, she is a lady of particular beauty. She cannot forget her flesh. The world will not let it be. It is the men! Often, she feels like a small polite princess lost in the woods, confronted by brigands: fearful they will snatch her tiara and jewelled brooch, then leave her stripped naked and sobbing.

'Gustav, dear man,' she observes one day, 'I notice that you never ask me to marry you. Or buy me a piano.'

'No,' he says. Just that. His 'no' falls like a single hailstone, transparent, hard and cold.

Well, she doesn't want to marry him. Not while she is beautiful and young. Only, she thinks it polite that he should ask and allow her to refuse. And a piano never comes amiss.

'Why not, Gustav?'

'If I were to marry, Lise . . .' he pauses, eyes screwed, mixing his yellows, 'it could only be to you. Or Emilie, Mitzie or Adèle. But, alas, I do not have an organ of fidelity. And I am happy as I am . . .'

She does remember this. He gives her an ambition. Oh, yes, what perfection, she thought, to feel happy as you are. Yourself. Content. At one.

You can see his summery contentment shimmering in the surface of his paintings, which are erotic, yearning, but strangely radiant, warm and serene. He knows what he knows. He wants what he wants. He is a lover of flesh. It is kind to him. His portraits command great prices. He is greatly admired, and very well loved. He has enough.

She suspects it is this good fortune, simple-minded happiness, that stops the Master from being truly great. For he lacks any fashionable *angst*. He never talks of agony or despair, like other, serious artists. And if he has any plans for suicide, he hasn't disclosed them to her. In the Museum Café, some gossips mutter that Gustav is a romantic lightweight, and is a fossil of a prior epoch. They says he lacks vitality. And that's the girl's experience. These last few weeks he's been less eager than before.

And I detect some change in his art. 'This painting, Gustav, it's meant to be me?'

'Yes, Lise, as Circe.'

'The body is exquisite, but the face isn't right. Normally you paint a good likeness, but this isn't quite me. The expression is lewd. It mars my pure beauty. You'd better repaint, to correct the bad impression.'

'No, Lise. That's how you look sometimes . . . when you have one of your wild turns. And you take it into your head to scratch.'

'Scratch you? I?'

'And bite.'

'Surely not . . .' I protest. Immediately, I'm sobbing. Oh God, the Other is betraying me again. And this provocative face is hers.

'I have a young friend . . .'

'Yes, Gustav?'

'What a draughtsman he is!' Gustav kisses his fingertips. 'But savage and wild. They do not understand it. His pictures show such anguish. I swear he will be great.'

'So, Gustav?'

'He needs models. And so I thought . . .'

'That I?'

'Exactly.'

'But we?'

'Almost finished, don't you think, Lise? Last portrait for a while. I have captured you often enough . . .'

'His name?'

'S—. First name Egon.'

Lise knows what he means. She is quick to feel.

'I'm no carcass, Gustav,' she howls, 'I am not a lump of flesh to be passed from man to man. Or traded like salami. I am not a hand-me-down or pick-me-up . . . I am not your gift. Lise Berg is her own. And her beauty too.'

'Lise,' he consoles, 'you misunderstand . . . . There,' he dabs my cheeks with the hem of his smock, 'we see each other still.'

'We do?'

'For sure. Some other times.'

I'd always thought of the Other as flighty and unreflective. Jumpy and greedy as a flea, with the persistence of a butterfly. It shocked me she'd the discipline to keep a journal. I found her self-indulgent, self-pitying jottings in one of my old notebooks.

106

Of course I'd never read another's intimate *pensées*. Only, if she scribbles on my sheets of paper, she can't plead for privacy.

—Pick, pick. Nag, nag. Why won't they let me be? Can't they understand? My suffering. The blood that's been spilled. Angry? I'll say. I'm entitled.

They don't care a jot for me. No! They only want to know that prig Lise. Some day I'll throttle the smarmy bitch!—

Whilst it's pleasing to read that one is well loved in general, it's frightening to learn a spiteful party has a jealous yen to harm you.

Beside the garbled self-pitying effluent were some guarded, coded diary entries that I was quite unable to decipher:

—18 Sat, G at K, $, **x2, mm!
20 Mon, T, H then S, $$, * and pq and pd, itchy!!"
23 Thur, F of Caval, *&mw, pit pr hrse.—

. . . and so on. It was clear she didn't want an intrusive eye to discern her comings and goings.

There is a flaw in the theatre. Its name is Director. He is like a worm in an apple or shame in the mind: a small wriggling thing that spoils it all.

Writers write well, sometimes. They rarely intrude. Often, they're dead. Actors act well, most times. Only the Director mars the craft.

He has finished his *Tafelspitz* and is sipping his wine. He is dining at the Sacher Hotel, run by the Sacher-Masochs. They are a distinguished family, writing two separate entries in the eternal ledger of sensuality. One side of the family creates *Sachertorte*, the other half perfects masochism.

The velvet drapes, scents of ripe flesh, bittersweet ambience are too rich for him. They provoke the Director into an act of imagination, lending him ideas.

'I know . . .' he says to himself, 'we will cast the play for dwarves on bicycles. No-one has ever done this before. It will be a novel interpretation.

'No! Better! We will set the action in a brothel in Barcelona. King Lear is Madame. The three daughters are whores. This will be sensational. It is Shakespeare's hidden intention. We get Strauss to write incidental music. And perhaps we have Grock play the Fool, and enter riding a cow . . .'

The Director smiles at his companion. He is flatulent with pride. He must burp his plan to his lovely companion. This other party is either actor or actress: they became intimate after the first rehearsal. It is necessary she keeps close to him, to put a brake on his imagination, protect her career and save the show.

This is a Secret Law of Theatre, whispered only in the dressing rooms. In every play, a member of the cast must become intimate with the Director. We share the work. We take it in turns. It is essential. You cannot leave him alone. There must be someone on hand, around the clock, even in bed, to distract him, or else say: 'Oscar, that is brilliant. But will it *really* work on stage? Sorry, I'm so stupid. Explain again the dramatic sense.'

This way, actors keep shaky control of their craft and save it from greater disgrace.

Lise's first engagement comes in 1912. It is a big break in Hofmannsthal's *Ariadne auf Naxos*. She plays a small mythical part to monstrous effect, quite upstaging Risa von Loehr, who'd supposed herself the star.

When you are strong and natural in a part, you enter a trance. It is disconcerting to come out of it to find yourself, volcanic with passion, shuddering your conviction, face contorted, howling your lines to the hushed hundreds, drawing their unseen eyes as you pad the stage, crazed as a caged tigress.

The composer Str— sees her performance four times and twice calls on her backstage. But his wife Pauline is a virtuoso of jealousy.

She smashes his metronome with a bust of Beethoven; or vice versa. Anyway, precious things are broken, vicious words are spoken. He never visits Lise backstage again.

Later, Str— turns the play into a musical, but she is not invited to sing in that. Soon after she is in Br—'s *August*, cast as Ilyona, the actress, who stings when she loves, and never marries the cad. She laughs, slams doors, rages, cries, roars for revenge, pours tea, knocks over furniture, kisses August, then curses him. All of this is scripted, condensed within a single scene. She ends the play with affected magnificence. '*Au revoir!*' she says. Lise will never forget this line. The curtain falls on her lightning exit, then sounds the thunder of applause.

Mamma and Pappa come backstage after the triumphal first night. Pappa clutches a bouquet of a dozen pink roses, tied with crimson ribbon. His gaze is down and his step is tentative – as if he fears a dog has done dirty business underfoot. His face perspires pink and radiates proud shame. The performance has cut fine new lines into his cheeks and brow.

'Lise . . .' he looks askance, 'you were most convincing and dramatic. And very loud. I wonder whether you understand the character. And yet you play the part . . .'

'Oh, Pappa,' she giggles, 'Georg, the Director, explains all that.'

'You were excellent,' says Mamma. Her enthusiasm is chilling. 'You act the loose soubrette too well. You play her with understanding.'

Georg sidles up and fondles Lise's rump: 'Isn't she the perfect little *strudel*?' He beams. 'Couldn't you just eat her?' He winks at Pappa. 'I could lick her all over,' he confides, then presses his lips to her cheek. 'I intend to.'

'Who are you?' demands Pappa. 'To manhandle this innocent girl?'

'The Director,' says Georg. 'And what dupe are you to protest her purity?'

'The *strudel*'s parents,' Mamma declares for them both.

14

NEXT day, worse happens. There are reports of the play in the papers.

For her dear parents, all publicity is notoriety. They would not mind her acting in theatre, so long as no-one sees or hears her.

". . . and the vivacious Liselotte Berg is a perfect floozie . . ." reads Pappa, ". . . combining highest self-regard with lowest virtue . . ."

Well, you can imagine this girl's delight. She has never been 'perfect' before, not in the *Neues Wiener Tageblatt*.

A hush falls around the breakfast table. Brother August's sneer freezes under Mamma's blenched stare. Pappa sits ramrod-stiff and bangs a clenched fist on the table, causing a clunk of porcelain and a tidal wave of tepid coffee. Some spills on the girl's new cream silk scarf.

'Very well,' he says, 'they retract or we sue.'

'Pappa!' she protests. 'This is a good review.'

'Disgrace . . .' hisses Mamma, 'how dare they!'

'Read, Lise!' shouts Pappa. 'It does not says you *act* a floozie. It says you *are* . . .'

'Pappa,' she pleads, 'the point . . .'

'The point is,' Mamma moans, 'it is published that a mother's daughter is a trollop. How can I show my face in Stammersburg? In the grocers, to Frau Krebs? What says Herr Pappenheim? When all Vienna reads that her daughter is a woman of easy virtue?'

In the second week of *August*, the author comes to see his play – to find if it survives its revival – and visits us all backstage.

'Ilyona,' he pecks at my cheek, 'bravo. You are very strong. A mite madder than I intended, but more powerful for that.'

'Thank you, Herr Br—.' I beam. 'But it is easy. This part is perfect for me. It portrays a secret side of me exactly.'

We would have parted there and then, only he frowns and asks me why I have pocketed his silver propelling pencil and his copy of the text.

'Please return them, Fräulein Berg,' he wheedles. 'The pencil has sentimental value. And I am very fond of this play, having written it myself.'

'Excuse me,' I say, 'but you confuse ownership and copyright. This book is mine. You may write the piece, but that doesn't entitle you to make off with a lady's lines.'

It sometimes happens that actor and writer wrestle for control of the text – but seldom literally. We both tug hard, and the book comes apart, ripped down the spine. I am left holding the early sections – in which I don't appear – whilst he's secured the final act.

The cast – now audience – have grown concerned. Georg intercedes. He never likes to see the leading lady and playright fight.

When we consult the title page, we find Herr Br— was right. The book bears his signature; also some pencilled notes in his hand.

Naturally, I'm inconsolable with grief to bring myself such public disgrace.

'I know how this looks,' I sob, 'but it wasn't me that did that. It was an Other. Pray forgive me.'

Herr Br— is uncontrollable with mirth.

'If you give me that asinine line,' he bargains, 'I will forgive you. And also buy you dinner . . .'

I was unfamiliar then with the way writers snout about in the dirt of blameless people's lives, like pigs rooting the good earth for truffles. Neither did I know that Br—, like Chekhov, is both author and doctor. Worse, his specialism is nervous disorders.

If he'd said as much, I'd never have confided my condition over *Gulyas* soup, *Paprikaschnitzel* and peach sorbet. But he encourages me to babble about myself and my art. Though it works out for the best, before it takes a turn for the worse, when I disclose about the Other.

'. . . she gets me into trouble . . .' I explain, 'and there's nothing I can do. She steals valuables, throws tantrums, flirts with my clarinet teacher, breaks things, disappears for the evening without a 'by your leave', consorts with strange men, gets me drunk . . . She is most awful when I strive hardest to be good.'

'Perfect,' says Herr Br—. 'For an absurd story like that you deserve a second bottle of wine.'

'Not too much,' I protest, 'or the Other will surely come.'

Herr Br—'s sad hazel eyes regard me over the gold frames of his spectacles. He lays down his fork, dabs his pursed mouth with a napkin, then commences to stroke his silvered beard. 'I do declare you're serious,' he rebukes in a mournful voice.

'Did you think I was a common liar?'

'A common thief but an uncommon liar, Fräulein. Or else a sick rose. I think perhaps the latter . . . You probably don't know enough pathology to make it up. Although your account sounds rather too pat . . .'

'Explain!' I demand.

'This "Other" is the part of you that you cannot bear to admit. Your mother and father are very strict. You are too inhibited. So you invent a persona to do what you want to. This way you can have some pleasure, and also keep yourself good. What do you say to that?'

'Nonsense,' I say, 'I'm a decent girl. I'd never dream of doing those dirty things the Other does. You sound as rude and foolish as Dr F—.'

'You consult professor F—?' The playright chuckles. 'And what happens?'

112

'He accuses me of awful, filthy things. By the end he gets over-familiar. My Other steals his fountain pen. Then I am too embarrassed ever to go back.'

'Perfect.' Herr Br— chortles, clapping me.

'Don't mock me,' I plead. 'It's not very nice.'

'Don't mock yourself, Fräulein Berg,' he cautions. 'Don't make yourself a laughing-stock or petty thief. And come and see me tomorrow at midday.' He hands me his card, disclosing his profession and consulting address. 'If you don't come punctually . . .'

'Yes?'

'I'll get Georg to sack you from the cast . . .'

'Then I will certainly come. It's a superlative part – despite some looseness in your writing.'

He warns me that I must be frank with him, and withhold nothing. Also I shall have to pay ten crowns an hour for the consultation. The money means nothing to him, he explains, but it's important I pay through the nose. A hefty fee invariably hastens a cure, by helping the patient concentrate.

'Can you pay?'

'Yes,' I mumble, 'I have 180 crowns in my savings account.'

'Only nine two-hour sessions. We shall have to rush. Now, Fräulein, tell me honestly, aren't I a greedy, bullying bastard? Would you like to spit in my face?'

'Yes,' I sigh, 'if you please. You read my mind exactly.'

'The "yes" is an improvement. But the "please", I'm afraid, is a relapse. Try harder, stupid girl.'

'Yes,' I hiss, 'I'd like to gob in your face. And . . .'

'What?'

'Box your ears.'

'Really, Fräulein! Too mild by half. Imagine you were writing lines for an angry woman of passion. . . . What would Ilyona say?'

Now a strange thing happens. Treat it like Theatre. Suspend your disbelief a while.

The time for my consultation comes and goes. Not until half-past three in the afternoon do I remember I must be at Dr Br—'s, and punctually, at midday. And there's a gaping, unreflective black hole in my time, that has swallowed several hours. I don't know what I've been doing to so distract myself.

Br— has threatened to lever me from his play if I don't show. So, you can imagine my shock and dismay.

I sprint down Berggasse into the Square, where I hail a fiacre. Seven minutes later we are at B—'s address. I race up the stairs to his second-floor appointment.

'Forgive . . .' I pant, 'please!'

'Back already.' He chuckles.

'I know I'm late. I'm sorry. Put it down to my condition.'

'But you came on time,' Br— assures me. 'More or less.'

'No, Doctor. You're surely confused!'

'But, yes!'

And so on. But he remains good-natured about the imbroglio.

'Sit down, Lise,' he waves me towards the ottoman, 'I'll explain what happened . . .'

'. . . you arrive ten minutes late without apology. I detect in your manner a confidence and nonchalance I hadn't seen in our prior meeting. Your voice, too, seemed changed – harsher, slurred at the edge. I suspected you'd been drinking. Your complexion is flushed. You wink and lick your scarlet lips. Your lashes are agitated.'

'"Fräulein Berg," I say, and reach out to shake your hand.

'"Call me Felice," you reply, "darling man." Then you peck me on the cheek, grim and purposeful as a hawk pecking at carrion.

'But I live to tell the tale, for you withdraw to perch on the chaise.

'I'm used to actresses. They are loathe to leave the limelight. For them, all manner of everyday encounters – buying a cabbage, drinking a coffee, consulting a clinician – hold dramatic opportunity. They speak rather loud. There are long pauses between their phrases, for theatrical effect, and in case any onlookers care to applaud. Oh dear, I think, this floozie's mind is still on stage.

'"Quit performing!" I say. "We have serious business."

114

"'Don't snap at me, pugface," you say. "I don't come here to be barked at."

"'Why have you come?" I ask.

"'I have a problem," you report. "I get paralysed by odd inhibitions. These are nervous attacks. For no reason I go all tongue-tied and timid, priggish and puritanical. A couple of times, it happens on stage. Sensitivity is a luxury an actress cannot afford . . ."

"'Fraulein Berg," I say, "you are quite contrary. When we had supper the other evening, you reported the reverse. You complained that an Other side of you takes over, goes wild, steals, acts lewd. And that you suffer some amnesia."

"'That's *her* . . ." you hiss, "this feeble, silly, sanctimonious bit of me. Cure me of it, please."

"'Tell me about yourself."

'Then you spin some unlikely yarns.'

'Doctor Br—,' I warn him, 'I think you're hallucinating. You need a rest, dear man.'

'No.' He smiles. 'Look in your jacket pocket. There's a letter I wrote for you.'

Sure enough, there is. A wax-sealed grey envelope addressed to me. I tear it open with frenzied fingers. Inside is a sheet of monogrammed paper with the hasty handwritten message:

'Fraulein, I met your Other. She's an entertaining character and insists on calling herself "Felice". Please come yourself, and I'll confide what she'd had to tell me. Yours etc. . . .'

I put my hands to my face, mortified. I begin to wail my shame.

'Don't worry,' Br— consoles. 'It's not so bad. . . . Now where to start? . . . Do you know about your Uncle Carl?'

'He's in Budapest?'

'Your clarinet teacher?'

'A beast!' I hiss.

'Your childhood accident?'

'I fell from the bridge at Stammersburg.'

115

'The game of Russian roulette.'

'What?'

'Felix's nose?' he continues his flurry of questions.

'It's gross,' I confide. 'Ugh, it looks indecent.'

'Listen . . .' says Br—, blinking, 'I'll tell you what Felice says about his snout. It will give you a flavour of her character.'

Cousin Felix accosts the girl in Augustinerstrasse.

'I'll wait no more,' he says. 'Decide!'

He has her compromised, has Felix. If he tells Mamma and Pappa of her comings and goings, they will manacle her at home. She'll forfeit her freedom, her career, her famous Gustav – who paints her for posterity.

She looks at Felix, and his comic *bratwurst* nose. He is so sensitive about this lavish appendage you must pretend you are blind to it. But this tact is all one-sided. For he is always poking his nose where it never belongs. He is a gawky long-beaked bird of a man. He has the dignity and demeanour of a pelican.

Another thought occurs to the girl as she appraises Felix's features; then her rage quite subsides. A wry grimace splits her face. Suddenly she's resolved, if not entirely resigned.

'Very well. If you want me, you may have me, Felix.' She smiles. 'But you must promise never to betray me to Mamma and Pappa. And you must respect me. You must love me the way I wish to be loved . . .'

'Very well, Lise. If you will satisfy my desire, I shall gratify yours.'

He leads her briskly in silence to a small hotel off the Gurtel, close by the railway station. The proprietor knows Felix. Felice supposes he has brought others there before.

Ach, it is sordid. Perhaps, I spare you the details.

No, better I tell the piece – so you don't think bad of the child.

The cost of the room is two crowns for the afternoon. Fifty thalers more for towels and to have a fire lit in the grate. Felix economises here. It is a damp room with an iron-frame bed. Over the mattress are folded grey sheets and a stained beige blanket. To the side of the window is framed our Emperor, Franz Josef. He looks younger and thinner, but a blue-green mould has devoured his legs.

'Lie!' commands the gentleman. 'There, on the bed.'

'No, Felix.' She stands her ground, shakes her mane, smiles. 'A bargain is a bargain. I will tell you how we do it.'

She lift her skirts for him, and loosens herself beneath. He is too impatient. He tries to rummage in her blouse, where he has no rights or access.

'No!' she yells. 'No hands.'

Then he is tearing at his trouser buttons.

'No, Felix. Don't bother to undo me, or disarray yourself. We do this business my way. A promise is a promise.'

'What?' He is agitated and flushed. His gaze is distraught and unfocused, fearing a trick.

'Take me. Now, Felix. With your . . . *nose.*'

'My nose!' He brays like a thrashed donkey.

'Yes. It is proper. For you are always poking it where it never belongs.'

'No!' I howl at the Doctor. 'Stop telling stories.'

'Don't interrupt,' Br— reprimands. 'I haven't finished the tale yet.'

. . . Felix looks at Felice, stupefied. She never forgets his expression. Then he sinks to his knees, defeated.

His face reminds her of Manfred's, in Act Four of *The Enigma of Pastor Herz*, when it is revealed that the Cook has taken the Holy Manuscript to wrap fish – four haddock – which she has sold at market for fifteen thalers to a visiting Rabbi from Linz.

Shortly she leaves him there, the rims of his ears glowing crimson, his nose glistening moist and pink. His expression is sheepish and humbled, as he kneels on the bare boards, but he will not meet her triumphant eyes.

'God!' I gasp. 'She says *that*? The lying strumpet!'

'You don't believe it?' Br— enquires.

117

'Well . . .' There are some details Br— couldn't make up for himself, not without inside information. And recently Felix has been acting strange – distant, cold. No, absent, really. 'No, but it could explain some things,' I concede.

Is that why Felix is so changed? He shuns her house, as though it held contagion. No visits, no flowers for seven months now. And in January he'd written to her Mamma and Pappa, proud and formal, announcing his engagement to a Fräulein Martha Broch. He calls her his innocent blossom.

Also gossip was heard from Aunt Edith. Felix had grown pugnacious. If people look at him in the street, he challenges them. He accuses them of mocking his nose. *Ach*, it is sad. It is eccentric. Our nearly cousin is not quite himself. No good can come of it. It is a game of consequences.

One day he is walking down Rathausstrasse and takes offence at a pleasantry from a captain of Cavalry. Felix demands that the captain retract the remark about his nose. There is anger, then chill formality. Cheeks are slapped. A duel is arranged.

You guess the outcome? Felix is a virtuoso with a cheesewire, but the soldier is more practised with pistols. This captain, though, is stabbed by pity. So, instead of killing Felix, he just shoots through his thigh. Thereafter, her almost cousin must hobble through life.

Ach, often she thought of Felix. His name means 'lucky man'. Sometimes she felt responsible for his misfortune. Yet, mostly, she supposed, he deserved it.

15

WELL, I've seen August's and Egon's sketches of the pouting strumpet. Edie and Mamma eye me awry, on account of her doings. But Dr Br— is the first to win her confidences and report them back to me.

Dear God, can I never be free of her? I come to the doctor's to secure a cure, and she sneaks an appointment before me – just to discredit me with her horrid, vile tales, craftily bent to graze plausibility.

'That's the sort of hussy she is,' I whimper to Br—. 'She blurts the first thing that comes into her head, just to win attention.'

'Perhaps it's the truth,' Br— offers callously.

Sweet Jesus, he believes her. She's taken him in. He's trusting her word against mine.

'Dr Br—, you spoke to this trollop for a long while?'

'Two hours, Lise.'

'And you talked about me, I suppose?'

'No.'

'About what then?'

'She spoke entirely of herself. But it was most illuminating.'

'Which of us is your patient, pray?'

The question makes him hesitate. I think he gets my drift. He rubs his eyes, having lain his wire-rimmed spectacles on the desk before him. 'You are, Lise. Your need, I should say, is greater than hers.'

'So, you take up with some strumpet who wanders in off the streets? And give her my appointment? It sounds like you have divided loyalties here. And which of us do you charge for the consultation?'

'This character is a part of you, Lise. Your Other side.'

'So, we're related. . .' I concede. 'But what she says I cannot swallow. You meet her the once. I've shared a body with her for four-odd years. And a bed. It's no easy lay, I can tell you. No laughing matter.

'I warrant I know her better. And I warn you . . . her morals and her honesty leave a lot to be desired. Better check, if I were you, she hasn't made off with any valuables, and . . .' I prickle, fidgeting with the band of my bloomers beneath my georgette crepe dress, 'I trust there was no hanky-panky . . .'

'Fraulein Berg,' he says, stiff with starchy professional dignity, 'you are my patient . . .'

'But *she* isn't,' I remind him. 'I want to know how you get so intimate with her so soon.' Is there a twinge of jealousy, perhaps? And I sense in myself an unnatural reluctance to hear what she has to report. Whereas a sensible, curious girl would be avid to learn what her Other half does on the sly, in her hole-in-the-corner way.

'This Other knows aspects of your life that you, apparently, do not. Shall I tell you?'

'No!' I hold my hands before my face, as if to fend off a blow. 'Never. I don't want to know her better. I want her out of my life. Now.'

Br— nods quietly. 'It is understandable. If you wanted to know, you would have no need to invent her to protect yourself.'

'*I* invent?'

'Listen carefully, Lise. I'll explain what I know of your condition. You have *poriomania*. Kraeplin and Charcot have written about it.'

Writers! Unless it's already in a book, they doubt a thing has a right to exist. Shoot their mother, and the occasion will remind them of some sorry poem.

'It is a form of automatism. Your mind splits. One part takes over, and goes about its business. The other part of your character doesn't know. One side of you is too timid and restrained. The other side too rash and wild.'

'Cast her out, Doctor. I must be rid of her.'

'But . . .' he smiles warily, 'she wants to be rid of *you* too. She complains you intrude on her intimate life, and sabotage her acting.'

'*Her* acting? The bitch! She's claiming my talent now?'

'Any talent to talk of is yours *and* hers. What we must do is reconcile you both. We must search out the trauma that has caused this split within you.'

'No!' I howl.

'Why not?'

'If I know what she knows . . .'

'Yes?'

'It will kill me.' Already we share a body. If I know her mind, I'll become her. It'd be the end of me.

I know it's vain. I shouldn't ask. But one question gnaws away in me: 'Doctor, you've met us both. Be honest. Which of us looks lovelier? Tell!'

He lowers his spectacles down his nose to squint over the frame. The littlemost finger of his right hand arches to scratch rhythmically at his temple: 'It is a very even contest . . . the difference is of facial expression and voice. She is more animated and flirtatious. There's a wicked glint in her eyes. But you have this . . . elegant inscrutability . . .'

'And which do you prefer?'

'You, I think.' He smiles judiciously. Of course, I suspect diplomacy.

'So, best if I stay just as I am?'

'Oh no, Fräulein.' He frowns. 'Not if you desire to be happy.'

Ignore the jealous gossip and foul-mouthed rumour. I never slept with Arthur Br—. Never. Not in the summer of 1912 in Vienna, nor later weekends in Morbisch. Felice, maybe. Me, never.

121

No, but we get to be close and intimate friends. I tell him things that help with the background for his stories – lingerie, longings, suspicions and such. For his part, he slowly acquaints me with myself, and encourages me to worsen my character.

'You see, Lise, this "Other", as you call her, speaks your memories and desires denied. You try too hard to be saintly.'

'True, Arthur.'

'You must come to terms with yourself. Give yourself some pleasure.'

'I'll try, Arthur. Really, I will. I'm working on this already.'

'You must recognise your desires. They are strong but they are natural. Come to terms with yourself, and accept your imperfections. Speak your mind. Then you can be reconciled with the Other.'

'Imperfections, Arthur? What?'

'Well . . .' he sighs, rubbing his eyes, 'at heart you're a floozie, with incipient kleptomania. But none the worse for that. Also an excellent actress, not untouched by vanity. The stage and the cafés would be poorer without you.'

'Thank you, Arthur. I give you some advice in return. When you're excited, you spit as you speak. This isn't attractive. And your plays repeat themselves too much.'

'That's useful to know, Lise.'

We are very frank. We get along famously.

To please Gustav, I sit for Egon. So I get painted by both. Ah, it's not so strange. Several women travel this route. Gustav passes us on: Wally, Mitzie, Adèle and Lise.

Poor credulous Wally Neuzil loves them both in turn. Gustav passes her to Egon. She dotes on Egon for a few years. Then he ditches her to make a respectable marriage to one or other of the Harms sisters – Adèle or Edith. I don't remember which. Nor, say the wags, does Egon.

And poor Wally? Alas, her name sets the tone. She's dogged through life by wordplay, persecuted by vicious puns. She joins the

Red Cross as a nurse and contracts scarlet fever. This lady, who splits herself body and soul for art, for Egon, expires in Split, Dalmatia. Sad.

Wally always answered the door when Lise called at the studio in Hietzinger Haupstrasse.

'Oh, Lise,' she frowns, 'how nice. It's you.'

Then Egon despatches his Wally on some two-hour mission, across the Danube, or to his mother's house in Tulln.

'But will you be all right on your own?' she asks, her eyes rolling reproachfully, pleading permission to stay.

'Lise is a woman of the world,' says Egon; 'she does not need a chaperone.'

'Don't worry, Wally,' Lise consoles, 'I have no mind to steal your man.'

So, sniffing and misty-eyed, Wally trots off, with the weary resignation of a pony hitched to a milk cart, dragging her heavy load. She never complains, nor contrives a pretext to arrive back early. Oh, she made them feel guilty. Yet Lise always kept her promise, and never stole her Egon.

He is endearingly perverse. But a self-respecting lady could never love him. For he was so narcissistic, always gazing in his mirrors. Once, he draws the girl facing a mirror, as he watches her watching herself, behind her. But really he is watching himself. If you catch his drift. She was a mite offended when she saw the drawing. But you cannot see the image is of her, for he has narrowed her thin as a pencil. Her breasts are small as dumplings.

Egon likes young girls. How, and how much, no-one is sure. They say he draws upon a taste he acquired with his sister, Gerti. But maybe he's just immature.

When he stayed in Neulengbach there was scandal. The villagers say he gets too fond of the children, draws them nude, and encourages them to examine their bodies. The police visit and confiscate a hundred paintings. This attests to their taste, and beggars the rumour they don't like art.

Egon is aquitted of abducting and seducing a minor, but found guilty of exhibiting an erotic drawing in a place accessible to children.

The judge burns one of his paintings in court, and makes him stay three more days in prison. This is in May, some months before Lise meets him. The publicity helps sell his paintings. He is a rebel who suffers for art.

'In prison in Neulengbach, Lise, they gave me only one blanket. I was condemned to draw on toilet paper. And they denied me even a mirror.'

'So you could not observe your own suffering, Egon?'

'No. But I felt it, to be sure. Yet I was not so much punished as purified.'

'Yes, Egon?'

'To restrict the artist is a crime. It is to murder germinating life. *They* were the criminals.'

'Yes, Egon?'

'But for my art and my loved ones I gladly endured.'

'I am glad you were glad in the end, Egon.'

Egon cannot recognise wit when it touches upon his person, although he can see it strike another. If the girl had known she'd spend her own time in prison, she might not have been so facetious.

When she poses for him, Egon's art is in transformation. If you know about Expressionism, it is enough to report he is midway through his stocking period and emphatic with the finger. So he requires his models wear only bootees, stockings and garters; and he advises her where to lay her hand.

'Lise . . .' he chides, like a schoolmaster, 'haven't we forgotten something?'

'No.'

'A finger?'

'Shan't,' she says.

'Surely, Lise? For art?' he wheedles. 'Will you deny art an honest depiction of Woman?'

'You are a profound artist, Egon. Your work will live in posterity, God willing, so I will not go down in the history of art as *The Lady with a Finger up Her Fanny*.'

'Wally is always willing . . . whatever . . .'

'She is not Lise Berg.'

'But, Lise, you did before . . .'

Yes, I guess as much. I've seen the portrait. There is a suggestive glint to her vulnerable gaze. It's a lewd pose that's *hers*. Never mine.

'Not I. Never. You confuse me with another.' Because, frankly, if Lise ever chooses, at some ticklish moment, to finger herself, rub here, or scratch there, that is her personal business, for her own intimate satisfaction. She won't do it to man's command, to be captured in the luminous light of culture. And what would her Mamma say if she ever saw the picture?

Surely, a naked woman is exposed enough. Egon must permit her a modicum of privacy.

One afternoon in August I am sitting with Herr Dr Arthur Br—, the darling man, in the summer garden of Schubert-Stubel Café. Hermann the waiter is delivering our *Kaiserchmarren* and *Eiskaffees*. I savour the scent of mimosa on the breeze when Br— chills the air, raising a personal matter.

'August 13, 1909,' he observes. 'I calculate that was the start of it all.'

I push the plate of pastry away from me. My fork falls from my hand, clanking on the tiled floor. I want to retch.

'Felice confided this to me. She remembered the day exactly. Now, I think you're ready to hear.'

I am aware that my skin shivers with goosebumps. Yet my chest and belly burn. There is the ebb and flow of vomit in my gullet, a foul acid burn.

'It is a terrible day for you. Horrible things begin to happen. You believe it's your fault. But it isn't. Truly, you are an innocent and injured party.'

I am panting. A misty gauze veils my sight.

'Sit upright and breathe deeply,' Br— advises. 'I will order a glass of water. Be brave and hear me out . . .'

His hands reach across the table to feel the pulse of my wrists. Of course, I jerk away as if scalded.

'Never, ever hold me so,' I pant, 'like Pappa . . .'

'Forgive me,' Br— soothes, 'I'm sorry.'

We sit in silence as my heaving subsides.

Dr Br— asks me my Christian name.

'Lise,' I say.

'Good. As long as I'm talking to the right person. I will tell some events. If you want me to stop, tap your hand twice on the table . . .'

'. . . your Uncle Carl lives upstairs. You are fond of each other. But he is a sad, inadequate man. He develops an attachment for you which is not proper. Not for a grown man towards a young girl relative.

'One day he grasps you and kisses you. You know this is improper. It disgusts you. You run from his attic room.

'That night, your mother asks you to take Uncle Carl his supper, which he eats alone in his room. You refuse. Your mother and father demand to know why.

'In your childish way, you explain. Your parents' faces show you have touched on a terrible matter. They interrogate you closely on how Uncle Carl has touched you. You fear you've said too much. You begin to recant and deny . . .'

'Is there more?' I ask.

'Yes,' says Br—.

'Then I have heard enough for one day,' I tell him, knocking twice on the table.

'It's progress at least. Shall I order more coffees?'

'For me, no,' I say. 'My appetite is quite gone. I have a splitting migraine. And I feel unutterably sad.' Then tears well in my eyes. I'm sobbing convulsively, as though suddenly bereaved.

All day terrible shapes loom in my mind. It's too large for my mind to labour to admit it. But still the foul thing heaves. Something monstrous pushes to be born.

There's a reverberant thud, overlaid by a splat, at the front of the house, silencing the dawn chorus of birds – a different, dismal sound: hollowing an absolute quiet. A dreadful package has dropped from the sky. I am down the stairs and out of the front door without remembering my passage there.

Uncle Carl lies on his back on the paved patio staring upwards wide-eyed and startled, his brows and cheeks bruised purple, his swollen nose oddly splayed.

It is very chill. Time has gone elastic. This moment is as long as I care to stretch it. I'm unfeeling, but sharply aware. He's fallen. Forty feet, maybe, from the window of his attic room.

The back of his head is curiously flattened and leaky. There's a sluggish spreading puddle.

I kneel. I press my mouth to Carl's stiff, cool lips. Too late to kiss him better; but small gestures count.

As my hands clasp his temples, I feel him cling tacky to my palm and squidge between my fingers. And his life blood seeps through my nightdress, dampening my chest. My bare feet squelch in something. Dear God, I've trod in his mind. Unbalanced, dizzied, I topple, slithering in his sticky puddle. Pink, jellied smears of him, flecked crimson, cling to my rump and thighs. Then my hands and arms, as I wipe him away.

And I get the pulp on my cheeks and brow, as I clutch my hands to my face and howl. And my nose is clogged with the warm, coppery scent of newly slaughtered meat.

Some of him – smeared on my lips – gets into my mouth. Then I'm kneeling, spitting out a jellied glob, coughing out a grit of bone. He is cool and slippery on the palate. Though I spit him out, still the taste remains.

So there we are, inseparable, Carl and I.

I'm writing on the paving, sobbing, smeared in his pulp. And though I clamber up and away from him, still he clings all over, hugging me everywhere. Though I tear my nightdress off, I only spread the curdled mess.

Mamma doesn't recognise me when her scarlet daughter glides past her in the hall. She knows every naked patch of me. But now I'm wearing Uncle Carl, smeared in his juice.

127

It would be a quiet, peaceful thing, to fall and forget.

Poor Felice, darling girl. She's carried this alone all these years. Just to protect me.

And I've repaid her so badly.

Dear God, we Bergs are so unsteady. So many of the family have fallen.

16

WHEN Fritz Bohler begins to orate Hamlet's soliloquy, the rest of the cast are rendered speechless. There is such a chilling, demented quality to his voice. Max Rinser, the director, paces the back of the auditorium, his face in his hands, quite overcome. It is an electrifying theatrical moment. I never forget. For we are performing Belmyer's erotic comedy *The Chambermaid Confesses*. And Fritz is meant to be playing the Pastor in the wardrobe, and not the Prince of Denmark. Only, being liquored up he forgets his lines, and fills in as best he can. Such things happen in weekly repertory. You get eclectic drama when you are rehearsing two plays and performing a third.

Yes. Theatre was my education. You hear and see amazing things. I could tell you stories you'd never believe.

When I appear with Klara Moll in Reinhardt's *The Miracle* we become intimate friends, and chatter about all manner of things – clothes, food, directors, actors, rumpty-tumpty, and men.

One day, she confides her peculiarity to me. It happens this way:

'Klara,' I say, 'we are close; will you forgive me if I make a personal observation concerning your craft on stage?'

129

'Observe away,' she consents.

'You are a considerable artist, Klara,' I say. 'Only I think I detect a flaw.'

'A flaw?' She frowns, her voice turning one notch chilly.

'That holds you from perfection. A small fault, only. Just a splinter sticking out from the fat plank of your talent. A tiny fishbone in your delectable *bouillabaisse*. Nonetheless, it sticks in the throat.'

'Tell, then. Cough it up. Don't spare me!'

'Well . . .' I hesitate, 'you sometimes make a small yelp or whimper during the performance. It distracts from the action. And it isn't in the text. Once, it happened in my main speech, otherwise I should never mention . . .'

'Oh, Lise. Is that all? Listen, there's an intimate explanation.'

She told me this much:

'Long story, Lise. I have a medical condition, a little peculiarity. It is not life-threatening, but it is distracting.

'I will explain by way of illustration.

'There is a French writer called Marcel Proust. He tells how one day when he is grown up he eats a sponge cake like that he had as a boy. One taste, and all the memories of childhood come flooding back. It is the same with me. Small things bring back fond feelings. I am a sensual woman. Memory works too strong in me. I tumble back.'

'Yes, Klara? Be specific!'

'All right, Lise. I will lay it on the line. You know how you go to the opera with a gentleman. He tries to fondle you in your box. He gets overexcited, then frustrated. Because Wagner sounds far too long . . .'

'I am familiar, Klara.'

'Patience, Lise. I'm getting there. After the opera you go to supper. The gentleman's mind is on his afters. He keeps massaging your knees under the table, then plays footsie if you pull away. His face may go rather red.

'In the fiacre home, he wrestles with you, and shows much impatience. He is perspiring and damp. His mouth is too much in yours.'

'I know it.'

'So he has been waiting six hours, perhaps. You could call him overwrought. By the time he sees the starter's flag, he's set to bolt, for he's already ahead of himself. Having got his delayed opportunity, he's finished before he's really begun. It is much ado about nothing, for both. You wait while he picks himself up.

'Maybe he goes apologetically or ashamed. But I never mind. Don't bother yourself, Heinrich, old man, I say. I am satisfied already.

'But I don't tell him when I became satisfied: once at the end of Act II, and twice more during dinner.'

'Klara, you mean . . .?'

'Yes, Lise. I am like man in general and Proust in particular. The mind works in strange ways. Memory is always fingering me; I am constantly surprised by brisk spasms.

'The least thing can set it off – the touch of a peach, the smell of a certain cologne, the sound of popping buttons. I go moist and warm. I flush. Presently, I'm all aquiver.

'This is why, Lise, when you invite me for a bicycle ride to the Schonbrunn Palace, I really must decline. I'm happy to sit on a bicycle, but it never gets me anywhere. For it presses too hard on my memory. It has a very evocative touch. Anyway, I fear, if I started to peddle, I would get distracted, lose my balance and topple on to my back.

'Men still move me, of course. Only I don't feel a need for new lovers so much. My memories keep me warm. For the recollection of past affairs pays compound interest. It is like having big savings in the bank.

'All manner of unlikely things can tug my tiny, hairsprung trigger. The odour of lilies, the aroma of a certain hair oil when the clock strikes two, the taste of rum and peppermint, *Harold in Italy* when the viola strikes up, or a line of text that echoes some romance in my life. Memories come streaming back. They set it off. Even on stage. Often, I can't foresee . . . So when you say *that* line in the script . . .'

'What line Klara?'

131

'I won't repeat it. I'm not in the mood. And I know you, Lise. If I tell you, you will tease by shouting it twenty times.'

'So, Klara, when you yelp during a performance . . .'

'Exactly, Lise.'

'Well, I never,' I gulp. 'Forget I ever mentioned it. Yelp away to your heart's content. Even in my speech.'

Well, we all have some peculiarity. Mine is of a different kind. I quite lack Klara's facility. I could never decide if I envied her. Probably not. I like to be in control and have everything in its proper time and place.

The girl has to mislead her family regarding her whens, wheres and whys. It is difficult to please inquisitive parents whilst also leading a life.

A girl's inclination is 'yes', but Mamma's reprise is 'certainly not'.

'Lise,' she enquires, 'where did you sleep last night?'

'Sleep, Mamma? I?' Yes, where indeed? I cannot tell.

She nods. She insists on knowing.

'Aunt Edith's, of course.'

'No!'

'No, Mamma?'

'No. I called on Aunt Edith this morning. She has not seen you for two days.'

This brutal inquisition moves the girl to tears. Besides, she cannot exactly remember. Not all of it. On Tuesday she got lost between the Hotel Imperial and Berggasse. Wednesday, a Hungarian string quartet entertained her over supper, but events went opaque on intoxication. She remembers a black cat crossed her path, and a parlour with a leather chaise longue. When she woke on Thursday morning, at dawn, wandering Stefanzplatz, she sensed a weight tugging her down. And when she pushes a hand into her overcoat, she finds the pockets are laden. In the left pocket there's a Browning revolver, with a single bullet in the chamber. In the right, there's a fat wad of fifty-crown notes. Also some dollars and deutschmarks.

This is typical of the Other. On the one hand she scares you silly. On the other she pays dividends.

'Everyone gangs up on me,' she sobs, 'no-one lets me live.'

'Is there trouble? With a man?' Mamma demands. 'Trust me. Tell me. I won't get cross.'

'No, Mamma,' she promises. 'Not a single man.' And, indeed, there is no-one special. Nothing so particular. 'Only, I go in the evenings to Klara's, so we can practise our lines. We rehearse too long. It is too late for the tram. So I sleep on her couch.'

'Look at me, Lise!' Mamma stabs the girl's breastbone with a forceful finger. 'This is not theatre. This is serious. It is life . . . I'm not a gullible audience in the stalls. I am your mother. I do not pay to laugh at you. Instead, I give you birth . . .'

She is very strong and naturalistic. Lise has never heard her orate so powerfully. Often before she seemed hammy. The girl had wondered where her dramatic talent came from. Now she sees it's from Mamma.

'I give you suck, I change you when you are wet, I bathe you, I rock you asleep. When you are ill, I sit eight months at your bedside. Poor Lise – I weep – my child has gone strange in her head . . .'

Mamma has an intuitive grasp. Many novices begin too loud and emotional, and leave themselves nowhere to go. They find themselves at the summit whilst still they need to ascend. But Mamma knows better – modulating wickedly, while winding the ratchet slowly.

'I tend you for one whole year. My wrists are swollen from arthritis. Always they ache. But do I ever mention it? No, I have my duty to do. . . . Now what? My daughter acts like a *maderl*. Do you think we are put on this earth to enjoy ourselves? To do whatever we want? To take pleasure? Have fun? . . .'

Ach, a pity. At that moment Mamma loses her balance. Having stepped in a lump of text, she slips. Of course, the girl laughs. She would never advise that Mamma philosophises, actors write, or writers act. We should stick to what we know best.

The highest peak in Austria is *Grossglockner*. It is also a theatrical term. Sometimes a character will equip himself with rope, icepick and crampons, in order to climb on to a tram.

'Mamma,' she giggles, 'you are wonderful. Do your duty, by all means, but leave the acting to me!'

'God forgive me!' Mamma gasps, slapping her daughter's face two-handed, howling at the pain this brings to her poor, arthritic wrists.

The next day, Lise leaves home. It is a big break for her. She has the lead, touring Bohler's *The Ungrateful Daughter* to Innsbruck and Salzburg. She'll never return home to live. When they get back to Vienna, Minna Levy and Lise share rooms.

Because Mamma and Pappa have brought her up well, given her confidence and good values, she is unafraid to leave. Besides, let them try to stop her now. It is 1913. These are modern times. And she's a mature eighteen, and has an income of her own.

Also there was Oskar K——. It was my reward, to be painted by three good artists.

Lise never betrayed their confidence, given in the confessional of their canvas, whatever their provocation.

Myself, I'm bound by no such reticence. The intervening years free me, courtesy of the statute of limitation. I tell you this much at least:

Oskar makes a lifesize model of Alma Mahler to keep him company in bed at night, saying it is more companionable than the real thing. But Gustav and Egon never sleep with dummies.

Gustav paints in a smock. Oskar has no fixed attire. But with both – you can rely upon it – the lady model wears less than the artist. Yet Egon sometimes wears his birthday suit. So, if you're in the uniform of shoes and stockings, you're more concealed than him. It can be disconcerting when he pauses in his painting, to fondle himself distractedly in front of the mirror. It is as if he finds *his* nakedness more alluring and poignant than your own.

Gustav and Egon never fight in the War. Oskar joins the cavalry, is badly wounded, but survives. Whereas the other two both die of

134

influenza in 1918. Strange. You never can tell how best to live. Should a man stay dangerously at home? Or flee for safety, by fighting in the army?

Oskar delights to make mischief and scandal. Gustav and Egon are artists of the erotic. Gustav is profound and superficial. He reveres a lady's surface. It does not concern him that we are all blubber, bones and offal beneath the skin. With Gustav there's complicity; he wants to show the shimmer and bloom of your beauty. He is like a great theatrical costumier, or doting dresser. He wants the lady to look exquisite in her role, when she appears to enact the Myth.

Egon is dissatisfied with the healthy flush of flesh, the wholesome gloss of skin. He wants to rub you raw, then cut away beneath. Give him a rosebud, and he will start tearing off the petals. He hopes for a maggot within.

He thinks you are withholding your beauty from him, if you cannot show him some blemish, pock, scab or scar.

'Sorry, Egon,' Lise tells him, 'I'm flawless, as you see.'

But, of course, he cannot. His is a tortured, deforming eye.

Perhaps you know *Recumbent Woman in Violet Stockings*. Yes, that emaciated, hollow-ribbed pubescent girl is meant to be me. Compare it to K—'s *Studied Innocence II*, drawn six months before. There, you see! Ask yourself, how does a healthy growing girl mislay her bosom and hips?

Intimacy with Egon? She finds it remote, distant or cold. She has never before met a man who thinks to make love with a woman when he is standing with his back to her, and she is sprawled in the opposite corner of the room.

'Does this excite you, Lise?'

'*Ach*, I can take it or leave it.'

'Won't you join me?'

'No. You just please yourself.' She sighs, more bemused than appalled.

Or he asks her to do insanitary things.

'In my *mouth*? Certainly not. I don't know where it's been.'

Frankly, they disappoint each other. He desires her to play doctors and nurses, or act a dirty girl to his naughty boy.

135

They lay flesh on flesh a few times. But though they grasp each other, their aesthetics never clinch. He requires they do it like some doggies he sees, humping in the gutter. This way he need not look her in the eye. It is all very chill, impersonal and passionless. Also wry and dry. All the while he watches their reflection in the mirror. He wears an expression of pained perplexity on his taut face. It is as if he is struggling with some problem of composition and hasn't resolved the perspective.

With Oskar it is frantic and turbulent; with Gustav deliciously languid and slow. Some things are very private. These she cannot tell.

Anyway, with Egon there was a happy ending, as his paintings show. Wally perseveres with him. Then he marries his Harms. By 1914 he is painting women with curves and swells. Shortly after, there is a man in the picture. In 1917 there is *The Embrace*: the couple are entwined, facing each other, in bed. A year later there is *The Family*. The naked couple crouch with a child. Sweet. Every picture tells a story, as the saying goes. Sad: that he promptly dies of flu.

I still have a letter he wrote to that girl that once was me.

> 'You will be so proud to have known me . . . . All beautiful and noble qualities have been united in me . . . I shall be the fruit which leaves eternal vitality behind even after its decay . . .'

But I'll say a good word for Egon. He forgave. Whereas the kind man, Gustav, never did.

Once, when I pay a surprise affectionate call to Gustav at his studio, I interrupt him. For he is busy at *bumsen* with Mitzie R— on the chaise.

I should not mind so much. They are adults. Both are avid to consent – gasping 'ah's, 'yes's, and such. Only he has the very same expression on his face that he wears when he is loving me. Also he is repeating with Mitzie exactly what he does with me. It is as if he cannot tell his women apart, or remember which is who.

And they are doing the business before my very eyes. For my portrait is facing them the while. So I am made to watch them, scowling out, from the canvas of *Jealous Actress II*.

'Forgive me, I disturb,' say I. 'But Dr Br— prescribes me to act forthrightly, and never bottle up my feelings.'

—Go on!— an inner voice prompts, —You know what to do.—

So – thus encouraged – I hack diagonally through the canvas of my portrait with the green-handled palette knife. There is a clean ripping sound. It feels as though I'm cutting, too, our long liaison.

'There,' I observe with satisfaction. 'Now you can be free of me. You lose me and my likeness too. I think you will regret . . . whereas I feel better already.'

You know what? He quite ignores me. He is hunched over the frame of my picture, fingering the frays of the cut, mumbling to himself, his whatnot visibly wilting.

'What?' I howl. 'Speak up!'

'Actresses, shopgirls, dancers, these are cheap. Five a thaler. But that effort, infatuation, light. . . .' He drums his temples with his fingertips. 'Those I can never replace.'

You've heard of Pygmalion, maybe?

There. I rest my case.

17

'LOOK, Arthur, my caster-sugared cherry dumpling, flambéd in kirsch, under a mound of melting double cream,' I remark to Br— one afternoon, as I lie candidly sprawled on the chaise in his consulting room. 'I take all your advice. I dump some hard-won morals. I speak my mind as I find it. I'm forced to remember foul things from my past . . .' I gulp. 'Won't you offer me any coffee, with maybe a small slivovitz? I love your darling new curtains. The duck motif is very droll . . . but my condition gets worse, not better. Perhaps you've given me some bum advice . . . or failing that, perhaps a small cognac.'

'What's happened, *kleine* Lise?'

'Last Friday afternoon, I wake up naked in a strange bed. Fritz W— is lying beside me, smoking a cheroot and wearing no more than a smug expression, and a signet ring on his little finger. I don't remember for the life of me how I got there. And I've to rush like a demon to be on time for my rehearsal and, by the way, do you like my new alligator-skin bootees from the House of Floge's? Aren't the diamanté buckles vulgar? I'd never have bought them myself. But Felice threatens a tantrum if I don't treat her.'

138

Arthur frowns and tweaks his ear. 'Fritz W—, who wrote for *Die Fackel*, the author of *Sexual Deprivation*, *Love Affairs in Bygone Days*, and *Ezekiel the Foreigner?*'

'All I know is he has a port-wine birthmark on his belly, and shares Irma Karczewska with Carl Kraus. Once I go to an art exhibition with her and she starts stroking Apollo's bronze privates, so I scurry away and hide behind the Danube Nymphs until she has satisfied her curiosity.'

'I don't suppose Fritz mentions, by chance, how much Egon Fleischel advanced him for his new novel?'

'It didn't arise, Arthur,' I wince, 'but you are showing the curiosity of a fellow author, not the true concern of a lady's doctor.'

'Excuse me, Lise.' He goes quiet, frowns.

'Well?'

'Your poriomania. . . .' He shakes his head from side to side, and adopts a mournful expression. 'It's an *extrem* condition, bewildering for clinician and patient alike. We're getting closer to the source of it all. But there's a complication . . .'

'Yes?'

'It's Felice, I fear she's misleading us.'

'You're still seeing that bitch — behind my back?'

'She called on Thursday, Lise. She told me some confidential stuff . . .'

'Yes?' I feign disinterest. I'd much rather not hear. Yet I itch to know. But can't bring myself to listen. This Felice mixes humiliating lies and corrosive truths. It's always mortifying.

'Felice is trying to trick us.' Br— breaks the silence, rubs his closed eyes.

'I warned you she was sly,' I remind him, all self-righteous.

'This story of your Uncle Carl's suicide . . .'

'It's true. I remember it.' My eyes moisten. I shudder.

'Yes? When I ask her details, she goes shifty and evasive. I'm sure she's concealing things. She's protecting someone. Herself, perhaps, or you.'

'Dear God.' My left cheek begins an involuntary quiver. My hands are wrenching the fabric of my dress. 'There's more? Worse?'

'I'm sure.' Br— nods. 'Don't worry. We'll find it.'

139

'Worry?' I wince a smile. 'Who's worried?'

Hannah Stein and I share a dressing room for Goldmann's *Fables of the Riverbank*. I play a nubile Watervole in an exotic costume of leather and fur that dramatises my chest and legs. I get to speak a long and poignant soliloquy on the squalid perils of rodent love; whereas poor Hannah, as Second Shrew, only gets to squeak through a hood. *Ach*, it is not art, but it symbolises something significant about social decadence. Gregor assures us so. Anyway, it's work.

'Lise,' Hannah says, one night after the performance, 'I am invited to supper at Palais Schwarzenberg. There will be Hussars, a poet, a string quartet, and my cousin Carl – who is quite a character. Also champagne and forfeits. Would you care to come along? The poet has asked especially if I'll bring along the furry vole. He has written a sonnet about you.'

Well, it is pleasant to be asked to the Schwarzenberg. This girl holds nothing against admirers. Neither will she decline to dine *gratis* on crayfish tails. So she doesn't pause to consent.

She gets seated between the poet and the cellist, opposite a Captain of Hussars. This soldier is introduced as Carl Fallehn. This excites her somehow. She cannot remember exactly how, but she's heard this name before. It carries an emotional *frisson*; of danger and passion stirred. She senses he is an enemy in some way; but otherwise a friend. He is a long, thin man. Maybe two metres. His bony fingers are obscenely sensual, massaging the tablecloth, stroking the bowl of a spoon, patting the arm of his chair, twirling a breadstick, caressing the rim of his wine glass. It is as if he must touch everything to confirm that it is real.

He has close-cropped black hair and sombre ebony eyes. The effect is more riveting than handsome. When his eyes arrest you, clinical and searching, you quickly blink and look away. He quite reminds a girl of her brother: with his lithe build and surly manners.

Fallehn observes the company with rapt derision.

'Oh, sweet, quivering vole . . .' commences the poet, skimming Lise's arm with an impudent finger.

140

It is a short ode, remarking upon her ivory teeth, shining eyes, lustrous fur, and dark clandestine burrow. She detects satire and innuendo, but is distracted by Captain Fallehn who makes every pretence of insouciance and, in some private defiance, never salutes her general charm and major beauty. Instead he stares at her with unblinking insolence.

'You aren't so beautiful as you suppose,' Fallehn informs her. 'Women like you expect men to frolic at their heels like puppies.'

'You aren't so singular as you suppose,' she confides. 'Men like you confuse boorishness with originality.'

She's unused to the indifference of men. Perhaps, she supposes, the soldier prefers his own gender. That would explain his steady-eyed contempt.

'Do you have poetry in you, Captain?' she asks.

'Well . . .' He spreads his open hands, gesturing his helplessness. 'A little. But, of course, I cannot compete.'

'Please,' coaxes the poet. 'Open your sensitive soldier's soul to us.'

So Fallehn coughs diffidently, then speaks:

> 'There was a toad who fancied a vole,
> And tried to delve in her hole.
> Alas, he was left on the shelf.
> For she only had eyes for herself.'

'Sir!' she protests.

'Really!' gasps the wounded poet. The verse has moved him, and he is temporarily the worse for words.

'It needs more work,' concedes Fallehn, frowning. 'It was composed recently in haste. The rhymes work, but the scansion is awkward. It is a realist work of social observation. It is the first part of a trilogy.'

The party has gone quiet. All eyes are swivelled on the triangle — poet, actress and soldier — its corners, obtuse and acute.

'If you don't like it,' Fallehn smiles at the poet, 'tell me and I'll make amends.'

'How?'

'I'll encourage you to eat your words,' says Fallehn, 'by force-feeding your thin volume down your scraggy throat.' He lays the poet's book next to his plate of grilled pike. 'This is known as autodigestion. It is a new form of literary criticism I recently invented. For I can't abide envious poets who snipe at their colleagues' work.'

'No . . .' the poet is quick to assure him, 'yours is an excellently sensitive little poem. Very condensed. And the imagery is very delicate. So exact.'

'Good,' says Fallehn, beaming as he rises. 'It is a pleasure to give delight. Pray manage without me for a moment. A pastoral muse moves me. I must go piss an ode in the snow.'

As the girl watches his victorious retreat, his motion lithe and willowy as a dancer, she remembers why she knows his name.

She leans across the cellist to confide to Hannah: 'What a coincidence. Now I remember . . .' She chuckles. 'How droll! Your cousin Carl is the shit who shot my cousin Felix in that duel.'

She's formed a strong impression of the man – for he is an unusual and pungent taste. The two occasions she hears of him, he's threatening violence to another. So, it occurs to her, that entertaining Fallehn in society is like admitting a fox to a chicken coop.

When he returns to his place at the table, Fallehn's eyes are phosphorescent, his hands are dancing more wildly, but his manner is muted, polite and calm. He intends irony, perhaps.

He demands to debate Goethe with the poet who, once bitten, has gone coy, and is as forthcoming as an oyster. But Fallehn insists on prying him out of his shell, peppering his preposterous observations with brotherly phrases like 'writers of our stature', or 'we explorers of the human soul', or 'we pygmies in the shadow of Heine'.

'I believe it was Goethe himself who advised that poets should write with chisel on stone, rather than with pen on paper,' Fallehn reminisces.

'Really?' the poet enquires.

'That way they strive for economy of expression, get some healthy exercise, and don't clutter up cafés.'

'Indeed?'

142

'Captain,' Lise hisses, 'you're a bully.'

'Perhaps . . .' he concedes, '. . . because when I have fleas, I scratch,' then he falls to a morose silence, staring at his plate, toying with his fish.

She almost feels sorry for him. He is not house-trained. His moods are too extreme. He has too thin a skin. He is a poet of violence. The bleeding beast cannot help himself.

'Don't be bothered by Fritzie,' Hannah comforts. They are locked in a cubicle in the cloakroom, to compare camisoles and confidences, and not be overheard. 'He gets like this when he takes cocaine. He calls it "powdering his nose".'

'The poor man.' Lise sighs. 'Can no-one help him? Surely, some woman . . .'

There! You guess already? Yes, she feels the oddest desire for him. This girl isn't calculating in her affection; nor can she ration her passion.

Over brandy and *petits fours*, Fallehn tells her strange and alarming things. It is his opinion there'll be a war.

'Nonsense,' she says. 'Someone would have mentioned it before. Besides, Georg would not have booked me for a European tour.'

'Mark my words. In six months or a year – whoosh . . .' He grins inanely, spreads his arms, displaying his open palms, as if warming his hands at a fire.

'You sound as if you *want* a war.'

'I'm a soldier, Fräulein. A war would suit me very well.'

'People will get hurt,' the girl warns, wiping her moist palms on her organdie sleeve.

'It will burn away all this . . .' he scowls about him, '. . . decadence, corruption, rot. Then we can live in an age of honour.'

'Decadence?' she enquires. 'Where?' All she can observe is the lush dining room of the Schwarzenberg, chattering and canoodling couples, slurred, staggering comings and goings.

He intrigues her, this sullen soldier, with his talk of decadence and corruption. It is like hearing there's a backstage party to which she hasn't been invited. Maybe he knows interesting places she's never been taken.

'Show me,' she challenges. 'I demand some corruption.'

'First take my hand,' says Fallehn.

She remembers all of the subsequent hours, even though she drinks too much – there was tango dancing at Zum Binder, dwarf-wrestling at Grinzingers, satirical cabaret off Cobenzglasse, and an exotic and unlikely skin show in a cellar in Fleischmarkt.

'I recall it all,' she brags to the soldier, 'I never blacked out once. I stayed aware and awake throughout. Really, I enjoyed myself.'

'Good,' he says. This is the complacent nonchalance of a man used to keeping women awake past their bedtime. 'I'm glad.'

'Usually an Other takes my place,' she explains. 'When it gets down to the sticky business with skin.'

'I'm pleased you stayed,' he says. 'I didn't want another. I only wanted you.'

'Truly?'

'Promise.'

'But why do I choose you? Of all people?' she whispers into the secret pink curvicules of Fritzie's ear. 'Why us? How does it happen?'

It is dawn now. There are glimmers of light round the hem of the brocade curtains. This is room 77, the Hotel Dionysus. It was a fine augury that they spend the night here. The girl is superstitious. Seven is her lucky number.

She is lying on his chest. They are stuck by sweat. As she rises to rest on her elbows, their skin sounds a rip of protest as they tear apart.

'Once upon a time . . .'

'Yes, darling man.' She licks his salty shoulder to encourage him.

'People were round and proud. Each had four legs and arms, and two sets of private parts . . .'

'Isn't that overdoing things?'

144

'It's true,' Carl protests.

'Who told you?' she demands.

'Aristophanes, a wise old Greek.'

'All right . . .' she concedes, 'as long as you're not telling me fibs.'

'And these round people please themselves and are very smug. They get very haughty and snub the gods.'

'They'd better watch out,' she guesses.

'Exactly!' Carl agrees. 'Because here comes Zeus with his carving knife . . .'

'Ouch,' she gasps, wincing, 'he never does?'

'Yes. He cuts each and every one in half. From then on people have only two arms, two legs, and one set of sexual parts. All of them are horribly torn. They spend their lives forlornly searching for their missing halves.'

'True,' she must admit.

'Those that were doubly woman are women who yearn for the woman they lost.'

'So that's why . . .' She nods. 'Poor girls. They'll never find the one they want. There are too, too many laps . . .'

'And some were double males. Now they lust for the missing man.'

'I know,' she squeals, 'I work with them in theatre. They never give a lovely lady a second look.'

'But most . . .' Carl yawns, 'were half woman and half man. As we were, pursuing the other sex to complete themselves. A fortunate few, like us . . .'

'Fritz!' She jerks up straight with a start, plonks her buttocks on his chest and peers down at his darling sullen face. 'You mean that we . . .?'

'Yes, Lise.' He reaches out a languid arm, drawing a cigarette from a silver case. 'Once upon a time . . .' he lights it and exhales smoke upwards in her face, 'once *we* were *one*.'

'How can you tell?' she demands to know.

'Our bodies knew,' Carl says. 'They recognised each other immediately. The moment they met.'

'But our silly heads didn't understand?'

'Exactly!'

145

'But we are so different, Carl. Is it possible? When I am soft where you are hard? And you are sour and I am sweet. And I am lovely and you are plain? And you are clever. Whilst I'm as froth-headed as a lager – everyone tells me so.'

'Just so.' Carl nods his conviction. 'It is because we are such perfect opposites that they are completely one. We complement exactly.'

The girl knows there is something to this; that they are a profound couple, Carl and she. She never wanted a man before as she wants him now. If they are parted, she'll be less than herself. It is beyond truth. Though she's acted many classical parts before, she's never lived a Myth.

'I know what, Carl. Let's try again . . .' She wriggles down alongside, wraps her legs about his waist and draws his head on to her. 'I give you my body again. See if yours can guess what she most desires.'

18

THEY take lunch at the Red Hedgehog. They are both thrilled: Carl especially, having taken some cocaine powder to keep his sinuses clear.

His impassive face blisters with sweat. His body seems to vibrate as he squirms in his chair. The waiter stands hunched, awaiting our order, his palms pressed together as if he were a penitent at prayer.

'What will you eat, Lise?'

'Something expensive, Carl. I leave the choice to you. And some champagne to drink. Whatever vintage you prefer.'

'Bring the lady something overrich and vulgar,' Carl bids the waiter. 'Make sure it's garishly garnished and prohibitively priced . . . I demand to wince when I see the bill.'

'Lobster in Armagnac. Then suckling-pig *en croute* with truffles, perhaps, Captain?'

'Exactly so. And consommé and a plain omelette for me.'

'You're a rich man, Carl?' she asks him, and watches the waiter slide away sideways, as if rolling on casters.

'Beyond my dreams. Now I have you.'

'Sweet man,' she says.

'But, Lise, I fear I love you. . . .' His tone tells it as a fatal infection. His eyes flicker closed in pain.

'Why fear, Carl?'

'Love is lethal.' Carl laughs mirthlessly. 'It is a crushing yoke of honour.' He groans and rolls his eyes. 'It is crippling to carry. I shall have to lie awake at night. Think of you all hours of the day. Go insanely jealous. Make foolish, extravagant gestures. Be seen carrying you flowers. Accuse strangers of staring at you and demand they duel. Be polite to your girlfriends. Attend your plays. Admire your garish clothes. Laugh at your lame jokes. Forego my other lady friends. Wear that tawdry necktie you'll inevitably buy me. Have you intrude in my rooms, even . . . I shall became a laughing-stock at the barracks. My companions will shun me . . .'

His is a long list of complaints. He is bending a fork back and forth, till it snaps with fatigue. His voice has risen loud. The surrounding tables are hushed audience to his melodrama. The girl is startled by this vehement grievance. This man is spitting in the face of their mythical love.

'Isn't it romantic?' she observes, to distract him. 'My almost-fiancé is the man who shot my almost-cousin Felix in an affair of honour. It is as though we were destined. And won't Mamma be tickled pinkish when I introduce you?'

'God, no!' howls Carl, turning to the sommelier. 'There is a *mother* too. It's worse than I supposed . . . I'll have to be polite to the crone. . . . What in God's name can I do?'

'Sir?' The man looks down the crease of his trousers to his patent leather shoes, and coughs.

'I pick up an actress at dinner,' Carl explains, as if tutoring a foolish child. 'We spend the night in a hotel. When I pause to examine myself, I find I've contracted a social disease.'

'Sir?'

'I'm in love,' moans Carl. 'This stupid girl has rifled my heart. And see how she looks at me, with those lovely wide cow eyes! What's to be done?'

'A drink, perhaps,' soothes the sommelier, 'to be going on with.'

'Is that the best you can offer?'

'Alas, so, sir. I can recommend my wine. But my advice is banal. When it comes to love, I'm an imbecile. If it's any consolation, sir, I'm married myself.'

'Champagne, then, fool.' Carl waves him away.

'I'm tired of hearing, Lise.' Arthur Br— shakes his silvered head, narrows his eyes, tapping hard on his desk with his fingers. 'Carl this. Gustav that. Do you intend to spend your life sleeping with Carls and Gustavs? Just because your uncle . . .'

'Silence!' I command. 'I don't want to hear.'

But the doctor won't be told.

'You throw yourself at worthless men.' He fingers his cravat, and picks some fluff from his sleeve. 'It's as if you're repaying a debt. There's some voracious guilt that gnaws at you.'

'Guilt?'

'Enough to make you try suicide.'

'When?'

'Lise! Surely even you must see.' Now he is knocking his temples with his knuckles. 'Is there anyone at home?' he enquires, 'in that lovely head of yours?'

'Tell!'

'Your childhood accident. You didn't fall from a bridge. You threw yourself.'

'For why?'

'I think you know.'

'No!'

'Then I shall give you a prompt. Your brother is involved. Also your father. There are falsehoods built upon lies.'

'Br—!' I howl. 'You are a dirty, filthy man. The things you suppose are vile. Do you think I waste my money on consulting you for this? When I can bathe in a sewer for free?'

'And the risen corpse?'

'Charlatan,' I scream, 'quack. Hack . . .' I am quivering frightfully, as my eyesight explodes in golden shooting starbursts.

149

Acting is poorly paid, selfless work. But someone has to do it. With musicians, artists, poets and writers, actors are the guardians of the Soul of Humanity.

Lise knows herself a fine actress because she can feel so forcefully. Also she sympathises excessively, and empathises extremely. Actresses are very feminine. Actors are less so.

Theatre is unjust to women. There are more women than men who aspire to the stage. Woman is more talented at voicing passions. Her feelings are finer, and her sensitivity sharper. It isn't just Lise who thinks this; poets too remark upon it. Yet, on stage as in life, men are awarded the more prominent, powerful roles.

Lise is outraged. She sees actors speak Hamlet who lack the finesse to play Mute Maid with Limp, or Grandmother Snoring by Fireside. So the actor sounds like a double bass playing against the actress's violin. He ponderously plucks his few, deep notes.

Another travesty. The actress must be trained to act. Then she only gets cast to play herself. The director will not trust her to imagine. Worse. He slowly explains to her, in insultingly simple words, how a woman acts and feels.

Or, like sheep, actresses are judged by their fleece. To play the romantic heroine, a girl should be blonde. With dark hair, a lady can dip to emotional depth. She can even be devious or depraved. Redheads, like Lise, express turbulence and passion.

Height is crucial. If you are as tall as a man, forget acting. Better join a circus as a freak.

But if you are very short, with a pretty, bland face, you can play little girls until you reach fifty. Then you must grow up. The creases in your complexion deepen. They swallow the make-up, but still they show. So you are forced to graduate to a mature repertoire – of Mother, Aunt Mimmi or Maid.

Minna Levy has black hair, sharp nose, and a stoop. Don't worry,' a director tells her, 'there'll be plenty of work for you as a Character, as soon as you turn forty.' Only, when he says this, she has eighteen years to wait, so the promise has a dispiriting ring.

To hold herself from heartbreak, and to cling by her fingertips to the cliff-face of ambition, Minna bleaches her hair, smears her

150

smallpox scars with pink greasepaint, lies about her age, and follows Lise to auditions. She smiles suggestively at the Director, but he has seen this desperate face too often before.

Lise considers herself fortunate. She knows her face is lovely, her body luscious, her voice mellifluous as a clarinet. She is often cast to play the scales of her passions.

Despite the contrast of their appearance, character and talents, Minna is convinced she is competing with Lise, accusing the girl of stealing her parts. She believes the girl should share her leads – as if it were a matter of gift, not graft.

'I don't get it, the part of Psyche.' Minna shakes her head, bewildered by this further prejudice of fate.

It is poignant and sad. She cannot understand the part, nor herself. For, to play Psyche, a lady must portray ravishing beauty. She mustn't have a speech impediment. Ideally she shouldn't slouch.

'I know. Georg tells me. He gives it to . . .' The girl fears to widen the wound.

'Who, Lise? Tell. I bet it goes to some talentless tart he sleeps with – all cleavage and pout.'

'Me, Minna. He casts me.'

'Congratulations, Lise.' She stirs her coffee furiously. Centrifugal forces fling droplets on her shawl. Her lids drop, her teeth slice into her lower lip. 'I'm not surprised.' Her felicitations sound sour as a curse.

Sad. For they are greatest friends. But their art threatens to wrench them apart.

All evening Minna slumps lethargically in the wicker chair by the stove. Lise's eyes and nose agree. There is supper prepared – a beef broth with liver dumplings. Yet Minna will not stoop to pick herself up, warm the pot and serve Lise.

'. . . bed,' Minna mumbles, too weary to start her sentence, eager only to end it.

Presently, Lise hears muffled gasps and sobs from the bedroom. Minna lies shivering beneath the quilt, her sorry head stowed beneath the pillows.

'Minna, darling, what is . . .?' Lise strokes the heaving back and pats the quivering mound of pillow.

'I'll never get a lead part,' the mound splutters.

'Nonsense, Minna. Be patient. Soon will come the right role for you – Witch, perhaps, or Jealous Sister . . . Anyway, if you want, I'll wangle it so you can be my dresser.' For Minna is always so willing, tidy and efficient, washing Lise's sheets, folding and ironing her clothes, polishing her boots, tidying her cosmetics, mopping up any spills, discovering her lost garters, reminding her what's happened, darning her stockings, delivering up a cup of coffee just as she desires it.

She does this anyway, so it is better that she gets paid for it, and they make the arrangement formal.

When Carl is not shaming the girl in a public place, he makes her weep and flush in private. He is maddened by nature, cocaine and love. A quite impossible man.

An example: his games with guns. She is brushing her hair when she hears Carl's tread behind her, then feels the press of cold metal to her temple. It is his revolver. The clank of the trigger sends shudders through her skull, and shivers through her chest.

'Don't play with guns,' she howls. 'I won't have shooting in the bedroom. One day you'll make a mistake, and the gun will be loaded.'

'But it is loaded, Lise.' He breaks the pistol open and shows her the single shell and the five empty chambers.

'One chance in six,' he observes gravely. 'A reasonable risk.'

Then he spins the chamber, pokes the barrel in his mouth and his finger twitches on the trigger.

'Don't!'

Clunk.

'Dear God . . .'

Clunk.

'No!' she howls. For she will not have it. She tells him if he shoots one of them, she'll never forgive him.

'Lise,' he chides. 'It's safe. It's a trick.'

152

'How?'

'Gravity,' he explains. 'The weight of the bullet pulls the loaded chamber down, away from the barrel.'

'Always?'

'No,' he concedes. 'But it is very likely.'

'Likely isn't good enough. You'll be the death of us.'

Maybe she encourages him. For when he lays down the revolver, her gratitude and affection overwhelm her.

Ach, but men. They think they know all about the business, and every way to make love. When the girl proposes some radical foreplay, they look askance, perplexed.

'No, Carl. Lie doggo. Like you're dead. Still as a corpse. . . . Open your mouth. Stick out your tongue.'

'Lise. The sheets!' he grumbles, as she pours the red wine cascading down his chest.

She licks the rivulets from his chest and belly. She ravishes the poor dead man.

Lise watches Carl as he pants in his sleep. She wants to locate in him the lie of her love. Dreaming, he shivers, twitches and mutters. The sardonic mask drops away. And beneath lies the puckered scowl of an anxious child.

She pulls down the sheets to regard his length. When she tickles him midway, he pumps his legs, as if off on a bicycle ride.

She doesn't understand it, how this surly, unkind man satisfies her, or resolves herself and an Other. Just look at him!

But his nakedness reveals nothing. She cannot solve the enigma of her desire. His surface doesn't disclose. It is merely the sealed envelope. And she wants to read the letter. She yearns for the knowledge beyond the carnal: an intimacy beyond reach, under the skin.

Perhaps its because he's contrary like her – part lovable, part atrocious. He speaks to her, and also to an Other. Maybe she's met her match.

When she nuzzles his shoulder, he turns on to his belly and leaks a polite, perfunctory moan.

It was the same with Aunt Edith's Pomeranian. Touch a certain secret place, and over she'd roll.

It pleases Lise to have Carl so: sleeping naked alongside. He is so vulnerable and docile like this, in the pathos of his sleeping flesh. Whereas awake he's a different man, a prickly package, a demon — who'll shortly do an unforgivable thing.

19

O F course, when I find it, I'm poleaxed by shame, sinking into my bed, panting desperately. When I've recovered my composure and colour, I scrawl a quick apology, seal it in an envelope with the item, and despatch it by messenger. Arthur is always so kind and attentive. It's a poor way to repay him.

'Dear Arthur, sweet man,
Forgive! I found your wallet this morning in the left-hand drawer of my dressing table. I can only suppose that unspeakable woman took it when my back was turned. A thousand apologies on her behalf!

Thank God there was nothing of value in it for her to steal — except that photograph of ugly old me. How sweet of you to carry me so close to your heart.

Again, I trust to your kindness and discretion. Imagine, please, my hot wet kiss on your big fat nose.

Your dear friend Lise'

Within an hour there comes the curt reply:

'Fräulein Berg,

Consider our relationship – professional and personal – as irredeemably closed.

I have made all possible allowances. I have given you every benefit of doubt. Now, no doubts remain to benefit.

The theft of a thousand crowns I could pardon. It is that other wound I can never forgive.

I fear you are quite mad, or incurably depraved. There is nothing more I can do for you. Only a sentimental compassion stops me informing the police.

Arthur Br—'

When I hurry to Br—'s apartment, Oscar his secretary, frosty with hauteur, tells he has strict orders not to admit me, ever.

'Why?' I enquire.

'Because you are a rank pestilence, Fräulein,' Oscar says, without any spontaneity or warmth, as if coached, 'and less welcome than a dose of dysentery.'

'Perhaps I've done something to annoy the dear Doctor,' I hazard. 'I expect by tomorrow he'll be ready to forgive.'

— It usually only takes a day. —

Oscar stares impassively, silently closing the door on my anxious smile.

And when I see Br—two days later in the Frohner Bar of the Hotel Imperial, he snubs my greeting and strides past as though I'm invisible.

So I must have done something *extrem* to tease him. I know not what. And I wonder, too, why his nose is smothered under such a swathe of white bandaging.

—Snotty bastard. —

'I've annoyed him somehow. What can I have done?'

— Only bit his nose about a bit. —

'You never?' I gasp. 'Sweet Jesus.' I cross myself.

156

—No big deal. It's still in one piece. . . . The shitbag deserved it. Always snooping in our affairs.—

'He did make some vile suggestions . . .' I concede.

—We're well rid of him. He was trying to split us up.—

'Maybe. He called you some nasty names.'

—I know what. . . . Let's get plastered. Properly pickled. Pissed as a . . .—

'The Museum Café?'

—Sure, to start off. Then I'll show you a good time at Pink Willi's. Do you know Ludwig the contortionist?—

We are too far apart, the girl and I. It is hard to sympathise. This woman–child knows nothing yet. Nothing. All her philosophy, psychology, poetics, wisdom, tact, are still to be learned. All she understands are cosmetics, acting and fun. Oh, yes: and taking a tram without paying the fare. But she left her mark on me, this girl, an indelible reminder, lest I ever forget.

Consider her young character. It will help you understand.

She is a mite perverse. Impatient too; impressionable and immature.

Take pastries, for example. She can't resist. No sooner has she taken a mouthful of the first than she fancies the next. Ditto wine. One sip, and she's worried: will the second bottle come in time?

She doesn't drink to forget; yet, sometimes, it helps that effect. A few times she opens her blinking eyes with surprise. Then it is some moments before she realises where she is sleeping, with whom and why.

One morning Minna shakes the girl awake, complaining of a pig in the parlour, snoring on the chaise. Minna claims Lise is to blame.

'Tell him to mind his manners,' she moans. 'No. Tell him to go home.' Sometimes in bed in the morning you desire no more than to be left alone.

'No,' says Minna, 'a *proper* pig.'

And so it was: a snorting, pink-eyed piglet, the size of a dachshund, only slightly higher off the ground.

157

She must have picked him up the night before, being suckered by his frisky, snuffling charm.

Later, she finds Anton asleep in the bath and, wakened, he accounts for it all, bringing her memory up to date. This is no ordinary pig. He is half of a satirical cabaret act, topping the bill at Mischa's. They'd shared a cab home. In the revelry this piglet – stage-name, Professor Leerlauf – gets parted from Igor, his partner. In theatre, you help fellow artistes in distress. So Lise offers piggie a spare bed for the night.

She likes a good story. But jokes bore her. You have to wait till the end for the punchline. You've invariably heard it before. And people expect you to laugh. Call her impatient, but she likes to know the denouement from the start.

So when she is sent a new play, she reads the last page first. And imagines her applause.

Often, she never gets beyond the last chapter of a book.

And she's ravenous for confidences. Suppose a gentleman says 'Good evening, Fräulein . . .' and winks, she is frustrated by talk of the weather or some novella of Thomas Mann's. She wants to get straight to the intimate chat. —Who do you hump?— she itches to ask; —Do you like my hair this way?— or —What was the most embarrassing day of your life?—

But the curious girl mustn't say as much. Instead she bites her tongue.

She's strong-willed too. She resents being imposed upon or taken for granted, tied up or settled down. Some men, having known the transport of her bed the once, suppose they have a season ticket. These she'll promptly disabuse. She won't be won, once and for all. Each day a lover must earn her anew.

—No! Klaus. Hands off!— she says. —I have loved you once. It was too often. I am more than you deserve. —

So, loving Carl, she resents his tug. Resentments she can't abide. They make her regret. Regretting, she begrudges. Grudges, she repays.

She's sprawled out on Georg's silk sheets, but Carl comes to mind. He ruins it all, itching away in her thoughts.

It is a prickly bedfellow, guilt. It will not let you lie content. It's worse than crumbs on the sheets.

158

'Have you cast Jocasta yet, Georg?'

'No, Lise. Why do *you* ask?'

'Only wondering, darling.'

Georg disconcerts her as he massages her neck and shoulders. She is a lump of clay he is shaping. He seems to read her mind.

'Who is this Carl?' he enquires.

'Carl?' she says. 'I barely know one.'

This is the trouble with Georg. His intuition is quite uncanny.

'Odd,' he observes, saucy with disbelief.

'Look,' I demand, 'who ever mentions a Carl? And in what regard?'

'Your left buttock mentions him.' Georg chuckles slyly, and slaps her rump. 'Albeit briefly, in regard to affection.'

'What?'

'The tattoo.'

She's never left a bed so quickly before. There's mocking laughter behind her. Having bolted herself in the bathroom, she is frantic to see for herself.

Did you ever try? To urgently examine your bottom? It's no easy task if the only mirror is screwed to the wall at head height. She must squat backwards on the rocking edge of the porcelain basin, and peer upwards through her legs. Then decipher the backwards writing, reading from right to left.

She get a new perspective on herself. She views herself in a different light.

Sure enough. Too true. A telltale buttock bore a message. Bald and brazen.

lraC dna ecileF esiL, it said. Below this, the outline of a heart, enclosing the legend EVOL lanretE.

Naturally, this girl is beside herself. At her wits' end.

She must erase the disclosure. The barefaced cheek.

But soap and water cannot efface it. Nor will pumice or scrubbing brush.

The more she rubs, the brighter it shows: indelibly purple against a glowing pink.

159

She sits on the wooden lavatory seat. She sobs some. She wonders back.

No sober and sensible woman will turn herself into a billboard, or have a man sign himself on her butt. Perhaps it happens one night when she's drunk.

She storms Carl's rooms.

'Bastard!' she greets, when he opens up, blinking through the chink of his front door. 'You took advantage when I blacked out . . . What gives you the right to scribble on a lady's bottom without her consent?'

'Calm yourself,' he hisses, ushering her into the gloomy hall. 'Explain.'

He greets her account with smirking disbelief. 'I insist on seeing your evidence,' he says.

'Here!' she howls, lifting her rustling clothes to expose the naked truth. 'The butt of your joke.'

'Lise, my love . . .' he sighs, pressing his lips to the spot, fingering between the split of her legs, 'you did that for me?'

She knows he is to blame for this. Only when he is guilty can he muster any innocence.

'Never again . . .' she swivels around, and swings her palm on to his cheek, 'do you have a place on my skin. Never.'

Even if she wanted to, she couldn't turn the Other cheek.

She consults a theatrical tattooist on Schleswigstrasse.

'Fräulein, you cannot suppose that I'm guilty of *that* . . . I'm an artist.'

'It isn't good?'

'Competent. But lacking in finesse, and devoid of ambition. And entirely two-dimensional.'

'Look,' she tells him, 'I don't come for an appreciation, or to display myself. Quite the reverse. I want it removed.'

His lids drop. He shakes his head. 'Ours is not a frivolous or ephemeral art. When we paint a lady, we colour her for life.'

There she envies him. The stage performance, or act of love, is always too, too transitory.

'Is there nothing to be done?' she asks.

'Well . . .'

'Please, dear man.'

'I could mask it with something else.'

'What?'

'A Hapsburg eagle, maybe, or a spider's web. Or would you prefer the head of Goethe?'

'Think feminine,' she advises. 'I want something pretty. And discreet. I don't intend to make an exhibition of it. I won't have it become a tourist spot or conversation piece.'

'A flower!'

'An orchid, then.' She selects her favourite bloom. Well, better that than bear the brand of a man.

The tattooist's breath comes in fast hot gusts on her rump as he peers close at his task. 'Pardon me for asking,' he says, 'I do not wish to intrude on your private business . . . but are you certain about this Carl? You're sure you want him erased?'

'Utterly. Completely. Blot him out . . .' She winces at the piercing prick. 'Delete him from my life.'

All day she is tetchy as a bear with a sore head, nagged by a distant, insistent ache.

Carl lurks on, like his tattoo. Though she no longer sees him, he will not go away.

'More flowers from Carl,' Minna says, as she locks the dressing-room door behind her. She squints around a florid exuberance of ribbons, fern and blooms. 'Perhaps you should see him. He's trigger-happy, and threatening to shoot Georg.'

161

'One more day of siege,' she says, 'then Captain Fallehn must stop threatening the theatre and leave us to our art. He is transferred to Military Chancellery, and must escort Archduke Franz Ferdinand.'

'Far away?' asks Minna, her face creasing hopefully. 'For long?'

'No secret,' she confides. 'Bosnia, via Trieste and Herzogovina. To inspect troops, greet mayors, snub Belgrade and so on. They end up in Sarajevo.'

Ach, but that's another story. Only she thinks it proves her point. Carl and trouble have a special affinity.

As she gets experience, a girl soon discerns. She detects a pattern to men. I'd first supposed, as Mamma asserted, that they were all the same underneath. But I think she'd only really known Pappa, and generalised from his singularity, as she often made personal observations about him and declaimed them as general laws.

'A man likes his spats cleaned for him on a Sunday,' she'd declare, or 'A man can't abide soggy dumplings'.

My own observations of men were of a different order. I'd begun to notice variations around the theme; to map out man's miscellany, and find an order of sorts. Often you see them coming. Klara and I would compare experiences and christen the various types.

'When you do *bumsen* with Carl,' she asks, 'what is he like?'

'He is a Hero of the Mattress, Klara. He insists on Doing His Duty. But it is very military and disciplined. Intimacy shouldn't be a contest of strength. If he wants to wrestle, he should do it with his chums. . . . I prefer him to Georg, though, who must always direct, even in bed. There's a lot of the Dancing Master to him. He is forever pushing and prodding a lady into the Correct Posture, or getting her to arch her back.'

'I had a Professor of Philology like that, once,' Klara says. 'When he wasn't rearranging my arms and legs, he was correcting my pronunciation . . . I called him the Puppeteer.'

'Have you come across any Explorers?'

'Explain,' she demands. 'You don't mean Fumblers?'

162

'No. They are Tourists. They leer. They want to get to all the obvious places as quick as they can. Two palaces and a cathedral, and they're on to the early train home. . . . No. The Explorer is adamant to survey you thoroughly, from parting to toe. You recognise him by his intense, bemused stare. He is conquering new territory. Not just for himself, but for the Emperor too. He keeps stopping to take his bearings. Or he talks to himself about the terrain, as if you were out of earshot, or simply not there. He is determined to discover the entire continent of your surface. Sometimes he takes an inobvious route, or gets lost. He is crawling down your back the wrong way. Or wistfully prodding your bellybutton. Then suddenly – for reasons best known to himself – he starts massaging your shins or peering into your ear . . .'

'You don't mean the Doctors?' Klara frowns. 'Who want to conduct an intimate examination with very cold hands . . .'

'No,' the girl shudders, 'but I know who you mean.'

Klara is a woman of cosmopolitan experience. She tells tales of Acrobats, Basso Profundos, Confessors, and so on, through the entire Roman alphabet of men. And in a year spent in St Petersburg, she learned some Cyrillic besides.

20

JUNE 28, 1914, is Ascension Day. By midafternoon news has been telegraphed to Vienna that Archduke Franz Ferdinand has been shot dead in Sarajevo. Countess Sophie too, though folk are less concerned with her. Sad, bad timing. It was their wedding anniversary.

For many days, public buildings are draped with black ribbons, and black flags flutter forlorn. All the theatres and opera houses are closed. But the cafés are crowded. I'm struck by the public indifference. Though all drama has been cancelled, and an Archduke annulled, the city's appetites are uninhibited, its chatter is unconcerned.

Perhaps she takes a special interest because Carl Fallehn is involved. She buys every paper to read all the reviews.

Carl is one of those who arrest the assassin. In that famous photograph, he is wrestling the boy's arm, third from the right. Also he testifies at the trial. It's a strange story that unfolds.

Someone gave explosives and guns to boys. Cabrinovic lobs a bomb at the royal car, but it rolls away into the gutter. Grabez has another bomb, but can't bring himself to part with it. He sincerely wants to kill an Archduke, but fears to draw attention to himself.

Princip has fled from Appel Quay. He is slouching outside Schiller's Delicatessen. His revolver is stowed beneath his overcoat. He is sweating in the midday, summer sun. His game is up, for the alarm is raised. He came to shoot a Hapsburg. Now, facing the salamis and schnitzels in Schiller's shop window, his parting breath condenses on the glass.

But fate is more fatuous than Feydeau. If Princip can't get to the Archduke, then – the drama demands – the Archduke must come to him.

The royal car takes a wrong turning up a narrow cobbled street and brakes to a halt. The chauffeur calls out for directions, the limousine pops and purrs.

Princip turns around to look. Over the fumes of grilled pork fat come the fragrances of leather upholstery, gasoline and chypre. There are rumbles of peeved hauteur.

At arm's length from Princip sits the Countess Sophie. Alongside, the Archduke barks his complaints, his face wincing amid a swarm of flies who suspect he is dead meat. It does not please the Imperial dignity to be parked outside a butcher's or to slide downhill in reverse.

Count Harrach rides the running board, to intercede his body between bombs, bullets and his royal charge. Only, he's on the wrong side of the car.

So, there's the farcical coincidence of schoolboy, revolver and royal prince, outside a sausage shop.

If I were playing in this melodrama myself, I'd advise the author to rewrite so as not to abuse the audience, who are never so credulous as Brecht may suppose.

'Which way to the Quay?' the chauffeur enquires of the assassin. 'Quick now, you are delaying royalty here.'

Princip promptly answers. Drawing his gun, he fires twice without aiming. One bullet tears through the car door into Countess Sophie. The second passes through the Archduke's bulldog neck.

Sophie flops forward, folding at the waist like a marionette when the strings go slack. Her head rocks between her husband's knees.

165

I'm no doctor. I don't know if a man can talk when a bullet has ripped through his windpipe. But it is reported that the Archduke then makes a Royal Pronouncement. Opinions divide as to his words.

According to Count Harrach, he said:

Stopherl! Stopherl! Don't die. Live for my children.'

But Colonel Bardolf reports the adieu:

'God save Franz Josef. No Serbian bullet can hurt the Empire. Chauffeur, drive on!'

But an adjutant tells in confidence (to Captain Vogel, who tells Klara's brother, who confides to her, who discloses to me) there was just a fine spray of blood, the hiss of compressed air escaping in an extended, blathering 'aagh . . .'

'Like a baby's fart,' Klara assures me, 'or when you slowly deflate a balloon. It's a strangely contented, satisfied sound.'

'Aagh!' I say.

'Yes, almost,' Klara advises, 'but you inhale deeper and first moisten your lips. Also impose a rattling glottal stop on it. I recommend you practise. May be, one day, when you are required to act shot on stage, then you can die true to life.'

This is the way in theatre. No experience is wasted on us. Ours is the alchemy to transmute suffering into art.

It is a fortunate faculty. Soon there'll be a deal of suffering. How to start? How to tell it? So much happens so fast.

It is believed the assassination is a Serbian plot. Yet there's no definite proof. Kaiser Wilhelm promises us support if, when we threaten Serbia, Russia takes sides. We threaten Serbia. Russia says she'll defend the Slavs. Bluff and bluster from all sides. I am cast as Electra to tour in Paris and Brussels. Minna and I buy a new set of Morocco leather suitcases. Russia starts to mobilise her troops.

If Austria fights, Germany will support her. If Germany fights Russia, the French will join the fracas.

The generals look to their rulebooks. They have plans to attack but not to defend, so it's necessary that they get offensive.

166

France can mobilise faster than Russia. If you fight France and Russia together, you should beat the French first. But the French borders are heavily fortified. Better, then, to get to France through the open door of Belgium. But if the armies enter Belgium without knocking, Britain will come in to defend her. And Belgium declines to give free passage.

If the German troops go to Paris via Brussels, our acting troop cannot. Our tour of Sophocles is cancelled. Oedipus wept, broken-hearted. Minna and I are philosophical. We try to return the suitcases, but the Emporium Sohne will not refund our money, saying the cases are used and the leather grazed. 'Hardly,' I say. 'Only the smallest, which I took for a brief weekend in Morbisch. Better blame the porter or the bellboy. I never hump my own luggage. Maybe my friend Felice has borrowed it without telling . . .'

Germany gets peeved with us. 'Look, Franz,' says Kaiser Wilhelm, 'you start all this trouble. Then you just sit on your butt, break wind but *do* nothing. Declare war on Russia. Invade Serbia, why don't you?'

Brother August is conscripted. Oskar K— joins the cavalry. Egon guards Russian prisoners of war.

'Don't worry, Irma, sugarplum,' Pappa consoles Mamma, '*Gott straft England*. August will shortly return a hero. I'll join the reserves. You and Lise can knit wristwarmers for the troops. If we Bergs make a special effort, and all pull together, it can all be over by Christmas . . . . We shall be round this table together – eating a fat goose for dinner. Touch wood.'

And Pappa knew a futility when he lived one, and had an unerring eye for a lost cause – always selling his stocks the day after they tumbled on the exchange. If he'd been in charge, it might have all turned out different and briefer. Instead, matters are in the hands of Joffre, Conrad, Moltke, French, and Archduke Nicholas. They intellectualise it all, pushing pins into maps, drawing clean smooth arrows with indelible pencils.

It is too much Greek tragedy: with Prologue, Chorus, (several) Episodes, then Exodus. Only there is no *deus ex machina*. God is never lowered on to the stage to untangle it.

167

'Bertolt . . .' I remark to this playwright I know, 'do you ever notice how life imitates theatre? We live by the scripts that we know. Suppose you write a new kind of epic, to help us live better, to spare us from history. Show how we can shape events with our very own hands. Save us from Tragedy.'

One evening in 1927, when Max B— was entertaining me to supper Chez Rainer in Wiedner Hauptstrasse, I excuse myself from the table between courses to take a leak. And who should I find in the cloak-room, powdering her puffy Pekinese face in the mirror, but Margi Wittgenstein.

'Sophia, darling,' she invites, 'come back to Steindglasse with Willi and me and you'll meet Alma's friend Herbert, whose brother is a famous conductor.'

'Wait while I get my cape and parasol,' I say. 'I'll be with you promptly.'

'But you were having supper with *me* . . .' Max protests, when I meet him a few days later in Ringstrasse.

Of course, I'm horribly shamed: 'Forgive me, Max,' I plead, 'I knew I left something behind me at the table. I quite forgot it was you. I didn't remember you till two in the morning. Then it was too late to go back.'

'Lise!' he scowls horribly, 'you're impossible.' Then he looses all manner of synonyms: like mindless, heedless, scatty and irrespons-ible, as if he's swallowed a thesaurus and it's started repeating on him.

'Fair comment,' I concede. 'Come buy me lunch at Kern's. I've got a good excuse. There's a simple explanation to satisfy a theorist. For I'm a rare species of person not unknown to science.

'I have my eccentricities, Max. But I believe I am entitled . . . . Maybe you'd be forgetful if you'd fallen thirty feet on to your head from the bridge at Stammersburg.'

'I am sorry to hear this story again,' says Max.

'This is why I am as I am,' I continue. 'My brain is as scrambled as an omelette. It's a wonder I'm half sensible.'

'Indeed,' the physicist sympathises. 'Which half is that? I can never tell.'

He's a shy laconic man. We have a division of labour by which he pays for the meals, and I provide him an intimate cabaret.

'On top of that, in the winter of 1915, my eggshell noddle gets cracked a second time. We give a charity performance of Sophocles' *Oedipus Rex* to cheer the troops home on leave, and a lead weight drops from the raised curtain and plummets down, striking me a fearful blow on my head, fracturing my skull, sending me headlong and breakneck into the first row of the stalls, where I fall into the lap of a Battery Commander of the Fourth Imperial Artillery – name Fritz Langermann, by the way – and dislocate my shoulder on his wooden crutch in landing, and I'm unconscious and no mistake, and the prompter cannot rouse me, although this is only the first act, so that Georg has to take my place as Jocasta, reading from the book, but dressed in gauze wraparound and wig, to general amusement and wolf whistles from the regiment of infantry, because my stand-in is drunk on a bottle of *marc* that a German Colonel brings from France, and Katherina J— has conveniently lost her voice, but the show must go on without me, because they know I'm a real trouper and wouldn't have it any other way, besides it was far worse for Johann when they insist he performs two hours after his wife dies in labour, saying "pull yourself together, now you've got a child to support", not through callousness, but because Doctor Theatre is a wonderful healer, and if you must return the customers' ticket money everybody goes short at the end of the week, and how would we then pay the rent, so all in all my head has been struck two terrible blows, not mentioning some fearful traumas of an emotional kind, and though it's hard to see on the outside that anything's amiss within, because all I have to show for it are two bumps either side of a depression on my scalp, but these never show through my hair.'

'Really?' says Max.

'Truly,' I say. 'Here! Feel my horns.' And I guide his long white fingers on to the bumps on my head, so he must realise I'm telling the gospel truth, and no exaggeration. 'So, if I'm sometimes strange, it's because life has struck me some savage blows, causing my mental condition.'

'What condition is that, Lise?' he enquires.

'Several,' I tell him, 'six or seven, maybe, including disorientation, sometimes. Impulsiveness, if the fancy takes me. Automatism, some evenings, associated with amnesias and paramnesias. Occasionally full-blown poriomania as described by Kraeplin.'

'You have my sympathy,' he promises. 'You are a helpless victim of your whims.'

'Exactly. But the strangest thing is that the second blow to my head is therapeutic. It cures some of my former illness. That stage weight that strikes me during Sophocles's immortal tragedy is sent from heaven to restore my health. So if you think I'm scatty now, think yourself lucky you never knew me before . . .'

'You're saner now?'

'By far. Usually a blow to the head does a person damage. But this second clout works wonders. Like when you bash a crackling wireless set.'

'That was fortunate, Lise.' He raises his eyebrows in this sceptical expression that is an affliction amongst scientists. I'd seen the look often before on the face of a certain zoologist who studies the reproduction of snails. Snails do sado-masochism in a big way – pushing calcium darts through each other's soft tissues, to perk themselves up for the slimey business. There's worse, but I don't like to tell tales about snails.

'No,' I explain. 'Fortunate it wasn't. I was a happier, healthier woman when I was sick.'

'You were?'

'Forgive me if I get technical, Max, but a metaphor is in order. I don't know if you scientists are familiar . . .'

'I've dined with them before,' he reassures. 'Also similes, metonyms, zeugmas and so on.'

'Very well. You know those performers who swallow razor blades? It's a horrible sight when they start to pull them out of their mouth – all those sharp edges joined together on a string of thread. Well, you're wincing in sympathy a moment. Then you cannot look. That's how it was with me. My head was full of horrible, wounding, cutting items. And I started to draw them out.'

170

'Better out than in,' says Max. 'And how is your veal?'

A bang on the head can cause amnesia. Anterograde or retrograde. You forget what happened before the blow, or forget what happens after. Not that there's choice. The whack decides all that for you. It's got a mind of its own.

When I fall from the bridge, I get both forms of forgetfulness. Trust me to be complicated. But when the weight strikes me on the stage of the Burgtheater, I begin to remember that forgotten past. Terrible things get loosened.

Can't life be a bitch?

Take it as a warning. You're never alone with yourself. There's a continuous record of your life in memory. The camera is always whirring.

It will come back and slice you open, despite your thinking you shut it out.

So six years after my fall, I'm back at home in my sickbed, with Mamma in attendance. It looks so different, this selfsame bedroom of my childhood, shrunken, shabby, dulled. The once plum velveteen curtains are faded a blotchy pink by the sun. The rug worn threadbare is in the centre. The silvering of my wardrobe mirror is pocked, blistered black and blind round the edges.

Felice and Sophia, my dolls, sit splay-legged on the armchair, their porcelain faces yellowed and cracked by age, watching me with spiteful unrelenting eyes. I abandoned them. Now their glassy glares repay me with pent-up bile.

'Lise, daughter . . .' the bed sinks with Mamma's weight as she sits at my side, stroking my brow through the swathe of bandages, '. . . your poor, sick head.'

Poor, dowdy Mamma, only forty-six but waxy-faced, jaundiced as parchment, her hands knotted by arthritis, her dry lips browned, her hair streaked grey, her daughter stricken again, her son fighting

Russians, her husband gone bellicose and boozy, her attic room locked, her picture frame staring empty on the mantel, dust settling in her parlour.

'Is the attic room still locked?' I ask Mamma.

'I leave it so.' She nods.

—Poor man,— comes the sigh. —Killed by a lie.—

The war goes badly on all fronts. Most personable gentlemen are called up to fight. Theatre shrivels – as if *our* drama didn't count. The standard of cuisine in restaurants tumbles. Henri, the majordomo at Kern's, says he just can't get fresh, reliable supplies. Not flesh, foul or fish.

Then the tragedy strikes home. Brother August is badly wounded.

21

I FIRST entered the Marie-Thérèse Military Hospital one drizzly Tuesday afternoon in January 1916 to visit my brother August. The sky oppressed me that day, trapping me cowering in the gloom of its pewter dome. All life lay torn in a tangled fester. It was indecent of me to smell of musk and health, rather than iodoform, pus and Lysol. It seemed a blasphemy to be so exquisitely unblemished. But the crippled soldiers had no mind to blame me. No, instead, they wrestled their blankets, strained against iron bedheads, to gain a fuller view of me. They loose a Blitzkrieg of winks, whistles and leers. Lust is a wonderfully resilient thing. Or its prosthesis is very lifelike. These incomplete men – who want for so much – remain partial optimists.

I don't blush easily. I am used to applause. But I affected a limp as I walked the ward. I was apologetic for my lovely, worthless, stage-prop, actress legs. For there simply weren't enough limbs to go round. Nor eyes, either. If I could have detached my parts, I would have shared them, there and then, with August and Klaus, his friend. Between the three of us we have only five legs, five eyes, four arms, and a single hope.

I stayed two days and a night, tending my brother at his bedside.

173

August lay blanched and muttering, till he suddenly stiffened and gasped – as if startled by a stranger.

'Sir . . .' he gulped. I believe he was saluting death.

So he passed on. But, myself, I stayed two years.

I surprise myself. The first few weeks after his death I feel chill, dutifully sorrowful. Nothing *extrem*.

But then I go weepy. For no sensible reason, I find myself muttering his name; and detect, in the mix of my voice, tones of regret and distaste.

He comes to me at night; as the boy he was at fifteen. For so long I barely thought of him. When he dies, I cannot keep him out of mind. We never spend a night apart. It is a terrible, disconcerting thing – to have erotic dreams of your brother.

—I loved him. The filthy bastard. —

'Of course, we loved our brother . . .'

—Oh, August . . . —

It's all in the mind. The problem is recollection. Some cutting images come to me: incidents and such.

'Let me see your little purse!' demands stiff uncle Adolf. 'And I will show you something to put in it.'

'Mamma is ill,' says Pappa. 'I'll bath you instead.'

It is a painful thing to write of – this family business. I try many times. Time is short, life is precious. You buy a box of 500 sheets of paper, but already you're running out.

174

Some experiences are stranded beyond confirmation or denial. The truth is lost to you. It's so many times overwritten, like a pedant's blackboard. All that remains is the smudge on the palimpsest of skin. Maybe I just have a dirty imagination.

Suppose you have a tattooed message on a private part of you. You have it overlaid, so the original can never be seen; only the florid deceptions of its mask. Then you can never read the trace again, or even confirm its existence. So, though you can regard it nevermore, still it will remain, lurking there unseen.

Or suppose there is a cellar in your house. You cast some squalid stuff into the gloomy cavern, then quickly bolt the door and scurry upstairs. For years you never open up, or even think of it. You quite forget it's there.

But years later, the door to the cellar creaks open in the night. You sniff the air with alarm. There is a putrid stench. It begins to permeate the house.

Yet you can never recover what you left there, only poke its rotten remains.

'Look . . .' Uncle Adolf beams and points, 'what I've got . . .'

I knew this, at least. Often enough, I'd dreamt it.

A boy and girl lie amid the golden corn. And how they cling, shivering, inseparable, legs entwined, thin-skinned, flat-bellied, bony-ribbed, abandoned and abominable, in a wickedness, a sour relish they cannot name.

His old eyes stare blank and forlorn. The girl shudders, licking her lukewarm tears, smeared salty on his hot boy's chest.

This girl has my sympathy. Sometimes I wake sobbing. It is bold to be so depraved. The sourness is stinging. The pure pungency of sin is enough to make you gasp.

They are corrupt, this boy and girl. They have cast ourselves out.

They trudge through the field, the straw parting crackling to their crushing feet.

175

'Come, children!' Their mother turns on her picnic blanket to watch their sullen approach. 'You were gone so long, we feared you were lost.'

In my ward of the Marie-Thérèse Military Hospital there are many intriguing cases, particularly gunshot survivors.

'What those?' Major Andreas Roth asks me. 'Nose holes?'

'Nostrils,' I say, 'noss-trills.'

'Lise holes,' he chuckles, reaching up to palp my nose.

You have to be patient with him and repeat yourself. This young man is practically dumb.

'Head hole . . .' he rolls those slate-grey eyes, shivering, 'makes hurts.' He rubs at the bandaging that swathes his temples.

'Don't touch!' I yell.

I must be strict. For his sake. It's best to distract him. Show him a different hole. He's potty about them. I got a sieve from the kitchen for him to examine. You could not get him to part with it for several hours. He was enraptured. He'd never seen such a profusion of holes, so densely packed.

Though he tires of any particular hole, when familiarity renders it stale, he remains besotted by the genre.

'Look . . .' I grip him by the chin to direct his gaze. I fold a sheet of paper in half, then fold it again, and again, then tear a semicircle from one edge. I open out the sheet. His face creases in delight. He cannot believe his luck. His fat red tongue, sputum speckled, flickers in and out.

'Much holes!' he giggles, rocking forward and back, clasping his thighs.

'How many?'

'Lots . . . seven,' he guesses, 'or twenty.'

Andreas has a problem with numbers. One, two and three he can recognise in many manifestations. Beyond that, numbers blur to 'many'. Although I've taught him the names of all the cardinals up to fifty, he can't discern their meaning. This will prove a problem if he

176

gets well enough to handle money. Ten and fifty are the same to him. I don't trust the world not to cheat him.

Poor, dear man. Terrible things have happened to him. And yet he cannot remember.

I'm teaching him, by rote repetition, the names of his body parts whenever it is my turn to wash him.

He is more at home with the sinister side of his body than the dextrous. So he can immediately name his left foot, but hesitates to label the right. But, if I place his two hands together, his mind is nudged by their similarity. So he can quickly christen them both.

'Hand . . . hand . . .' Then he claps them together to applaud himself. 'Good-boy, And-rus,' he grunts.

As I introduce him to his body, so he develops an interest in mine.

'What those?' he asks, 'chest-knees?'

'Breasts,' I say. 'Don't touch.' The notions of politeness and rudeness are alien to him. These will form a future, tortuous lesson.

'Breasts.' He jerks his head approvingly. 'One lump. Two lumps. Nice. Good number.'

He is an enigma, this man–baby. He cannot feed himself. The first meal, I gave him a fork and turned my back. When I return, his shoulders are sodden from gravy and the lumps of his stew lie in the basin of his lap. I also see prong marks in his chin. He tries his best to reach his mouth, but keeps stabbing his cheeks and neck.

He can't fit his feet in his slippers, either. But there's a miraculous feature to him.

You wouldn't believe.

His virtuosity. This man is a consummate pianist. After supper – which is a lengthy, spoon-fed, dribblesome business – he likes to play Schubert or Brahms on the Steinway in the conservatory. Sometimes I sing and he accompanies. In a few weeks, I shall be good enough to hold my own without embarrassment. It is widely told I was an actress, so I insist on performing with panache.

I plan that we give a recital, a week on Saturday – of Mahler's *Rückertlieder* – for the staff and other patients. Already I'm selling

177

tickets. Proceeds to buy a gramophone for the Field Marshal Mackensen Wing for Chronic Military Trauma.

It is important for me, for Andreas, that the doctors see him at his very best. He has adapted the orchestral score for solo piano with no aid but his memory. I believe there is too much there, locked in his strange, still mind.

'*Nun will die Sonn'so hell aufgeh'n* . . .' I begin to sing. This is a lament for dead children.

Andreas slumps lower over the keyboard. His moist eyes close and – over his pianissimo playing – I hear his urine trickle on to the floor. I do not know if he is weeping for music or shame, but I stroke his shoulder to console him.

No matter. A man who understands Mahler like this can piss on the parquet whenever he likes. Later I can mop his eyes and the floor, then get him to name his toes, ankles, knees and thighs, when I change his napkin and tug him into dry nightclothes, and tuck up his sleeping mind for the night.

He took a single bullet through the head somewhere. It made a clean entry by his left ear, and a wider exit wound in his right crown. Bullets, like heavy drinkers, are blunter on departure than arrival.

I have learned a deal about bullets, these last two years. Bayonets and mustard gas too. I have seen a lot of punctured men with their insides outside. Nakedness never disconcerts me. But it is shockingly intrusive to witness a man's internal organs, which come as a surprise even to him. They pulse and quiver horribly. Their lurid colours and viscous gloss seem scandalous next to skin. You cannot wait for the livid healing scab to come. And the gauze only reminds me of that fabric butchers use to wrap hams.

Some of Andreas' faculties were sprayed out of a hole in his head. There is a foreign field where are spilled for ever his numbers.

'What has been lost can be recovered . . .' Dr Kiss advises, 'perhaps. Another part of the brain can take over, and learn the lost capacity. But there is also compression damage to the remaining tissue. Splinters of bone are scattered widely. A bullet in the brain is not straightforward. It is not a problem for the simple-minded or empty-headed. We are dealing here with delicate matter. He has serious complaints – aphasia, agnosia, acalculia, ataxia . . . a lot.'

'All the 'a's,' I say. 'Not forgetting some 'in's.'

'He has a lot of deficiencies, First Class Assistant Auxillary Nurse Berg. This is a man without a lot.'

'But he has a personal guard, Civilian Doctor Acting Head Neurologist Kiss, darling,' I observe. 'Unlike other patients. Why is that?'

Before Andreas, I only knew of a Staff General to have a permanent sentry with him.

'It is a military matter. Major Roth is important to the army. It is not our business to know more than that. Ignore the guard entirely. Do not question or mention him again. . . . Will you come for a nightcap later, Lise?'

'Yes. Perhaps he is a hero, Karl, but not before eleven-thirty.'

'Perhaps I can lay my hands on a bottle of rum. It is a mistake to become too attached. Whilst there is so much dying, at least. Dismiss.'

Sad. To be important and a hero. And yet not know it. And have people pity you so as they pass – because you are always blinking your surprise at the world, are incontinent, incompetent and incomplete, and walk like a limping baboon.

Karl and I are tangled on his office couch. We glimmer in the dark as a mosaic of golden glints – teeth, chin, curves of skin – reflecting the flickering flames of his fire.

On duty, he is twenty-seven grades my superior, in the hierarchy of this hospital. By strict protocol, I can address him only through three intermediaries. But intimacy can't speak so indirectly. It resorts to taking liberties.

Naked, our status is much reversed. Though I affect not to notice this – his bald crown, pocked cheeks, arched belly, stork's legs, splayed feet.

179

I am fond, in a tender, indulgent way. Despite his medical diplomas and doctorates, there are facts of life, bodily truths, he never knew I cannot withhold them.

He is a gentle, quizzical, whimsical man. I enjoy his orchidacious mind. But I never envy his wife.

In German, there is no pun if I succumb to a Kiss. I should not like to think I am provoked by coincidence, or seduced by a linguistic whim.

Favourite with me is when he wraps my eyes in surgical bandage before we do rumpty-tumpty. Then – blindfold – I can imagine all manner of things. It's never to his taste. He complains, then grudgingly complies.

There are plenty of vacant coffins in the corridors. Size G is very capacious. I always itched to try one out for size. *Ach*, just a girl's idle fancy.

'Please! Just once.' —You beneath. Me on top.—

'Lise,' Kiss groans, 'don't be perverse.'

'It's a theatrical tradition,' I coax. 'Sarah Bernhardt would make love in nothing else. Won't you indulge an ingenue's whim?'

But he never does. 'Sometimes, Lise,' he observes, 'I think you love death.'

He is more original and enlightening making conversation than making love.

'Tell me more about a man's mind . . .' I sigh.

'There are two hemispheres. No bigger than these.'

'Why two?' I ask. Then I chuckle, having caught myself talking as foolishly as Roth.

'Because nature loves symmetry and duplication. So, Lise, do I . . .'

'Are they different? The left and right? I need to know.'

'In the left, there is more language function. Imagination, calculation, visualisation are more in the right. Also, there is a crossover of function. The right-hand side of the brain controls the left-hand side

180

of the body, and vice versa. Vision is more complicated. But . . . and I speak roughly here . . . the right of our sight is conveyed to the left, and the left to the right. Somewhere they are fused. . . . This is a sight for sore eyes. There is an immaculate union. You cannot see the seam.'

'How can a man like Roth make sublime music but be unable to speak his name?'

'Different parts of the mind have different functions. One part of the man is touched by God, another part is shot by man.'

'It's common? You've seen it before?'

'Never quite like this. But I've met the reverse – *amusica* – a tragic case . . .' Kiss unwinds his limbs, ends his embrace, starts to explain, buttons his shirt.

He tells how Kohler, the violinist, bursts a blood vessel in his brain during an interval. It causes him a slight headache. But the concert must go on. His assistant hands him his Stradivarius.

'What's this thing?' says the great man. 'This wooden box contraption? What am I meant to do with it?'

'Play Bach's *Partitas*, Maestro,' the assistant coaxes. He is used to the virtuoso's whims.

'Look,' says Kohler, 'I don't know this Bach from Adam. Tell him to go to hell. If he wants to play, that's his concern, not mine.'

The assistant winces. He is progressing towards panic. The orchestra are into the last movement of the *Prague* Symphony. Soon it will be the maestro's turn.

'God Almighty!' At last Kohler hears the enormity of music, and protests, 'What's that dreadful noise?'

'Mozart's concluding,' the assistant confides.

'Amateurs, amateurs!' Kohler rages. 'Can't he conduct his business without making a din?'

'But, Maestro . . .'

'No! Either he's silent, or I'll have him dismissed.'

A small stroke wipes out his music centre, his genius and craft. Kohler has lost a lifetime of study and practice. Extinguished, his divine gift. Whoops. All gone. He never plays again. But otherwise he's exactly the same – haughty, petulant and vain. Arrogantly possessed of the genius he's lost.

181

Kiss has a store of anecdotes like this. All my psychometrics, psychiatry and neuropathology I learn from him.

A person's mind is a delicate thing. Men should understand this, before they start shooting guns.

And it is a strange thing to be alive and intact. In the lottery of war it ranks as top prize. I don't deserve.

22

TODAY I suffer some from aphasia. Word-weariness. It comes and goes. Worst when I'm *fatiguée*. Then words won't work for me. They hide away, and I can't find them awhile. *Noms*, worst. Verbs, awkward. Adjectives, mainly faithful. Prepositions and *prénoms*, no problems. Nonagenarian disease, I suppose. And English my third language, after German and French.

It itches away horribly when I can't nab the AWOL, *déraciné* term. And I've no-one to ask — except Desmond in the Spa Grocers, colleague drinkers in the Crown and Woolpack, or strangers on the streets.

When it's the *mot* simple — so most embarrassing — I ask a *policier*. They're hard to shock and always stop to listen. Desmond always understands, if I can't secure the law.

'Excuse, Desi, please help an old lady.'

'Tin of sardines?' he guesses. 'On tick again?'

'Nothing like it!'

'A pack of ciggies?'

'Completely wrong,' I giggle, 'it's a fruit. French for it is *pample-mousse*. What is English?'

'Pardon?'

'Citrus fruit. Colour of lemon but larger than orange. Shiny, pocked skin like Ludwig Webern's.'

'Grapefruit,' says Desmond. He shakes his head wearily. 'But we don't have any in stock.'

'*Ach*, no matter,' I reassure, 'don't trouble yourself. I only came in for the *mot juste* – the word alone. Thing no use to me. Grapefruit I never eat now. They always give me . . .'

'Yes?'

'Help an old lady. What is it when you have acid pain here?' I pat below my sorry heart. 'Feels like someone's twisting your stomach with metal pincer things. There's another word for those.'

'Indigestion, Lise. And pliers.'

'*Exactement*,' I agree. 'Desmond, *tu es un véritablé* . . .'

And he leads me by the bendy-part-of-arm like a man-suffering-inconvenience-without-show-of-temper, all the way to metal-framed-glass-sheet-swinging-thing-in-the-wall designed for comings-and-goings.

Better I take a kip. Rest my noddle.

I haven't mentioned Andreas' looks. He's a beautiful man–child – flaxen hair, sea-grey eyes, umber freckles, high-cheeked, firm-chinned, two metres tall, lean, smooth-skinned, hard-muscled, steel-sinewed. Every morning I brush his locks, wash him, clean his teeth. Twice a week I give him a bath, then pat dry the lithe length of him. It is like being a child who is given the largest, prettiest doll.

So there are two men in my life. Kiss and Roth. The clever, unsightly man, and the beautiful foolish child. It strikes me as contrary and droll that I spend my days chattering to the idiot and my nights humping the ugly one.

Andreas' mother hasn't visited him, for she's too far and fragile with a broken hip in Schallaburg. She has hopes to come in March, 'when we are both entirely recovered to our former healthy selves, and this sorry war is over'. This I know from her letters. No matter if he doesn't understand, still I'm moved by obligation to read them

184

aloud. Then, if no sense penetrates, the sounds can caress his ears. Maybe he'll recognise the fluttering, skittering patterns of her mind.

'"Andreas, my dearest son . . ."' I begin.

'What that?' he asks. 'Who says?' His brow is creased with concentration.

'Your mother.'

'What that? Mother thing?'

Well, how to explain a mother? She is a difficult thing to understand. To grasp her, you must know some rudimentary biology, see a glimmer of gender, comprehend relational terms.

'Mother . . .' I begin, 'is a woman.'

'What that?' Andreas interrupts, 'Wo-man?'

Ach, there is so much he has to relearn.

Still, we are making progress. When I first took charge of him, Andreas couldn't speak a word.

By April, he can feed and dress himself, and speaks complete sentences, with adequate grammar, like – 'Why are men crying?', 'Is this dream or awake?', 'I want alone with piano,' or 'Why is this place?'

He tends to the sensual and concrete. Abstractions make him crease his brow and roll his eyes in pain.

'What love?' he moans. 'Where is it?'

Also he makes personal observations about me.

'Your hair is fire,' he suggests, or, 'My eyes taste yours.' 'Your laughter smells of jasmine', or 'Your beauty is too loud'.

'Synaesthesia . . .' Kiss explains. 'The circuitry is tangled. His senses are scrambled. He confuses touch, taste, hearing and sight. But he makes good progress. His coordination is considerably improved. Overall, he functions like a five-year-old. I would never have believed . . .'

'I tell you what he does that surprises me.'

'Yes, Lise?'

'He becomes agitated whilst he is eating. The holes of the salt cellar are clogged, so he starts hammering it like a gavel on the table. Then he starts examining it, transfixed. He begins nodding wildly, laughing, clapping his hands. 'This Andreas!' he shouts. "Andreas this! Salt is word. Word is salt. Salt is word." He is quite adamant about this. It is as if he has solved the meaning of his life. He keeps pointing to the clogged holes of the salt cellar, then to me. Of course, I pierce them for him. Then the salt flows free.

'But this isn't enough. Now he starts tapping his head. "My holes," he screams. "Do my holes. Salt open. Make words. Make words. Open salt."'

Kiss is twitching his fingers madly. He is nodding like an epileptic. He has caught Andreas' disease. He's beaming at me like an affective disorder type. 'You goddess, Lise. So you brought him paper and pencil. And then?'

'Paper and pencil?' I say. 'What do you prefer? That he writes a philosophical treatise or makes architectural drawings?'

'Auxiliary Berg!' Kiss mutters his disgust, seizing rank, discarding friendship. 'Do you not recognise a phenomenon? A case amongst cases? Take him writing materials now. Immediately. No, sooner. Please. Don't delay. I would come myself, but I'm summoned by the Surgeon Major. Note carefully whatever he does. Report back to me. I believe we may have productive aphasia without agraphia . . . Why didn't we think?'

Ach, doctors! Why don't they talk German like everyone else? What he means is that, perhaps, Andreas can write despite his speech being impaired.

At first, it is quite as I supposed. Andreas looks perplexed at the pencil, then sucks the graphite tip. I have to stop him chewing it.

'No, like this . . .' I show him. I write my name.

Andreas screws his eyes to watch, then nods his recognition. He is quivering now. He seizes the pencil. Then he starts to scribble – more eager than any writer I have ever known.

What do you expect? A miracle?

'You are beautiful, so let your looks do the talking, Lise. That's my advice,' Maria Magdalene von Losch always told me. 'A girl can say too much.'

'But these "talkies", do you think they'll catch on, Maria? Maybe it will be difficult for us German-speaking girls.'

'Nah,' she says, 'don't have a care, Lise. You're a serious actress. Don't waste your talent on these American films. Your place is on the German stage.'

This is in 1927. Maria Magdalene and I meet at an audition. We both go up for the maid's part in the film *Madame Wunscht Keine Kinder* – too true. It is to be filmed in Berlin. Alexander Korda directs.

'Do you want this part, Maria?'

'It's a bitsy role, Lise. Who cares? Perhaps I demand something bigger. In films, you must always push yourself . . .'

Then Korda calls me in.

'I have read the script,' I tell him. 'I play Elyane or nobody. I cannot accept the part of a maid.' Nothing ventured, nothing gained.

'It cannot be, Fräulein Berg, I have already promised the lead.'

By coincidence, he offers it to Carla, his wife. As things turn out, she accepts.

Maria Magdalene gets the maid's part, wisely declining her own advice. She disappears to Hollywood, Los Angeles, America. The next I see of her, she is speaking fluent English as lead in *Dishonored*, blonder than before, on account of the bleaching Californian sun. America has been kind to her. She used to be a Plain Gertrude. Now she looks attractive, in a masculine, monkeyish way, like Ignatz Hauser when he's dressed up in a frock. Her Christian names she combines to Marlene; new surname Dietrich. A cute woman, that. She sees the main chance. Maybe I'm better at tactics, but she was sounder on strategy.

She ends up top billing on the big screen with Gary Cooper, while I'm in a small political cabaret off Ringstrasse, appearing as a satirical gooseberry in a spherical green furry gown, alongside a revolutionary ventriloquist and topical conjurer; but with my integrity intact.

Enough of that. No regrets or might-have-beens. And I don't have a bad word for Maria Magdalene. Hers was a great achievement. I like a girl who unsaddles herself from shame.

Later, she sings some; when her voice is too weak for acting. Did you ever hear '. . . can't help it . . .'?

I must tell you what Andreas writes to me. It is written in me with the indelible pencil of pity, and so I can quote verbatim.

'Thank you. Thank you. Thank you. These I can move instead of my mouth. In another time and a different place, I have handled a writing stick before. See how the white virgin lies still for me, blackening to my touch. Do you decipher the marks? Are they speaking in your head?'

'Yes, Andreas. Write more.' I push the paper back to him across the oak table.

'It is bad here in my head. Although I am not three stupid. There is more to me than I can say. But I do not have the words. It is all a matter of words. I do believe. Words can save us all. But they wriggle all slimy. I cannot grasp. Did you ever see a tray of eels?'

'Yes,' I console, 'I know what you mean.'

'My mind is tangled, slippery so. The words writhe like eels. Sounds slide from their meanings. There are sounds I cannot understand. Understanding slither without sounds. Much is lost through this hole in my head. I am part empty and part stuffed. I cannot see back before it is black.'

'I will help you. First tell me what you know.'

'Thank you, thank you, kind man.
    We are all sick with our holes. In the chest or face or legs. We must help each other. We must struggle ourselves to mend. If a

188

man falls silent. They take him away on a trolley. He never comes again. Another takes his bed. I struggle hard like you, so I never disappear.

Where is your hole? Does it mend? I seen your chest is swollen. You have bandages under your shirt. Heal your holes for me. What can I do for you?

I never see you wash or eat. You must not get dirty or hungry. Would you enjoy I wash you wet and pink like you wash me altogether before?'

'I wash and eat in another place. Thank you for your offer. Tell me what you know about yourself.'

'I enjoy you smile when I write stupid. This I forgive. Smile always. You are too loud. You mind I mention, pretty face?

There is too many to tell of myself. I have all my parts except some mind. My name is Andreas Leo Otto Roth. There is a number to my years which are many. My rank is Major of Cavalry in the Army in the war but these meanings I forget. My horse, Hercules, is also lost. If you meet him in another place, don't forget to feed him, please. Although, I already ask too many.

Before now it was black. Now it is light, except when I sleep.

Many faces and places come into my mind when I close my eyes, but I do not have all the names. I believe there was Clotilde in St Polten, and Sophia in Karlsplatz. Do you know them? They pee sitting down. Their skin is soft. Also I know Klaus in Bucharest with a big nose. And Johann in Salzburg, last name Timms. Hercules I mention already. In Constanza there are broken houses, silent men, fire and smoke.

Do you forgive me to stop? My heads hurts many times. Will you lay me in bed? Sorry. Please, come to me again in my dreams. You touch so kind. I never forget.'

All this makes my eyes moisten. But Kiss is ecstatic. For him it is science fiction; a message from another world.

'This is *a case* . . .' he proclaims, 'of a man who has lost almost all his knowledge and faculties and is gaining them anew. Imagine, Lise, if an infant was born able to read and write, interpret and perform great music – but is otherwise naïve. This is Major Roth. This is a man I must *write about*. He will be a legend in the annals . . .'

'What will become of him?'

'He's learning fast. If he continues like this,' Kiss spreads his arms expansively, 'in six months, a year, he could be fit to face his trial.'

'Stand trial? For what?'

'Did I never tell you . . .?' Kiss frowns. 'No, perhaps I didn't. Major Roth is to be court-martialled for mutiny. He sought his own justice by shooting himself. He intended to blow his brains out. Alas, he only half succeeded. The military want an example of him. It is decided there must be publicity and a trial.'

'And after a trial?'

'He'll be shot, I suppose,' says Kiss, who can't conceal his regret. 'This will be a loss. A phenomenon like Roth won't manifest twice.'

I care like Kiss, but in different ways. I am not going to nurse a man back to health just so the military can shoot him. And Andreas is my patient. I get very fond. I aim to keep.

It is hard to blunt an avid mind that struggles to learn. If a bullet cannot stop him, what hope have I?

One afternoon I find Andreas curled weeping on his mattress, his face bloated livid, the whites of his eyes webbed red.

'What is it, dear man?'

'Artur tells me . . .' Andreas' hands wrap his eyes, 'about the war . . .'

'What about the war?'

'Haven't you heard? Three men get killed . . . and a horse.'

'Oh,' I say, 'that.'

The next day, he challenges me. 'You're a woman,' he accuses. There's belligerence here, as if I've been withholding a secret guilt.

'I know,' I say, 'people have mentioned before.'

190

Normally, it's never my way to brag I'm a woman. I expect gentlemen to see this for themselves.

'Why you never tell me?'

'It's a difficult thing to explain – sex. Do you know the difference between man and woman?'

'Artur says some difference.' Andreas has a sly look. His darting eyes skitter away from mine. 'It's too strange. I don't understand.'

Darling man. You know what? I kiss him. He blushes.

One night as we are sprawled in the buff on the Turkish rug in his office, Kiss chides me for my melancholy.

'You're not yourself tonight, Lise.'

'Sorry, Karl. My other life intrudes. I'm otherwise engaged.'

I think back to home – Brother August, Mamma and Pappa, a certain cousin, an uncle. Certain images come to mind that I'd prefer never to mention.

'Tell,' he says. 'I don't understand.'

'Knowing things I shouldn't . . . remembering things I thought I had shut out . . . messages from the other side, from the left-hand side of life.'

'For instance?'

I shiver at the thought. 'Really, Karl. These are private things between a woman and her mind, a character and her past.'

'Trust,' he says, 'tell.'

'I tell you a case, instead,' I say. 'See what you think. . . . Do you know Schachter, in cot seven, with the missing arm and shrapnel in his chest? Watch him some time. Once a minute at least he scratches his nose.'

'So?' asks Kiss.

'He tells me about the night he is wounded. He is struck by shell fragments and starts to slither downhill into a crater. With his good arm he reaches out for a safehold. There is only a coil of barbed wire. Below him he sees a pond. Here lies his dilemma. It may be inches deep, or a quicksand of slime that will swallow him. If he slides into it, he may be sucked from sight, or merely catch a cold in a puddle. Also he worries there may be mustard gas hugging the hollows. For

191

two hours he hangs on the slithery slope, clutching the piercing spikes of the wire. Then he develops an irresistible itch to his nose. The nag of it quite distracts from the hurt of his wounds. He clings on three more hours, waiting, wailing, till it is clear for his comrades to stretcher him back.'

'Explain,' demands Kiss, sympathetically rubbing the length of his nose.

'Some people would scratch, take their chance and challenge fate,' I say. 'Most others would be too sensible or afraid. Like Schachter. He has to wait an eternity to scratch his nose. Because, sometimes, it is impossible to tell a bog apart from a puddle. Now he makes up for lost time. And scratches just for fun, whenever he likes . . .'

'I don't get your point,' says Kiss. 'Everyone would cling on for dear life.'

'No,' I say. 'For some the pull of the pit is irresistible. The wager with risk is ravishing. Too alluring. With some corrupt desire, say, when the erotic worm wriggles. . . . They must let themselves go, and slither down that slope. To see if they sink, stand or swim.'

'You're perverse, Lise. I don't understand you.'

'You wouldn't, dear sensible man.' I tousle his hair and peck his cheek. 'You wear galoshes when it drizzles. Some people fear to get their feet wet. Others dare to be damned.'

23

I **NEVER** thought I'd do such a thing: kiss the chill glass of Cary Grant's grainy close-up on the television screen on a Saturday afternoon black and white film. Static makes me shiver. My cracked, leather lips go all aquiver.

No regrets. But strange – having loved so many, so much, I never bore a child. And what fathers my children might have had – K—, S—, M—, Ka— or B—. Yet I find ways and means to avoid motherhood. When I finally try for a baby, nothing doing. My tubes are rusted. The plumber can do nothing. Only cluck, ask intrusive questions, blink at my replies, and poke coldly with a speculum.

Now, at ninety-odd, I lack family, friends, lovers, romance. I've outlived them all.

Also, it is impossible in Finsbury to secure good coffee or adequate pastries – though there are plenty impersonations.

Ah, the confections of my youth! *Salzburger Nockel, Strudels, Kaiserchmarren, Guglhupf, Krapfen, Zwetschkenroster*. Ah, what alchemy can be worked with humble butter, flour, jam and cream. Also crush some nuts and sprinkle poppy seeds.

And in Vienna we had so many coffees. *Melange, Brauner, Turkischer,*

Mokka, *mit Schlag*, *Doppelschlag*, *Eiskaffee*, *Einspanner*, *Mazagran*, or simple, honest, *Portion Kaffee*.

Say what you will about us Viennese. You cannot convict us of poor appetite. We eat and drink well; but always with discrimination. Ours is the only city in the world where a McDonald's hamburger bar closes for lack of business. It's true. I read this in *Reader's Digest*.

One day, in a supermarket, I spy a tin of coffee labelled *Viennese Nights*. 'Ah, Lise,' I exclaim, 'this is the stuff of memory!' I buy three tins, despite the price. I hurry home. I carry it back, hoping it returns the favour by transporting me.

It was not so funny. To tease an old lady like that. When all she wants is a palatable cup of coffee to warm her frigid flesh.

I warn you, it is part of a wider plot to filch life from under your nose.

There is a new tendency. First they find something good. Then they discover what makes it work. Then they take out the active ingredient. Then they package the emptiness, for sale in shops. You buy wine without alcohol, coffee without caffeine, sausage without fat, music without tune, hamburger without meat, books without plot, jam without sugar, newspaper without news.

This way you get experience without intrusion of life. You are very welcome. Don't mind me if I die soon.

The afternoons, I drink in the Crown and Woolpack. I have a special arrangement. If I buy my first five cognacs, the sixth they give me for free. With a packet of crisps, *gratis* too – flavour of my choice: prawn cocktail is my favourite.

Today I notice developments when I go to the lady's lavatory. I find Malcolm T— has had installed a contraceptive machine. Of course, no practical use to me now. At my age, I never make love like I used. I barely think. But I buy two packets for nostalgia's sake.

When I get back to my table, I promptly examine them. You never guess! They have peppermint and strawberry flavours now. In my day, there was only vaseline, talcum or rubber tang to rubbers. In those days, we swallowed our pride. No-one ever considered them good taste.

I tear open the foils and find that the whatsits are coloured – green, yellow and red. What's the point? Surely, they're gilding the lily. Do they think a lady has eyes in the back of her head?

At the next table, the young couple have started to watch – a boy and girl of forty, maybe.

'You want?' I smile. 'Take two. I don't need them.' Then I chuckle in reminiscence. 'No. Treat yourself. Take all six.'

'No, thank you,' says the girl. She screws her face in distaste. But her boyfriend looks wistful.

'Sorry,' I say, 'no offence.'

'It's kind of you,' says the girl, 'but I don't need a stranger to tell me when, and how often, to have sex.'

'Wise girl,' say I. The kids today are smart. Prickly, too. I never turned down a prophylactic in my life, if it was proffered in good faith. In my day, they were worth something. Waste not, want not. In Berlin in 1945, a GI could buy a choice girl for a packet of condoms. She had to invest to accrue.

Malcolm has been listening with interest. So he wanders over to chat. I've unrolled a rubber, stroking its oily iridescent length, as if to caress it to life.

'Lise! For Christ's sake, what are you doing?' he asks.

'*Ach*,' I confess, 'just reminiscing. It reminds me of someone I used to know.'

I calculate that the less I teach Mayor Andreas Roth, the slower his mind will mend. If he stays in his state of semi-idiocy, he never can stand trial. But other patients on the ward give him information it would be better for him not to know. Also he tries to read, but I confiscate unsuitable matter, on medical grounds – substituting poetry for newspapers and journals.

'This war, Lise,' he informs me, 'is a wicked thing. We must end it. Too many are hurt already.'

'What can we do?' I ask.

'Complain to Matron,' he says, 'tell her it must stop.'

'It's worth a try,' I remark. 'I'll tell her what you say.'

So Roth, who, as a Major in the Cavalry, it is rumoured, incites his troops not to fight, is, in his new incarnation as a child, preaching pacifism again.

But this is dangerous talk that only attracts attention.

A few days later, when I arrive for duty, I find a huddle around Roth's bed. There is something sickeningly reminiscent about the dull jangle of brass, creak of leather, squeak of tight seams, and waft of citrus cologne over the tang of moist serge. Yes. I see again the back of Carl Fallehn.

'. . . like a child,' I hear Kiss report.

'Nonetheless,' Fallehn clicks his heels, 'we shall interrogate him again.'

'I must insist against it,' says Kiss.

'As you wish, Doctor. But we have charge and jurisdiction. So I humbly advise, sir, you go jerk yourself off in a corner.'

'Still a bully, Captain,' I say.

He spins around, teeth clenched, his eyes slits. Then his face slackens to a sour smile of recognition. 'No, Lise. Now I am a full Major.' Sure enough, he has the epaulettes, baton and sash to show so. 'And you too are promoted in life,' Fallehn observes, licking his lip with relish, observing me from head to toe. 'Now you're an auxiliary nurse. Whereas when I knew you before, you were merely a *prima donna*.'

'Be gentle on Major Roth, Carl, dear man,' I whisper, clutching at his braided cuff. 'He means no harm. He's no more than a foolish baby.'

But when Roth is brought back in the early evening, he wears a shocked expression. They've bruised the left side of his face, split his lower lip, and loosened an incisor.

I dry his eyes with gauze, dab his swollen cheeks with witch hazel, and apply clove essence to the gum of his wobbly tooth.

Fallehn always likes to leave his mark on another's skin.

'What did they ask you, Andreas? Tell me. Now.'

'Don't hit,' he jerks away, 'Andreas good boy.' He rolls his eyes in alarm. 'Stab the slimy Limey. Slit the French in their trench. Crush the Serbs.' Then — at pains to please — he commences, but with scant conviction, a mournful song they have taught him. 'Dawn of day, dawn of day, to early death you lead me . . .'

'Stop it! I demand. 'What did they say to you?'

'If I die in foeland, in I fall in Poland . . .' he sings in faltering falsetto, rubbing his swollen cheek.

Two days later — a Tuesday, August 1917 — I lead Major Andreas Roth for a walk in the hospital garden. We are dressed in our uniforms, as nurse and soldier. He still limps, so I clutch his left forearm to steady him. We wander down the slope of the lawn, around the ornamental fountain. Looking back, I see the sentry watch us from the terrace. I wave and smile. Corporal Goldhammer makes no reply but turns his eyes right, concealing his cigarette in the cup of his hand. It is a pretence of his that he is not guarding Roth. So I never mention to him that Kiss gives me permission to take Major Roth for an excursion.

We take the gravel path behind the hedge, leading to the side gate on to Schubertstrasse.

'No,' says Roth, tugging me back by my starched white cuff, as I open the screeching gate, 'too far. It's the end . . .'

But he doesn't know what it's the end of.

'Trust me,' I say. 'We've permission to go out.'

He winces, and the side of his mouth twitches in spasm. He fingers the buttons of his tunic and stares at the ground between our feet. 'Trust you,' he concedes reluctantly.

'Good. We'll elope for the afternoon. See the world. First we'll get lost.'

197

'Easy, peasy,' says Roth, relieved to be back on familiar ground. 'I get lost three times every day.'

Roth is insatiably curious and constantly demands that we pause on the way, to gawp at the satin gloss of a buttercup, some entirely commonplace rusted bicycle spokes, ladies' lingerie at a market stall, a flyspeckled melon rind in the gutter, a crate of beer bottles here, a chipped enamel café sign there, some gentleman's hat. He insists on fingering and sniffing. Then I'm called to act the diplomat.

'Forgive him, sir,' I say, 'the hero has a head wound. It affects his manners. But he's more sensible than he seems. And very curious. . . . He doesn't mean any harm by sniffing at your moustache.'

'Here,' says the indulgent burger reaching into his pocket for some coins, 'buy the stoutheart a beer.'

'I am Major Roth', Andreas volunteers with a grin. 'I have lost my way, my past, and Hercules my horse. This is Lise, my nurse. Never mind, it's all a game.'

'That's the idea.' The gentleman taps his shoulder. 'Keep smiling, brave lad.'

The major business on Roth's agenda is to search for his missing horse.

'Her-cules. Hercu-lees,' he shrieks to the summer breeze.

We cross a stile into a meadow. When he's frisked some more, we lay out a blanket and lie awhile, listening to the birds and insects, or the wind rustling the shivering grass.

His surreptitious sideways looks begin to disconcert me, aimed as they are at my chest, hips or lap. I know he is pondering flesh again.

'In the hospital, Artur talks about you. Other fellows say too.'

'What do they say?' I swish the hair from my eyes to watch him.

'They say you are lovely. They admire your looks.'

'And?'

'That you do things with Doctor Kiss.'

'What things?' I prickle and flush, crossing my legs.

'Dirty business.'

'No,' I say severely, making him blink and look down. 'Nothing dirty. Only friendly.'

198

Besides the Look, he is learning the Touch. Whereas he used to jerk my hand to get my attention, now his fingers linger on my wrist, or gently graze my cheek. This laying on of hands is sensual and exploratory.

'I touch woman before.' A straying finger tickles my wrist. 'Sophie, maybe.'

'Tell me.' I suspect he remembers more than he says.

He frowns at the clouds, his forehead puckered in concentration. 'Woman different . . .'

'True,' I agree.

'Breasts,' he reminisces, 'thighs. Nice places.'

He reaches out slowly and runs his hand down my hair, then coils some strands around languid fingers.

I show him how to plait it, and he spends an hour with my locks in breathy absorption. He conspires to press my breasts with his elbows, or skim the slopes with a palm. His eyes are avid for the triangle of skin between my neck and blouse.

'What are you staring at, Major?' I ask.

'Nothing,' he says, drawing his hand from me, reaching out plucking the grass. 'Nothing interesting.'

Truly, he's progressing. For he's woven some guile into his slyness. I suspect him of intentions.

So the forgetful leads on the amnesiac. They wander the winding paths back at arm's length, pondering their adjacent desires. Their desires meander in perfect parallel. But they never touch.

He stops at a ditch to pick me some flowers: marsh marigold, buttercups and daisies. His eyes are cast down as he offers up the blooms in the cup of his hands.

'Thank you, Andreas. Beautiful.'

'Pretty smelly flowers,' he gives a sly smile, 'for pretty smelly woman.'

'Next time . . .' I suggest, 'pick stalks too.' For he's delivered into my moist palms a heap of crushed flowerheads.

I do believe he's courting me; sketching certain designs on my frame.

199

Roth knows I am withholding soft skin. He's itching; stung by the nettle of desire.

'We're alike, you and I.' I smile.

'How?'

'Hurt in our heads. We forget too much. There are painful things to remember.'

But I never mention that his condition is worse. I lose some casual hours, here and there. He's mislaid his life.

A special trust. I must never abuse it.

'Hold hands, Lise?' He reaches out, and his heavy, humid hand squeezes mine. 'Nice to touch,' he whispers.

He reminds me of the boy I first loved. His innocence molests me.

'Touching, Andreas,' I advise, 'is like talking. Our fingers speak. To squeeze is to shout. Touch me quieter.'

His grasp loosens. A languid finger circles my palm.

'Better,' I sigh, 'now I hear you.'

'Hand wants to feel you,' he says, pressing my hip. 'Wants to say hello. Everywhere. All over.'

'You know it is rude to stare?'

'Yes.'

'Use your hands like your eyes, Andreas. They mustn't stay too long in one place, or rest too hard.'

And, clever as can be, his fingers skim my waist, then drop away.

'Look at me!' I demand. We stop in the thigh-high rye grass. He turns to watch me, and his eyes take a skittery tour of my face, glancing, avid, shy.

'Good boy, Andreas. Learn to touch like you look.'

'I want . . .' His touching fingers graze the naked skin of my shoulders. But the poor man cannot voice the doggerel of his desire.

'We cannot have what we want whenever we want.' Then I break into giggles. My God, I sound like my Mamma.

Ach, poor man. He has so much to learn. You forget how little he knows.

We pass a couple of boys on the road, herding back a strayed cow. They salute Roth who, for his part, panics the beast by patting its haunches.

200

'Big dog. Small people,' observes Roth, conversationally, as if confiding a small insight.

'Children,' I say. 'They'll grow tall and strong like you.'

'They will? Why don't I grow?'

I briefly summarise the human lifespan – omitting the lurid parts, but mentioning the major comings and goings.

'Seems strange,' Roth's face creases at the complexity, 'all this borning and dying, growing, talling, fattening and olding. Better if everyone stays same size and age like us. Be happy for ever.'

'You were a baby once.'

'When?' He's startled to disbelief.

'Thirty years ago.'

'Oh . . . then . . .' He's reassured it wasn't yesterday. 'Far time and black. So I forget.' He excuses his natural lapse of memory – eager not to be thought absent-minded. He gets frantic if he mislays a spoon or apple, for his memory for the here and now is always very sharp. 'Nice people? Babies? Nice as big folk?'

'Oh, yes. But funny, stunted things.'

'And where do they come from, babies?'

Ah, but that would be telling. We've had too many facts of life for one day.

We are in the centre of the barley field as we kneel. Roth's flaxen crown is level with the golden heads of corn.

'Lie,' I urge, 'so no-one can see us. Let's hide.'

Brother and sister play such games, flattening the stalks rolling, giggling, together then apart. You can see down the dark cracks in the parched earth. A beetle eyes me from the sheer face of his chasm. I roll on to my back and squirm to press flat the prickling stalks. You want to sneeze on the dusty, bready scent of the corn. Above, the clouds are stretched thin and translucent, like sheets of *Strudel* pastry. You lay your elbow across your eyes to shade them from the dizzying madder yellow sun. The world's gone gold. The straw, tangled hair, the boy's stubble, sparkling glints on his cheeks and chin. And when you close your lids, the sun burns through your lids as a sulphur-yellow disk. The tips of corn rustle, chafing in the wind. But you're becalmed, below the breeze.

201

You wriggle, then go still, but your outstretched fingers have grazed against him, then are entwined with his. You pretend a dazed drowse. But you're listening to the breaths: yours and his.

You sigh. Enough said.

You're lying there so serenely warm, you feel your skin belongs to the sun. All cover is concealment.

The comes the touch. A hand rests flat on your hip, a calculated inadvertence. The shadow falls over your closed eyes. There's the scent and close tremor of another's skin. Open eyes regard you, you sense. Your twitchy lids stay closed.

You feel the hand move upon you. Upward first, over the flat of your belly with a skimming grace, running up along the ridges of ribs, then over a swell of breast. Pray God, he doesn't kiss; to that you must respond or resist. Acknowledging the touch, or forfeiting with accusation. For brother and sister should not lie so. The girl should know better. No matter she's only a child.

It's not that you desire him. You'd never thought to bear his touch. Yet it's intriguing to sense what another can rouse in you, to feel yourself through borrowed, trespassing fingers.

It is a charade of tact. That you do not flick open your eyes tells enough. Lying still is consent enough.

'Aah,' you whimper softly, in pretence of satisfied sleep, a whispered encouragement.

A finger circles a breast. There is the hammer of heart beneath it. Your pulse sounds too loud, pop-pop in your ears.

There's fumbling perplexity. I have to guide him a little, regarding what fits where, and how.

He's startled by an outcome and slumps, eyes closed, head rocking. Then he sinks his moist brow on my belly, and encircles my thighs with his arms.

And the effluent comes gushing back into my mind.

How brother August came to my room at night. You fret he'll come. You fear he won't. You lie waiting, imagining the jolting shock of touch.

First, there sounds the creaking door. Then shuffling feet on the rug. You hear his intake of breath.

'Lise, can I lie with you?'

The girl stays mute as her hidden hand draws back the quilt.

The mattress sinks beneath the weight of another. They roll together. He presses hard against her hips. She shivers against the chill, tugging the sheet over again.

'Brr . . . brother, your hands are icy.'

A mouth nuzzles her neck and a darting tongue leaves dewy dots. Then her lips part for his, then her legs.

Rude, they are, his ticklish fingers, rousing twitches, tingles, prickles, cold creeps, an itch, wetting an ungodly taste.

The girl's eyes are closed. He feels. She allows. They never discuss. They barely speak. She doesn't know what he intends by it, or why he's so curious below the waist. He's a boy – when all's said and done, growing to be a man. Only, she knows he wants.

She shivers, quivers, trembles, to permit; a cold unfeeling girl, inflamed by skin.

'Aah!' his hand observes. 'Here!' It tickles.

'Oh!' Her chest judders. 'No!' Her jerky thighs rejoin.

'Yes!' He presses on, insistent.

'No!' she gulps.

Outside only. Inside is too far. Only touch.

But he wrenches in, plunging on, his panting breath gusting in her ears, thighs jerking fierce and frenzied, like a berserk clockwork machine. And when he's shortly done, she's smarting, shuddering a stinging shame. Bruised open, poked and skewered.

'Lise,' the boy coaxes, 'don't cry.'

'August,' she shivers, 'what have you done to me? An awful thing.'

'Why cry?' Roth looks up, squinting against the sun.

'My brother gets shot,' I sniffle, 'and my uncle falls.'

'Sad,' he mumbles. 'Dead?'

'Dead,' I confirm. I tousle his hair. Poor Andreas. He was shot too. By his own hand. Only his knowledge was spilled with his sense.

'What are you thinking of?' I sniff back my tears. 'Remember anything?'

Because you can never tell what will jog a man's mind. Perhaps love has opened a way, leading him through the maze of life past. For once he knew a Sophia in Karlsplatz, and a Clotilde in St Paulen.

'Mmm . . . nice game. Love . . . better than playing piano . . . warmer than a bath . . . stranger than numbers . . .' he mumbles. Then I know from the throb of his chest on my hip, and the tempo of his breath, gusting between my breasts, he's dreaming innocently of something or other.

24

'SURPRISE, surprise!' Elli shrieks, all wide-eyed and breathless. 'Rudi's back from Strasburg. He bought a talking parrot. It sings the first verse of *Allons-y, Chochotte*.' Or, 'You'll never guess! That red-haired Gerti, the waitress at Kern's with the limp, is up the spout by Fat Otto, the bassoonist.'

But it takes more than that to surprise me. I've guessed stranger things in my time. And promptly forgotten them because reality can bear a grim grin, facts can be stubbornly brutal, and brass tacks pierce you. Truth's a cruel prankster, and memory a frightful sadist. Trust make-believe to thwart them. And absent-mindedness helps.

Thomas M—, the scribbler, would waste whole days hunched over his desk, sucking the blunt end of his fountain pen, blinking through the smeared lenses of his spectacles, snow-blinded by the blank white paper, trying to peer back to his youth. He'd suddenly sigh and break into a burst of demented scrawling. There's this infuriating scratching sound, like a mouse in the wainscot, for the ink won't flow fast enough to lubricate the nib.

It's a dry, parched pastime. You're resigned that the best portion of your span is ended. Your life is become a dusty archive, and you've

205

become a dull historian of yourself, librarian of your life. Committing slow suicide by autobiography.

'When I was fourteen . . .' he'd cluck all confidential, 'I saw my governess in the nude . . .'

'Ugh!' I'd cut him short. 'Can't you stop this morbid remembering. No good will come of it!'

Because I used to fear reminiscence, its phantasmagoria of ghoulish dancers.

I was overprotected as a girl. Felice kept my sordid memories to herself, leaving me blissfully unaware.

Poor girl. You can understand why she's maddened. She suffered so much for me – like a Prince's whipping boy.

Trouble comes when she starts sharing her recollections. A sanitary barrier in my mind starts crumbling. Cack starts slithering through the cracks.

—How do dead men walk?—
'Say again . . .'
—Mamma must have known.—
'What?'
—Oh, Pappa!—

You don't understand what she means'. Only you feel distant pain like the throb of an abscessed tooth as the dulling novocaine wears off.

You feel the bones of your skull resonate. A monstrous thing is knocking to come into your thoughts. There's a flickering at the dark edges of your mind's eye. Soon some lurid footage will show. You watch the rushes, appalled. You wonder who is this crazed cinematographer, and how he gets the right to project in your mind. Then you recognise the girl. That young face is yours. And you're there in a role you never remember playing.

The continuity girl's worked wonders. The finest detail is authentic. 'Look,' you sigh to yourself, 'it's the cameo brooch I lost that Christmas at Klosterneuburg. This must be the summer of 1909.'

And the flashback jolts you, and no mistake. It tells its own story, of course. But it puts a new perspective on later events you know already. It plots to rewrite you: cutting and pasting the pieces of your life into a repulsive collage.

Ach, let's get it over and done with. Better I tell you, at last.

*

'He did what?' Pappa growls.

'Only kissed me and pressed my bosom,' I whisper. 'Uncle Carl never meant any harm.'

There is pounding, crackling silence in my ears. Pappa and Mamma's glances jerk and fix upon each other. She is blanched, whilst his face glistens a mottled crimson.

'It's just he's lonely,' my voice breaks the solemn stillness. 'No-one has kissed him for seven years.'

'Lise?' Mamma entreats. 'Say this isn't so.'

'Seven years,' I repeat mechanically. 'Ask Uncle Carl. It's true.'

'Go to your room, Lise,' Pappa mutters. 'Your Mamma and I must talk.'

So I know I'm in disgrace, through my uttering a terrible thing. I slope, feet scuffing, up to my room.

Prone, tearful on the floorboards, my ear to a crack, I half hear awesome, awful things. I've unleashed pandemonium. It's a terrible tempest, as Pappa's gale batters Mamma's squall.

Sweet Jesus. Let every man in the house touch me in turn. I'd prefer that to this.

What have I done? That Mamma howls and Pappa roars. Porcelain and glass are hurled to the floor, and a father howls he'll gouge out an uncle's eyes, and hands strike faces, and you hear clothes get ripped, and unspeakable things are shrieked, for the entire household to hear.

Then comes the thunder of Pappa ascending the stairs, past my door, upwards to Carl's attic room.

The membrane of my ceiling quivers. You hear furniture topple, squeals in time to rattling blows to the floor. Then muffled squeaks.

207

All is quiet for a full quarter-hour, till Pappa descends alone, sounding a limp on the stairs, as if he's hurt his foot.

Pappa has a fearsome temper. I fear he's hit out at Uncle Carl and shouted some cutting words.

Through the floor I hear Pappa's gabble urgent but garbled, and the clink of the brandy bottle on the silver salver. Mamma has commenced a desperate sound – as if she's wailing whilst retching, or maybe gargling barley gruel.

But from above I hear nothing.

Yes. I must slink up to console poor Uncle Carl, then beg pardon, *mea culpa*, beat my breast, cry till he forgives me. Penitence is the only balm. Oh, I'll be so abject.

There's no reply to my knock or muffled plea. Yet the flickering ribbon of light at the base of the door shows Carl isn't yet at rest.

I twist the chill porcelain doorknob, push open the door to his attic room. A warm gust greets me, spiced and stale, like when you lift the lid on the laundry basket.

Carl's lying on his belly by a toppled chair. His arms splay out from his sides – like a child pretending to fly like Bleriot. Those calm blue eyes look up to me, frankly bemused. A triangle of amber tongue glistens through gawping lips.

'Forgive . . .' I whimper. 'Don't make faces . . .' For I think he's reprimanding me with his unblinking, unrelenting gaze, and sticking out his tongue at me, till I see the line of blood from the side of his gaping mouth, swerving down his chin.

He lies still, except for some fine, upstanding hairs of his scalp, flickering in the breeze. There's an odd indentation on the back of his head, glistening with blood-matted hair.

From below sounds a laborious trudge on the stairs, pausing on the landing below, then treading louder up towards us. I believe it's the second coming.

The girl slithers beneath the bed, and peeps out between her fingers, behind the tasselled fringe of the eiderdown.

The intruder looks down, winces, rubs at the lids of his eyes, then pokes Carl's chest with an exploratory toecap. He kneels down and places an ear to Carl's frozen gaping mouth as if to coax some confidence.

'Carl,' the moving man shakes his sorry head, groaning his grievance, 'why can't you take a thrashing like a man? Why do you have to die on me?'

The live one kneels by the still one's head. They eye each other steadily. Of course, the living man blinks first. Death is such a resolute condition.

'What are you trying to do to us, you bastard?. . . Ruin the whole family?' asks one, shaking the other's shoulders. 'Get me locked up in prison?'

He pulls up the toppled chair and lays it upright; then, bending, wraps his hands beneath the still one's chest, straining to raise the dead.

'Up, you bugger,' he urges the corpse who, compliant, bends at the knees. 'Down!' he mutters to the spread arms, levering them back to the side. 'There's nothing else to be done. I fear you're due a terrible tumble. You'll not get the better of me,' he warns.

And the puppet is jerked stiffly up on to the chair. But it keeps rocking forward, as if to topple, until his chest is urged further towards the backrest, and his feet urged down to anchor his swaying weight.

'Now . . .' the live one grunts, 'then . . .' from his exertions. 'You'll do the right thing for once. . . .' He swings open the screeching window. The gauze curtains flutter in on the breeze.

He draws Carl up, head between arm and shoulder and, with an arm around the waist, drags him, feet trailing, limp as a collapsed drunk, across the room, drawing the trapped rug beneath him.

They wrestle at the windowsill. The dead one lolls and sways uncooperatively, resisting with inertia and body weight, but the live one gains the upper hand and has Carl framed in the window, balanced on the seat of the sill, gazing bewildered at this scene in his room, his back to the night and the drop. Only his splayed elbows hold him back and in.

A push to his chest will send him swinging over and out.

The live one is the spit of Pappa. And yet he acts so cruel and strange.

The girl has clamped shut her eyes on the slow, demented drama. Myself, I lay alongside – observant and calm. It is a curious thing. I watch still and unmoved, whilst she begins twitching, clawing the boards with her nails. I hope she won't go loopy on me. We're in a big enough fix as it is.

'Uhh . . .' she bites her lips, stifling a whimper.

—Shh!— I chide, —He'll hear you. . . . Then where will we be?—

It's *her* fault. She should never have said that it was Carl who kissed her. For it was never him, but another.

But everyone blames Carl anyway. He has little enough credit to lose. And it's too shaming to confess that you let him do those things. And leave marks, signing himself on your skin. Kissing was the least of it. Only she never thought it would come to this.

It's odd to feel so split and separate. There's an awesome cleavage within. I am the innocent, uninvolved witness. The guilty girl squirming alongside is the cause of it all, and yet she turned away, and so never saw. And so my eyes are split from her heart. Hers is the blind, dumb guilt. Mine the blameless voice and vision.

She squeaks, biting her tongue, as we three hear the fallen thing strike ground. But the dull clump comes as no surprise to me. For I've been watching every move in sight, and guessed the hidden trajectory.

The moving man is shakily distraught, and gazes down on his trembly palms, then wipes them on the dusty seat of his trousers. He turns away, brushing busily at his waistcoat, and strides out of the room, as if he knows his way about our house.

*

We are rousing the patients one morning when Fallehn bursts into the ward without warning, in the company of four hussars. He strides up to Andreas' bed and stamps his boots on the boards. His shaded eyes glower beneath the peak of his cap. His nostrils twitch then flare. He glowers his disgust.

He does not speak his own mind, but unfolds a typed document which he commences to read aloud in an officious nasal drone.

It's a military arrest for Major Andreas Roth, on yellow paper, with two seals and a burgundy ribbon. It takes a full minute to recite.

I don't think Andreas understands a single, fine phrase of the indictment. His pain is in sighting Fallehn again. His cheek is twitching a spasm, and he's clutching my hand for comfort. Then it occurs to him to hide beneath the blanket. But his shivering outline and audible panting give the game away.

Andreas casts me bewildered backwards glances as they frogmarch him down the ward. I'm wrenched by a sense I've betrayed him.

That evening, immediately my duty is ended, I write to Major Fallehn, 'My Darling Carl', suggesting we take dinner together 'for old time's sake'. Why not the Red Hedgehog, next Monday?

'We've unfinished business, Carl. Don't you feel so?'

'Yes?'

'Indeed.'

Only I notice Fallehn is changed. He's acquired a platform of dignity to stand on. So it seems he's talking down from a height. There's more calculation and self-importance, less whim and wilfulness. And there's a peeved intimation from his manner that he feels somehow, sometime, I've wronged him.

I reach out to clasp his cool dry hands in mine. 'And this poor Major Roth,' I enquire, 'what can we do for him, Carl, darling?'

'Put the bastard in front of a wall and shoot him,' Fallehn smiles, 'that'd be best all round.'

'But he's innocent! . . . With the mind of a child. Whatever he did before doesn't matter. For now he can't remember.'

'Who cares?'

'I do, Carl. Call it sentimental attachment. I nurse him all these months. So, of course, I get fond . . .'

'Forget him. He's spoken for. He has an appointment with a firing squad.'

'Look, I'll be straight with you. It's important. I owe a favour in life. . . . If I can help Roth, maybe it evens the score.'

211

'What can I do?' Major Fallehn spreads his palms, all mock impotence.

'Lose his papers,' I'm quick to suggest, having asked myself that question already, 'or swap his identity with a dead man's. Have him transferred to another hospital, and mislay him on the way. Report him deceased – killed attempting escape.'

'There's risk to that. I'd need a motive. What incentive could there possibly be?'

'You'd know my gratitude.' I venture some fingers across his brow. Wriggling forward, I trap his knee and squeeze it mercilessly between my thighs. 'A girl can never resist a man who gives her what she wants.'

'Remind me of your gratitude, Lise. For the life of me, I can't recall it at all.'

'Oh, Carl, my sweetie, it's true as the flowing Danube. It is hotter than August in a bakery. It is lewder than the Fourth Artillery regiment after a year on the Russian front. It is more accommodating than Lotte Krebs, pickled on rum. And yet it burns slower than a Burmese cheroot . . .'

He blinks uncertainly. 'Perhaps, Lise, you'd better remind me . . .'

'Sweet man,' say I. Then I lean across to suck the lobe of his ear, intoxicated and flushed by my newfound saintliness.

We take a room in a cheap hotel nearby. It's the sort of place a subaltern takes his floozie. The merits of this place, neither visible nor hygienic, are of economy and proximity. So I sense I'm devalued stuff in the Major's regard. We undress languidly in silence, unruf-fled by any urgency or passion. And before long I find myself grown indifferent to his charms. Not that I'm unobliging; I make all the right noises, to be sure. Only I find something brutal and brisk in his routine manoeuvres. Time hasn't mellowed him. I sense he intends to hurt, as he plunges in and out.

'Oh, Carl,' I remark, turning my head away. The creased undu-lations of the stained pillow, the glistening opalescent crusts of dried lover's juice, remind me of the vista from Burg Kreuzstein when the slopes are under snow. I went tobogganing there once with Klara.

Afterwards, we took hot spiced wine to thaw our bones. When an American painter sits down to chat with us, we claim we are Russian Princesses. Klara confides to him that her maternal grandfather is Leo Tolstoy, then lectures him on the emancipation of the serfs.

Such thoughts cross a girl's mind when her passion's not fully engaged. Then glancing down, to the concertinaing space between his belly and mine, I'm moved to recall the pumping pistons on locomotive engines. All that huffing and puffing to build up a head of steam. Then the shriek of the whistle and the groaning strain. But still you've barely moved.

'Darling . . .' I observe, pleasantly enough, as Fallehn draws shuddering to a halt in his siding, 'was it as good for you as it was for me?'

A philosophical question, this, I know. Because I once asked it of Ca—, a well-known logical positivist: he talks about privacy and the impenetrability of our experience; I reply this is rum and rich, considering what he'd just done.

'Nostalgic, Lise,' sighs Fallehn. But there's sweat to his brow, trickling down like drips of rain on a windowpane.

Gratitude, or pillow talk, was never his *forte*. He prefers to smoke a Papirossi, or one of those wrinkled-skin stubby cigars. I watch him light up – and imagine, for my private satisfaction, in the absence of more compelling pleasures, that he's sucking on something obscene. And smile at his puckered baby lips. I watch the skeins of smoke drift up and diffuse.

Shortly, he gets amorous again. Rougher now and ruder. There's some anger he's venting on me.

Men do this. Men do that. A girl learns to cut herself off, disengage her mind.

*

'No, August! Please . . . don't!'

'I'll pinch . . .' he warns, insinuating a hand in the split of my thighs to lever my legs apart.

213

'I'll tell Mamma,' I mumble, 'this time, I will.'

'No,' he tosses his head, chuckling nastily, 'you won't . . .' he stares me out, his nose tip prodding mine, 'because then she'll know you're a whore . . .'

'It's you . . .' I splutter.

'Men can't help themselves. But tarts like you lead them on . . .'

He sits on my chest, clenches my wrists, then twists the skin till it burns. I feel his teeth nibbling my shoulder then, gripping skin, slicing in.

'No . . .'

'Say it!' he demands. 'Or I'll bite again.'

'Beast,' I blubber. 'Bastard . . .'

He reaches down to clench my buttock. Two pincer fingernails pierce me to squeal.

'Say!'

—I'm a whore,— an Other girl whimpers, —I want . . .—

'Lie still,' commands August. 'Open your legs . . .'

So I'm laid exposed and splayed, poker stiff, stubbornly straining, braced unbending. As he prods and pushes, forcing an entry, I'm unyielding within. Flesh may admit him. I never do.

For it's as if I slip out of my skin – just as he comes in – and I hover above, watching the spasmodic jerks of the girl's puckered face, her eyes clenched closed as she bites on her lip.

So I'm a detached, unfeeling thing. Above this dirty business. Really. It's as if it's happening to another – remote, quite apart – to an Other in a separate flesh, wrapped in an Other's skin.

When did it start? When I was ten, I think. This image comes to mind of his hand trespassing across her goosebumped maiden skin, as Felice and Sophia, my porcelain dolls, look on.

214

25

L AST night in the Crown and Woolpack, I was watching the television – the starfucker slot. A man with vinyl hair and smile is talking to a woman medical victim. Some plastic surgeon has hoisted her chest a foot too high, and pulled her face taut as a drum skin. Her complexion is latex stretched over a skull. The tension tugs her mouth open wide. When she pouts, her ears are jerked forward and down. She is wearing a silver-foil basque, and camiknickers made from a black plastic rubbish bag.

So she looks like a Dada collage. But the man says she's an actress, and this she confirms without shame. Then she tells some anecdotes about how she eats raw vegetables for breakfast, loves people, admires honesty, and broke a fingernail on a plane. This she delights in revealing, so we can learn and share.

Bernhardt was an actress. Elisabeth Bergner, ditto. Garbo too. But this woman I cannot believe.

Well, we all love people. But the public want to know who and how: and why, if you know. And to describe your breakfast is to tell too little and say too much. Better she stays mute or discreet. Otherwise, we'll mistake her as shallow. I think her agent should advise her.

My ears burn when I hear two men at the next table discussing my dead acquaintances, saying Thomas Ma— this and Franz K— that.

'Excuse me,' I lean over, 'you were on first-name terms with them? And yet you don't look older than thirty.'

'No,' says the fellow, winking to his friend, 'I didn't know them personally. Did you?'

'Some,' I concede, 'but I never know a girl who gets intimate with Franz, though he's such a beautiful man, and his very smile sends you all aquiver. . . . With Thomas, it's quite another matter.'

'Oh, yes?' says the man, distractedly rising to leave. As if he meets an intimate of legends every day. Or else he disbelieves. 'Anyway, goodbye.'

'You don't want I tell you about my picnic with Franz? I spill mayonnaise on his manuscript, but Milena licks it off?' I look melancholy at my empty glass. 'Or how Stefan Zweig and I share a bath in Zurich?'

These are good anecdotes. Worth a cognac at least.

'Sorry.' The man shakes his head. 'We're late as it is.'

'Once Oskar Kokoshka declares I'm a work of art and signs my . . .'

But they're gone.

*

I tweak a tuft of hair on Fallehn's taut belly, and finger a wedge of muscle below. So odd and brutal, how men are assembled. And that curious hydraulic block and tackle: like a boy's mechanical toy.

'About Roth . . .' I mumble. Best transact our business whilst he's soft and satisfied. And, after his brutal behaviour, a gentleman should feel guilty. It's no way to treat a lady.

'No!' he grunts. His caressing hand retracts, denying me too.

'No what, darling?' I pat his belly, so hard and unrelenting.

'There's nothing I can do.'

'So this?' With open questioning palms I point it all out – the warm tacky sheets, our flushed bodies, intimacy, friendship and trust.

'I'm always happy to give myself,' Fallehn smiles, 'to please an old friend.'

'Surely . . .'

'Really, Lise . . .' Indeed, he does! He smirks. 'Do you think I'd risk rank and reputation? Just for roll in the sheets with a skirt?'

My lapping tongue meanders down his salty belly. He murmurs a rising note of anticipation, a mixture of purr and growl.

That old scent saturates my twitching nostrils. You can smell the ocean from here.

Yes, I decide. Everything considered, I will.

Quelle joie! I've often had the whim to do that. Only I'll give him one last chance.

'Please . . .' I swish it with my tongue. Then nibble gently. Hot lick or sharp reprisal: it's entirely up to him.

'No,' he grunts, grown a hard and upright man.

So it was, I bit.

A symbolic vengeance, this; and deeply gratifying. For once in my life I've bitten no more nor less than I can chew. Somehow the revenge is sweeter, for I'm settling not just with Fallehn, but with others too.

The brave Major – twice mentioned in dispatches – emits a pitiful howl. He was wounded in the shoulder on the Eastern Front, but never *there* before, in bed. I cling on just long enough, against his crushing clubbing fists, to taste the hot spurts of blood at the back of my throat.

I gulp and swallow. Then sit up dazed and blinking, my ears ringing, to survey the scene. He gave my scalp a frightful drubbing, but it's clear I've won. For he's writhing on his back, howling like a child.

You'd never believe such a slight prick would leak so much. But – as we nurses learn, in Basic Circulation II – the male member is a domestic appliance empowered by a rush of blood. Besides, I got carried away, severing an artery, near slicing off the tip.

Fallehn squirms away on the sodden crimson sheets, cupping his wounded part in his hands as if it were the most precious thing on earth.

217

It's hard to to disconcert the law. For it bends to all convolutions, contorting itself even to cover some unlikely events that can happen in bed.

You'd blush to hear the legal precedents that get mentioned in court – like when a gypsy dancer bites off a butcher's testicle and swallows it. Not to mention worse.

In due course, I'm appalled to learn that – technically – by statutes 227, 1326 and 1447, (i)–(iii) of the Imperial and Royal Criminal Code – I've committed an aggravated assault, and Conspired at Sabotage against His Majesty's Forces. Never mind if Fallehn asked for it; no matter it was only his dick – an entirely commonplace item, and no conceivable loss to the Empire. The due process of law is loud, deaf and unrelenting.

At six the next morning, following my altercation with Fallehn, the police batter the flimsy door of my cubicle in the nurses' quarter. I slide bedraggled, bleary-eyed, from my cot and slip on my silk kimono to cover my *déshabillé* and shame, nagged by foreboding.

'Bad news?' I enquire, squinting round the door.

'Clink, I think,' says the sergeant, barging in, crushing my scattered lingerie underfoot, leaving his bootprints on my pink silk bodice.

'Some delicacy, please!' I protest. 'I know you aren't accustomed, but you're in the company of a lady.'

'We have a warrant for your arrest.' He smiles briefly, just this once, as he untangles some lace smalls from his ankles, fingering them with undue interest, which I take as overfamiliar.

'Surely not!' I gulp. 'What have I done?'

'Wounding a Major of the Uhlans in the Army of his Imperial Majesty.'

Really! As if the regiment matters.

'That was a private affair,' I confide. 'Intimate and confidential. An unfortunate bedroom accident.' I smile sheepishly. 'Least said, soonest mended.'

'No. There's a warrant.'

'The gentleman's pressed charges? When I wear his name tattooed on my left buttock? After all we've been through together . . .'

'Yes. Please dress!' the policeman barks, departing from patience.

'Turn your back. . . . Shall I dress formal or casual?' I ask. 'Where do you want to take me?'

'Prison!' he says, quite unforgiving.

And so it turned out. I get four years, for this and that. And conspiracy to do worse. Not to mention two lesser charges concerning my alleged nonchalance in leaving the scene of the crime.

But after serving a year, I appeal. And the sentence is commuted to twenty-eight months, on account of the persuasions of a gaggle of character witnesses my lawyer shepherds through court.

Dr Kiss describes my exemplary devotion to medical duty. Georg reports my generous good nature, and the loss I am to Theatrical Art.

Aunt Edie tells that I am a pleasant niece to be related to; sometimes impetuous, but never malicious or cruel. I'd only bite another person, she assures the judge, if possessed of a very sound reason. And this Fallehn, she lets it be known, once shot my cousin Felix. Men have their codes of honour. So, she sniffs, do women.

Finally, dear Doctor Flugel is brought shuffling and blinking out of retirement to pronounce his medical opinion. I'd been ambidextrous and cuckoo, he advises, ever since I fell on my head as a child.

The court take into consideration that, though I was once charged with theft, it's my first offence of this very particular sort.

Never mind. A girl lives and learns. You shame your parents. You make mistakes. You pay if you must. You learn what's there inside you and come to terms with your past.

To pass the time, you teach yourself French. Strange. Thoughts come swift and fluent off the top of my head to me in French. Feelings and sensations that I never entertained in German.

Gallic impulses move me. I swear at the warders in a foreign tongue, with *panache* and *savoir-faire*.

A Belgian *arsoniste* – a *parfait* sweetie called Rosalie, more sinned against than sinning – corrects your pronunciation. In return you perform your audition pieces, and procure *allumettes* for her from the kitchen.

In September 1918, Kiss writes me a kind, forgiving, consoling letter, regretting to inform me that Andreas Roth is shot, following a court martial. Though I couldn't save him, I'm glad to have loved him *en passant*. And the amnesiac did me a favour in turn — helping me remember family things and such. He was a dear man. An odd case and no mistake.

In prison there are angels and demons, riffraff and pussycats, same as outside. You get intimate with all sorts — because you live very close together. When the chill touches your marrow, you sleep two to a bed. You hear some rum yarns; meet some nice girls. Men you can live without, for a while.

You get to envy men, even. For they enjoy the pliant soft-centred love of women, whilst we girls squirm in the stiff harsh grasp of men.

The influenza epidemic of 1918 never touches us in Mauerbach. So I can count myself lucky I'm out of circulation. Gustav snuffs it first. Egon draws his death head, then shortly follows. Though I tell my intimacies to the Governor, I'm not allowed out to either funeral.

All the while in prison, raw memories strike her out of the blue. Make her shudder. I wince to recall: games of Russian roulette — winner takes all; making off with Aunt Edie's diamond brooch and Minna Levy's acrobat; getting overfamiliar with a Hungarian string quartet, and such.

Most of all, maybe, she regrets biting dear Arthur Br—'s darling nose, just to stop him telling tales about my past. He tried to tell me, but she wouldn't hear . . .

. . . that I feel guilty because Uncle Carl Gustav dies because of my lie: that I love Carls, Gustavs too, too much thereafter, as if to repay a debt: that I batten down the hatches to keep the lid on my past: you can deny a man your body, without him killing himself: that a girl's under no obligation to gratify a brother: that a girl can lose her innocence more than once: that there's more than blood, pain and debt to love: that I should love whosoever I like, regardless of his name: that even an Artur is lovable, viewed in a favourable light: that you can't stop men being shits by biting their dicks. I won't be told. Always I have to find these things out for myself.

She was a a dumb prig – *Kleine* Lise – the young woman I was, and no mistake. So much she refused to see, remember or hear. But bad, sad things had happened around her – frightening her half out of her wits.

The time I serve in Mauerbach kills her off. She barely bothers me again. I quite outgrow her. Memory was her exorcist.

*

I'm released in April 1919. The weary, stooped old woman who greets me at the gates is my very own Mamma. She says she'll strive to forgive, even if Pappa cannot.

—Bless you, Mamma, darling.— I kiss both cheeks and hug her for good measure.

She feels so scrawny beneath the canopy of her cape. Her hip bones jut like a cow's. There's not a pinch of fat to her. I've heard life has been difficult for civilians, this last year. Austria is wrecked. Money doesn't help. You need a kilo of banknotes to buy 500 grams of cheese. We're endlessly devalued. Foreigners flock in to flaunt their currency and glut themselves on our poverty. Seventy crowns to the German mark. So belching Bavarians stagger the streets, getting double drunk for the price of an apple at home. The *de luxe* hotels on the Ringstrasse are packed with the English unemployed, puffed up like barons, their pockets lined with dole whilst we are beggared. It's enough to make you feel Nationalist, or Socialist, or both.

—Here, Mamma. Take . . .— I reach into my overcoat pockets and start unpacking, —coffee. Two bars of chocolate. English cigarettes. Hungarian salami. Some Swiss francs. Also 105 American dollars.—

'Lise!' she winces, 'I hope you haven't been misbehaving in prison.'

—Easy come, easy go, Mamma,— I reassure. —I got lucky playing bezique and *vingt-et-un* with the girls inside. . . . And how do I look?— I demand. —And what do you prefer? Do I wear my hair down or up? And how are you? . . . And Pappa? Does Aunt Edie still need a lodger? And how is Mitzie the dog?—

She says my hair is better up in a knot, to show off my cheekbones, and tells that my complexion's pale as marble, but my figure's finer than ever. There's a maturity to my beauty now. I'm statuesque. Quite stunning. Also, she warns, I must try to behave.

—Sure, Mamma. *Absolument*. Understood. And does the Tunnel of Fun still run at the Wurstelprater? Shall we go take a ride for old time's sake? Before we drink ourselves blotto?—

But she tells that the Tunnel of Fun is closed up. They melted down the rails to make cannons and shells, to kill men. Shame.

Auntie Edie has a room for me. Theatre, though still unheated, is struggling back to its feet. Georg is casting for *Scandal*. He greets me as though we'd never parted. I must have given a powerful audition, because I get the lead part.

*

So, I'm off again. Saner? Surely. Maturer too, but never sedate. Although I've lived apace, I'm still only twenty-four, a fresh-faced and staggering beauty, not to mention my monstrous talent. I've got my best years ahead. There's too much I haven't tried yet. I aim to find myself pleasure and love – to make up for all the lost time. Maybe take myself to Paris. Perfect my French.

Live? I'll say.

'Only try not to shame us,' says Astrid. She's my big, solemn sister, older by two years. No, I never mentioned her before. Sometimes, to tell the truth most clearly, you must delete the inessential. If a sister is gratuitous, you simply cut her out. It's a principle I learnt from reading Dietrich's novel – her pretend autobiography.

Of course, life still ambushes me. There are vicious surprises; disquieting turns of affairs.

222

Two months after I'm released from prison, I chance upon a character I'm fated to live with awhile, an intimate from my past.

I'm crossing the Graben by the Pestsaule – known as Leopold's erection, though it really celebrates the plague instead – when I feel myself strangely moved.

You may have had a hint of the feeling if you've ever been on a binge. You get tiddly, then drunk, then venture beyond. After the world stops swirling, it goes eerily chill and still. Someone's tinkered with nature, for the laws of gravity and motion are oddly tranformed.

You keep drifting up, naked and weightless, towards the ceiling, gazing down bemused at your back. It's no use fastening your collar to keep youself buttoned in. No. You must attach yourself to some furniture, or grasp some solid gentleman by the arm, if you want to keep your feet on the ground.

If you try to walk forwards, you stumble on rubber legs. But, as luck would have it, you discover you can still go backwards, skipping nimbly and as friskily as you like.

You can't utter the briefest banality without slurring through leaden lips, dribbling your rum down your front. Yet you can sing *Freundliche Vision* with a precise and tender melancholy that makes Paula de Ahna sound coarse and harsh. And though you keep slithering off your chair, bouncing your butt on the boards, you still have the agile balance to win a bet by walking down two flights of stairs on your hands, even though your petticoat curtains your eyes, and your appearance is discomposed.

In short, you find yourself severed from your customary good sense. You've acquired unlikely abilities, but your habits just won't work.

So it was, that minute, for me, as I crossed the Graben. My feet were pattering to another's purposeful step. I found myself humming *Ah! Vous Dirai-je, Maman* without any sensible cause. Foreign feelings were welling up in me, misting my understanding. An alien impulse sounded in my head.

223

Let's visit Willi, in Dorotheergasse, it said.

'Willi?' I strain to remind myself. 'Which Willi?'

'*Willi Fischer, ma petite,*' a strange voice chuckles. There. In my mind. '*Willi the poet, who owes me 300 crowns, and never returned my mandolin.*'

Well, and I'm not even drunk! Experience has taught me a little at least. I suspect the worst. This voice sounds the breathless gurgle of a pampered darling, in frightful affected French.

My spine has gone all tingly. I blanch, I shiver at the sound of this wraith. I hug a streetlamp to steady myself.

Some gentleman stops to peer at me, raises his hat, creases his face in concern.

'Are you quite well, Fräulein?'

'Yes,' I pant, 'thanks.'

'*Bien sûr, Henri,*' adds the voice, all chirpy nonchalance.

The man saunters off with a smirking backward glance.

'Who's there?' I mutter under my breath.

'*C'est moi,*' she giggles. *Sophia*.

'Sophia?' I suspected as much. Call it intuition. It's the name I feared most to hear. 'Sophia . . . as in Lisellote Felice *Sophia* Constanze Berg?'

'*Who else would it be? Es-tu folle, chérie?*'

'So we . . .'

'*Exactement!*'

'Then my body?'

'*Of course, we share! Share and share alike.*'

And I'm suddenly twisting, posturing and gesturing, contorted against my will. For she rests my hands on my hips, and swirls a gandiloquent circle.

'I expect you're a lively girl . . . with a past?' I wince.

'*Comme ci, comme ça. I've lived and loved. I've been around . . .*'

Dear God, and so she had – as I learnt to my cost. And she leads me a pretty dance. I could tell you plenty of tales about Sophia you'd never believe. Never mind Constanze. But that's another story, and an entire new ream of paper.